UNDERWORLD
RISE OF THE LYCANS

D0880645

UNDERWORLD
RISE OF THE LYCANS

A Novelization by Greg Cox

Screenplay by Danny McBride and Dirk Blackman
& Howard McCain

Story by Len Wiseman & Robert Orr and Danny McBride

Based on Characters Created by Kevin Grevioux
and Len Wiseman & Danny McBride

POCKET **STAR** BOOKS
New York   London   Toronto   Sydney

Pocket Star Books
A Division of Simon & Schuster, Inc.
1230 Avenue of the Americas
New York, NY 10020

First Pocket Star Books paperback edition January 2009

POCKET STAR BOOKS and colophon are registered
trademarks of Simon & Schuster, Inc.

For information about special discounts for bulk purchases,
please contact Simon & Schuster Special Sales at
1-800-456-6798 or business@simonandschuster.com.

Manufactured in the United States of America

10   9   8   7   6   5   4   3   2   1

ISBN-13: 978-1-4391-1284-7
ISBN-10:   1-4391-1284-3

UNDERWORLD
RISE OF THE LYCANS

Prologue

From **The Underworld Chronicles** *by Selene:*

$\mathcal{A}$ war has raged for the better part of a thousand years, a blood feud between vampires and werewolves. It had its roots in the Dark Ages, when a great plague burned through Eastern Europe, turning all the land into a graveyard. Corpse wagons were piled high with the bodies of the victims, their lifeless faces contorted by the fearsome agonies of their deaths. Blackened flesh and swollen buboes hinted at the torments the doomed souls had endured before the Grim Reaper put them out of their misery. Their limbs and extremities were rotted from within. Pus oozed from open sores.

None was spared save Alexander, Duke of Corvinus. To him and his heirs, the Plague brought not death but life eternal. He became the Father of all immortals, beginning with his twin sons, William and Marcus.

William was the first to be changed. It began on a moonlit night in the Carpathian Mountains, when the two brothers rode their steeds fearlessly through a dense, black forest. Blessed with immortality, they feared neither beast nor man as they raced past ancient firs and pines. Pounding hooves tore up the winding dirt trail. Without warning, a great black wolf lunged from the shadows. Ivory fangs glistened in the moonlight as the beast leapt at Marcus, who was taken unawares by the wolf's savage attack. His horse reared up in alarm, whinnying in terror. All but thrown from his saddle, Marcus clung frantically to the reins of his panicked mount, unable to defend himself. The wolf snarled loudly as it went in for the kill, its hot breath steaming the cold night air.

The young nobleman would surely have perished had not his brother come to his defense with lightning speed. Yanking his double-edged sword from its scabbard, William struck out at the beast only moments before its fangs could tear out Marcus's throat. Tempered steel sliced through matted black fur. Blood sprayed from the beast's side. Dying, the wounded beast whirled about and snapped at William's outstretched sword arm. Powerful jaws clamped down on his armored wrist, punching through chain mail. The wolf's fangs sank deep into his flesh. . . .

William saved his brother's life, but at a terrible cost. Within hours, as his thrashing form was laid out atop a rough-hewn wooden table at the nearest inn, the wolf's bite caused the mutated virus within his veins to react in an unexpected fashion. Violent convulsions racked his flailing body as a hideous metamorphosis forever robbed him of all semblance of humanity. Snow-white fur sprouted from his agonized flesh. Bones cracked and twisted audibly. His skull stretched beneath his skin, transforming his once handsome features into a canine snout. Jagged fangs protruded from his gums. Hairy ears tapered to points. Claws slid from his fingertips. His hands and feet gave way to large, shaggy paws. His fine clothes and armor came apart at the seams. Bloodshot brown eyes turned cobalt blue and opalescent. An anguished scream devolved into the howl of a ravening beast. On that terrible night, before the shocked eyes of his brother, William became the first werewolf, a soulless monster with a bottomless appetite for slaughter.

His bloody rampages became legend. He and those he infected laid waste entire villages. Packs of marauding werewolves ran amok through the countryside, devouring the populace while creating ever more of their kind, much to the horror of his brother, Marcus, who in time became the first vampire. It fell upon Marcus to create the Death Dealers, an army of vampire soldiers dedicated to the destruction of William's inhuman spawn. Vampire waged all-out war against werewolf in a series of horrific battles—until William himself was cornered at last. Led by Viktor, the Death Dealers' ruthless military commander, the great white beast was finally brought to his knees—and locked away in a secret prison for all time.

But even after William's capture, his vile breed lingered for centuries. Death Dealers fought an endless battle against the beasts he had created in his own image. Like William, the werewolves were nothing but wild, unreasoning animals, forever trapped in the shape of monstrous beasts. Only upon death did they regain their humanity.

Until, one fateful night many years after William's downfall, *he* was born.

Lucian.

Chapter One

Hungary
The Thirteenth Century

*T*he werewolf whimpered in pain as its captors dragged it through the shadowy corridors of the underground dungeon. Silver barbs, embedded deep in the beast's bleeding hide, were affixed to heavy iron chains that weighed down the werewolf's shaggy black form; unlike their albino progenitor, William's successors were covered with fur the color of midnight. Even with its massive head bowed in submission, the monster's pointed ears brushed the low ceiling of the dungeon. Its clawed feet scraped against the dank stone floor as it staggered down the tunnel on its hind legs. Death Dealers, clad in gleaming black plate armor, tugged on the other ends of the chains, being careful to stay out of reach of their captive's razor-sharp fangs and claws. The immense werewolf, more than eight feet tall, towered over the smaller vampires. Additional knights, armed with crossbows and silver truncheons, warily escorted the procession, in the event that the beast was not quite as cowed as it appeared. Too many Death Dealers had seen their immortality end beneath the slathering jaws of an enraged werewolf; no one wanted to take any unnecessary chances with this prisoner until it was safely locked away in its cell. Even a chained wolf could bite.

Loathsome animal, Viktor thought. The regal Elder watched with satisfaction as his soldiers led the beast away. Piercing azure eyes peered from his gaunt, clean-shaven face. Sandy blond hair receded from his lofty brow. An aquiline nose distinguished his patrician countenance. A black velvet robe with golden trim clothed his narrow frame. He looked to be roughly fifty by mortal standards, although, like most of the inhabitants of the castle, his true age was measured in centuries.

Not for the first time, he pondered whether it was worth the risk to take these monsters alive. His alchemists and advisers insisted that they needed living specimens to experiment upon, in hopes of finding new means to combat their bestial enemies, but Viktor sometimes had his doubts as to whether their efforts were truly necessary. Fire and silver had always served the Death Dealers in the past. What more did they need to rid the world of these wretched beasts?

"This way, sire."

A jailor gestured to the right, reminding the Elder of his errand here tonight. A bizarre story had reached his ears, one that frankly beggared belief, but which had seemed to demand his personal attention. With Marcus and Amelia presently hibernating beneath the earth, enjoying two centuries of interrupted slumber, Viktor was the sole Elder in command of the coven. As such, it was his solemn duty to investigate anything that might affect their eternal war with the werewolves—even if, in this case, he suspected he was wasting his time.

Surely there must be some mistake, he thought. *Such a thing is not possible.*

"Lead on," he instructed the jailor.

The club-footed turnkey, whose pasty complexion was even paler than an ordinary vampire's, guided Viktor down a murky subterranean corridor. He held aloft a sputtering torch that did little to dispel the gloomy shadows shrouding the dungeon, while gripping a crossbow with his other hand. Heavy iron bars, reinforced with silver, guarded the dismal cells lining both sides of the passageway. Chains rattled as caged werewolves shuffled behind the sturdy bars. Low growls and angry snarls escaped the cells. Filthy straw littered the cold stone floors. Water dripped down clammy, slime-encrusted brick walls. Arcane runes were inscribed on the greenish-gray masonry. The fetid atmosphere reeked of sweat, piss, offal, and foul wolfen blood. Cobwebs hung from the ceiling. Rats and lizards scurried away from their approach.

Viktor's nose wrinkled in disgust. He seldom ventured into these noisome depths. "This had best not be an idle rumor," he warned the lumbering jailor. "I have better things to do with my time than go prowling through this cesspool in search of a drunken hallucination."

"No, milord!" the jailor assured him fearfully. His voice quavered at the prospect of incurring the vindictive Elder's wrath. He nervously licked his lips. "It's true, I swear it upon my life!"

We'll see about that, Viktor thought darkly.

They came to the mouth of an cavelike cell at the end of the corridor. A barred gate blocked their path. "Here, milord!" the jailor proclaimed. "You can hear for yourself!"

He struck the bars with the stock of the crossbow, producing a harsh metallic ring. Annoyed snarls greeted the noise, along with something else. To Viktor's amazement, the unmistakable cry of a newborn baby issued from within the cell before him. He exchanged a startled look with the jailor, who nodded in confirmation. After centuries of immortality, few things surprised the Elder anymore, but the inexplicable wailing left him speechless.

No, he thought in disbelief. *It cannot be. . . .*

Shoving the jailor aside, he stepped forward and peered through the sturdy bars of the cell. The stygian darkness beyond strained even his vampiric vision, yet as he squinted into the gloom, he thought he perceived a small pink shape clutched to the bosom of a squatting female werewolf. The infant's high-pitched squeal continued to echo through the subterranean recesses of the dungeon. The cries agitated the other werewolves, who barked and howled incessantly, raising an infernal racket that chafed at the Elder's patience.

"Open it," Viktor demanded.

The jailor hesitated. He seemed more afraid of his bestial charges than Viktor thought suitable. "Milord?"

"Open it, I say!" He snatched the crossbow from the jailor's trembling grip, barely resisting the urge to cuff the fool. The weapon fit comfortably within his hands, reminding Viktor of many a glorious battle. "And be quick about it!"

"Yes, milord!"

Depositing his torch into a nearby sconce, the jailor hurried to carry out the Elder's command. He grunted with exertion as he drew back a tarnished silver-plated bolt. Rusty hinges that sounded as though they had not been employed in months screeched loudly as the barred gate swung open. Chains clanked inside the cell as the she-wolf lurched up from the floor. A warning growl escaped her throat. Her hackles rose. Glistening black lips drew back, baring her fangs. She crouched above the bawling infant . . . like a mother defending her young?

Viktor could think of no other way to account for the baby's presence in the cell. Yet that defied all reason; werewolves bred, certainly, but they gave birth only to primitive animals such as themselves. No she-wolf had ever whelped a human child.

Until now.

Raising the crossbow, he stepped warily into the cell. "Take care, milord!" the jailor cautioned, remaining safely outside in the corridor. The bitch barked furiously and tugged at her chain. If not for the riveted metal collar clamped around her neck, she would have gladly ripped him to shreds. Her cobalt eyes blazed with murderous fury.

Viktor took the she-wolf's show of aggression very seriously. He knew full well how dangerous a wild animal could be when guarding its young. Should his lady wife ever bear him a child, he intended to defend his own heir no less zealously.

He took aim with the crossbow and squeezed the trigger. A silver-tipped bolt flew from the weapon, striking the werewolf directly between the eyes. She yelped in pain as the force of the shot knocked her backward against the far wall of the cell. Her mangy bulk collapsed against the straw-covered floor. She spasmed once before falling still and silent. Blood streamed from her sloping brow. Smoke rose from the silver arrowhead buried in her skull. The smell of burning hair and flesh added to the noxious atmosphere of the cell.

The baby cried out in fear and longing.

Was the beast truly dead? Viktor waited a moment or two, just in case the fallen creature was feigning death, until he saw her thick black pelt begin to recede into her mottled hide. The prone body of the werewolf contracted as much of her size and weight evaporated into the ether. The creature's grotesque exterior melted away until only the naked body of a dead peasant woman remained, sprawled lifelessly amidst a spreading pool of blood.

Viktor wasted not a moment mourning the she-wolf's death. Slaughtering her kind had been his life's work for centuries now. It was the infant that interested him. Lowering the crossbow, he crept farther into the cell, drawing near to the orphaned baby upon the floor. His probing azure eyes confirmed the staggering truth:

A baby boy, completely human in appearance, wailed piteously at his feet.

How can this be? Viktor marveled. He assumed that the bitch had been pregnant when captured, but that hardly explained why she had given birth to such a normal-looking infant. The child's plump pink skin had been licked clean by its mother's tongue. His toothless mouth shrieked to the heavens. He shook his tiny fists at the pensive vampire standing above him.

Viktor wondered what manner of beast had sired the child upon the she-wolf. Alas, the identity of the father had died with the mother, not that the mindless creature could have ever communicated that knowledge, even if Viktor had spared her life. The circumstances of the baby's conception were destined to remain a mystery forever.

What mattered now was deciding what was to be done with the unnatural child. Viktor raised the crossbow once more. Every fiber of his being urged him to slay the infant immediately, before its very existence overturned the immutable laws by which their twilight world was governed. Who knew what dire consequence might result from the birth of this seeming abomination? Best to dispatch the child now, the same way he had disposed of his mother.

He loaded another bolt into the crossbow and took aim at the baby's head. His finger tightened on the trigger.

And yet . . . the baby's birth was a miracle of sorts, albeit of a dark and disturbing variety. And perhaps a miracle should not be taken lightly? Curiosity as to the child's true nature and potential arose in Viktor's mind. Perhaps there was an opportunity here, as well as risks? Why rush to judgment?

I can always put the whelp to death later on if need be. . . .

For now, however, he chose to stay his hand. Putting the crossbow aside, he knelt and lifted the naked infant from the straw. The squirming newborn felt small and fragile within his arms. Innocent brown eyes peered up into Viktor's own. A small pink fist gripped the Elder's chin with surprising strength.

He prayed that he was not making a dreadful mistake.

Fifteen years later

Castle Corvinus was carved into the very face of a craggy black peak rising high above the surrounding forests and countryside. Its forbidding turrets and battlements stabbed upward at the starry night sky. The light of myriad torches and lamps shone through the fortress's lancet windows, making the isolated mountain stronghold appear to glow from within. Crimson pennants, the color of freshly spilled blood, streamed atop the watchtowers. Sculpted grotesques, in the shape of writhing plague victims, perched upon the eaves and ramparts. Flanking towers abutted the sturdy guardhouse defending the front gate. Armored

Death Dealers patrolled the tops of the high gray walls, which were more than ten feet thick in places. Rectangular stone merlons jutted up from the parapet like a bottom row of teeth. Flying buttresses reinforced the walls. Massive siege crossbows the size of catapults were mounted upon the outer palisade. Steel harpoons more than ten feet long were loaded into the formidable weapons, which were also known as ballistas. Steel winches were required to draw back the bow arms.

A slender youth, no more than fifteen years old, stood poised upon a parapet overlooking the drawbridge below. Dark brown hair fell past his shoulders. Coarse woolen clothing testified to his lowly status in the castle's hierarchy. His dirty brown tunic and breeches were torn and frayed. Piercing brown eyes peered out from a handsome face that had yet to require the touch of a razor. A brisk autumn wind rustled his unkempt locks. He gazed past the rampart at the precipitous thirty-foot drop before him.

Don't look down, Lucian thought.

Despite his sage advice to himself, the young servant could not resist peering down from his elevated perch atop the castle's outer walls. The drawbridge below looked impossibly far away. Any mortal man who attempted to leap from this height would be smashed to pieces for certain.

Thankfully, Lucian was no mere mortal.

I can do this, he thought. *Lord Viktor expects me to.*

He took a deep breath to steady his nerves, closed his eyes, and stepped off the parapet. Gravity seized him and he plummeted downward at breathtaking speed. The night air rushed past him, roaring in his ears. His eyes snapped open in time to see the hard wooden floor of the drawbridge appear to surge up at him like a battering ram. His brief, inconsequential life raced before his eyes as he feared that he had fallen victim to some cruel joke on the part of his undead masters. Would it amuse Viktor and the others to see his brains splattered across the mountainside?

Perhaps.

It's not fair! he despaired, only heartbeats before hitting the ground. *I haven't even begun to live yet!*

He braced himself for death, only to land nimbly upon the drawbridge in one piece. The impact didn't even knock the breath from his body, let alone kill him. He glanced down at his intact flesh and blood in astonishment. He gasped in relief.

I did it! he rejoiced. *Just like Viktor promised!*

His jubilation was cut short, however, when three beefy ruffians emerged from the shadow of the castle's high front gate. Lucian recognized the men as mortal laborers employed in the ongoing expansion of the fortress's dungeons. Their unwashed hides had been baked brown by the sun, compared to the paler complexions of the castle's more nocturnal inhabitants. Dried mortar splattered their filthy garments. Iron bludgeons in hand, they charged at the unarmed youth. Angry shouts and florid red faces made clear their hostile intentions. Their breaths reeked of strong spirits.

Lucian had no idea what he had done to incur the men's wrath, but he did not intend to be beaten senseless by the likes of these. They were just mortals, after all, and mere commoners to boot, not vampires whose harsh discipline he might be expected to submit to without resistance. Although he was nothing more than a serf himself, Lucian owed no deference to these drunken louts. A growl escaped his lips as he dropped into a defensive crouch. His brown eyes turned cobalt blue.

The men spread out around him, clearly intending to assault him from all sides. The first man—a bald-headed lummox with a neck like an ox—came at Lucian from the front. He swung his club at the youth, who ducked beneath the blow and butted his head into the human's chest hard enough to crack the man's ribs. Gasping in pain, the man staggered backward. His club flew from his fingers and Lucian effortlessly snatched it from the air. He smacked it against the man's skull, dropping him to the ground, even as he heard the second man—a sallow-faced brute with bad teeth—lumbering up behind him.

A backward kick sent Bad Teeth flying off the drawbridge. A startled yelp ended abruptly as he crashed down into the rocky slopes below, which were studded with jagged boulders. A high-pitched shriek gave way to agonized groans as the man was impaled upon a granite outcropping. He would have been better off breaking his neck instead.

Two down, one to go, Lucian thought. He spun around to confront the third man, who had attempted to way-lay Lucian from the right. A one-eyed stonemason who wore a leather patch over the empty socket, this one appeared both larger and cagier than his more impetuous cohorts. Swollen veins bulged atop his meaty thews. A mermaid tattoo suggested that he had once gone to sea. Daunted by the preternatural speed with which Lucian had dispatched his fellows, the cyclops took his time attacking. "Demon!" he hissed at the boy as they circled each other warily. "I'll send you back to hell where you belong!"

Lucian growled in response. He bared his teeth.

The stonemason's face blanched, and, for a second, Lucian thought he might turn tail. The man crossed himself fearfully but did not back down. Mustering his courage, he let out a ferocious whoop and raced at Lucian with his club held high. His boots pounded against the wooden planks of the drawbridge, but, compared to the boy's inhuman reflexes, he might as well have been slogging through heavy mud. Grinning wolfishly, Lucian sprang from the ground and leapt over the mortal's head, landing nimbly behind his foe. He spun around quickly, before the startled cyclops even realized what had happened, and kicked the man's legs out from under him. The man fell forward onto his knees. His club slipped from his fingers and rolled away from him. He frantically scrambled for his weapon, but it was already too late. Clasping his hands together, Lucian clubbed the man across the back of his head with both fists. Bone cracked and the stonemason collapsed face-first onto the hard wooden planks. Blood and brains spilled across the drawbridge.

So much for those ruffians!

In a matter of moments, the melee was over. Lucian stood triumphantly over the fallen bodies of his assailants. He wasn't even breathing hard.

Before he could fully savor his victory, however, the boy's keen ears alerted him to another threat. Something came whistling through the sky behind him and he whirled around just in time to pluck a speeding crossbow bolt from the air, only inches from his face. The silver glare of the arrowhead hurt his eyes, so he tossed the offending missile away. It rattled harmlessly onto the floor of the drawbridge.

A smattering of light applause came from the castle. Lucian looked up proudly to see Viktor and a small group of vampire courtiers and ladies gazing down at him from the grand balcony upon the central keep. The aristocratic vampires were clad in all their finery, wearing elegant gowns and robes of the darkest silk and velvet. Legend had it that the bite of a bat had transformed Marcus into a vampire; the flowing black raiment of his kind draped over their slender forms like folded wings. Viktor lowered the crossbow. He nodded in approval, plainly pleased by Lucian's prowess.

Of course, Lucian thought, as the reason for the mortals' unwarranted attack upon him became clear. *It was another of Viktor's tests.*

The regal Elder had taken much interest in the young man over the years, despite (or perhaps because of) his bestial origins. Lucian sometime wondered why so powerful a monarch concerned himself with the bastard child of a dead werewolf, but he was grateful for the Elder's patronage—and for the fact that he had not been put to death at birth. He knew that many in the castle wished otherwise; they made little effort to disguise their contempt and suspicion when they passed him in the drafty corridors of the ancient fortress. Nor could he blame them for their disdain. Despite his best efforts to prove that he was not an unreasoning animal like his savage forebears, the taint of the wolf still flowed through his veins. . . .

"What do you think, Sonja?" Viktor's voice carried from the balcony as he addressed his small daughter, who stood beside him behind the railing. The girl's birth, eight winters ago, had been a time of both celebration and mourning. Her mother, the Lady Ilona, had perished giving birth to Viktor's only child. "Shall we make more?"

"Of him?" The little girl was spellbound by the handsome youth below. Curly brown locks framed the child's angelic features. A black satin kirtle clothed her diminutive form. A crest-shaped pendant, centered around a polished turquoise gemstone, dangled on a chain around her neck. Wide chestnut eyes peered down at Lucian.

"*Like* him," Viktor clarified. "Lucian will be the first of a new breed. The first of the lycans."

Sonja nodded absently, seemingly more interested in the boy himself than her father's machinations. "Lucian," she repeated, trying the name out in her mouth. "Lucian . . ."

Pure-born vampire children were rare in the castle. Lucian wondered what she would be like when she grew up.

Lucian crouched nervously in his humble den in the castle's sprawling dungeons. A straw pallet rested in the corner of the cell, but there would no rest for him tonight. Viktor had other plans for him, plans that filled the boy's heart with trepidation. His stomach rumbled unhappily; upon the Elder's orders, he had not been fed for hours. His eyes were fixed on a narrow window cut high in the moldy stone wall before him. Naked, he waited apprehensively for what was to come. A capital V for *Viktor* was branded on his bare right arm.

He felt the full moon rising outside even before the first silvery beams invaded his lair. His brown eyes dilated, shrinking down to tiny black pinpricks. Blood pounded in his ears, like a tide crashing against the shore. His heart stampeded wildly beneath his hairless chest. Teeth and nails tugged at their roots. His skin felt hot and feverish. A sudden sweat drenched his body.

No, he thought, just as he did every month when the moon waxed full. *Not again!*

He wanted to shrink away from the moonlight, yet that would have been contrary to Viktor's expressed wishes. Iron bars trapped him inside the cell, making retreat impossible. There was no escape from the rising moon—or the beast it awoke inside him.

His face contorted into a hellish mask of pain as his innards twisted within his gut. Bulging veins throbbed beneath his skin. His eyes glazed over into inhuman cobalt orbs. Jagged fangs clenched tightly to keep from screaming. Convulsing, he collapsed onto the straw-covered floor and rolled into the pitch blackness at the rear of the cell, as far from the open window as he could get. He huddled upon the floor in torment, praying for deliverance.

Why must I be so cursed? I never asked for this!

But despite his prayers, the moonlight found him

19

out. A beam of cold white light slashed his arm and the slender limb turned dark and sinewy. His splayed fingers degenerated into claws. His bare skin thickened, becoming coarse and leathery. Muscles rippled across his back as his youthful frame seemed to absorb weight and substance from the moonlight, growing larger and more imposing. Bristling black fur erupted from beneath his febrile hide. Dark hair spread over his body, hiding his nakedness beneath a thick sable pelt. Bony talons scraped at the damp stones beneath the straw. His vision blurred, the color fading from his sight as the dungeon around him dissolved into fuzzy shades of gray. Tufted ears twitched atop his skull. His nostrils quivered, suddenly alive to myriad new smells. He choked on the overwhelming stench of dungeons, even as he bit back the howl forming at the back of his throat.

No! He fought against the almost irresistible urge to give voice to the beast. A canine snout stretched out his face. His clamped his protruding jaws together. *I'm not an animal! Not inside!*

But on the outside, it was a different story. The wrenching pain passed away as the hellish transformation reached its end. Little trace of the gawky youth remained; instead a great black werewolf arose from the filthy straw, standing erect on his hind legs. Moonlight bathed the enormous monster Lucian had become. He stared in revulsion at his own misshapen paws.

This isn't me, he tried to convince himself. *Not truly.*

Ordinarily, the worst of Lucian's ordeal would be over now. In the past, Viktor had simply kept him securely locked up on the nights of the full moon. But tonight would be different. Lucian found himself torn between apprehension and a strange, shameful excitement that he was scarcely willing to acknowledge, even to himself. His ears perked up at the sound of multiple footsteps plodding toward his cell. He licked his chops in nervous anticipation as his glowing cobalt eyes peered through the bars of the cage. Drool dripped from his jaws.

Within minutes, a dismal procession came into view. Flickering torchlight revealed a row of human serfs being prodded toward the cell by armored Death Dealers. Iron shackles bound their hands and feet. Filthy rags barely covered their undernourished bodies, many of which bore the marks of the vampires' whips. Lice infested their unkempt hair and beards. Heads bowed meekly, more than a dozen men and boys were herded like cattle through the fetid bowels of the dungeon. Their bare feet trudged wearily over the uneven stones. Captured in war, or sold into bondage by their feudal lords, they had no idea of what lay in store for them . . . until they glimpsed the fearsome werewolf waiting hungrily in his cage.

Screams erupted from the prisoners, threatening to unleash pandemonium. Lashes cracked against mortal skin, flaying flesh from bone, as the vampires brutally restored order and continued to press the unfortunate mortals toward Lucian. The helpless serfs whimpered and begged for mercy, but their frantic pleas fell upon deaf ears. Tears streamed from their eyes, and sobbing fathers clutched their children, as the lead Death

21

Dealer unlocked Lucian's cage. The barred door swung open.

Lucian was tempted to make a break for it, to take advantage of his wolfen strength and speed to flee what was to come, but he knew that the Death Dealers would strike him down if he made the slightest move to exit his cell. Or was that just an excuse to remain where he was? As much as he hated to admit it, part of him didn't want to go anywhere, not now. The smell of fresh human meat tantalized his nostrils. His mouth watered at the sight of the savory mortals.

The captain of the Death Dealers, a dark-haired vampire named Sandor, laughed harshly. "Feeding time, cur!"

A loutish peasant was yanked from the procession and shoved into Lucian's cage. Shrieking hysterically, the man fought his captors every inch of the way, but his mortal thews were no match for the superior strength of the Death Dealers, who chuckled as they cast him to his fate. The trembling serf found himself trapped between the merciless vampires behind him and the horrifying werewolf looming before him. Convinced that his end was upon him, he prayed fervently to the saints while wringing his hands in despair. He squeezed his eyes shut, not wanting to look upon his doom. His scarred body shook like a leaf. He lost control of his bladder. His bowels emptied.

"Mother of God, have mercy upon my poor soul. . . ."

The man's manifest terror stirred Lucian to pity, but it was not in his power to spare the stranger this ordeal.

Viktor held the reins of all their destinies and what the Elder had ordained must now come to pass. Lucian wished he could offer the anguished serf some words of comfort, yet his hideous new shape denied him the luxury of human speech. The growl that issued from his muzzle did nothing but make the condemned prisoner shudder even harder. The only merciful thing, Lucian realized, was to be quick about it. . . .

He lunged forward and sank his fangs into the peasant's shoulder. Blood gushed from the werewolf's jaws. The prisoner screamed in agony. The intoxicating flavor of the bloody meat filled Lucian's mouth as he tasted human flesh for the first time. His heart pounded in exultation. His mind reeled.

It took all his self-control not to tear the man to pieces. . . .

Viktor observed the grisly spectacle as, one by one, the shackled prisoners were led forward to receive the werewolf's bite. He gazed down at the proceedings through a metal grate covering the top of Lucian's cage. Death Dealers dragged the wounded slaves away from the werewolf once they were bitten. Metal collars, of singular design, were clamped around the victims' necks. Silver spikes, each more than an inch long, jutted from the inner lining of the collars, so that the tips of the spikes almost pricked the prisoners' skin. Writhing in pain, the bleeding men and women barely noticed the "moon shackles" being affixed to their throats. An intricate locking mechanism ensured that they would wear the collars for the rest of their lives. Branding irons marked their arms with an ornate capital *V.* The smell of seared flesh wafted upward.

Excellent, Viktor thought. *All is going just as I decreed.*

He was pleased to see that, thus far, Lucian had resisted the temptation to devour the hapless mortals whole. The orphan's discipline and willingness to follow orders boded well for the future of this entire enterprise. Viktor could only hope that his spawn would prove equally docile.

"Behold," the Elder said smugly. "The birth of a new race of immortals. Werewolf, but also human." No doubt many of the bitten serfs would die from the infection, but Viktor trusted that enough of them would survive the transformation to suit his purposes; if not, he would simply have to throw more humans between Lucian's gaping maw. "Unlike William's kind, this new breed can be harnessed to guard us during the daylight hours."

It had long been a source of concern to Viktor and the other Elders that the fortress was vulnerable by day, as not even the fiercest Death Dealer could withstand the burning rays of the sun. What if their mortal vassals rose up in insurrection, or a hostile pack of werewolves ventured forth after dawn? The castle's remote location and high stone walls provided a degree of security against such incursions, but he had always feared that these defenses were not sufficient. Viktor had been a veteran military commander even before Marcus made him immortal, and he knew full well that no fortress was truly impregnable. Indeed, he had razed more than few castles himself.

"Or so we hope, milord," his companion added cautiously. Andreas Tanis, the coven's chief scribe and historian, stood beside Viktor upon the grille. He was a slight man, with the deceptive look of a mortal in his mid-thirties. His mousy brown hair was slicked back to expose a high forehead. A slightly florid tinge to his face hinted at an overindulgence in mortal blood. His black brocaded doublet and satin hose were of lesser quality than Viktor's own regal attire, but the rich fabrics and fine tailoring befitted his elevated status in the coven. No warrior, he was a vampire of scholarly inclinations and distinctly hedonistic vices. Still, Viktor valued his keen mind and loyalty—to a point.

"You doubt me?" he said crossly, annoyed at the scribe's apparent lack of enthusiasm. A scowl crossed his face. "You question my judgment in this matter?"

"Not at all, Lord Viktor." The chastened scribe hastened to mollify his liege. "I trust your profound wisdom implicitly." Backing away from the Elder, he nodded at the gruesome transactions taking place below them. He raised his voice to be heard over the screams of the future lycans. "I'm just not certain that I entirely trust *them*."

Chapter Two

Two hundred years later . . .

*T*he horsewoman raced through the dark, primeval forest. The hooves of her ebony steed pounded against a muddy dirt road as she urged it onward. Skeletal trees, their jagged branches denuded by winter's chill, snatched at her flapping black cloak. Moonlight filtered through the dense arboreal canopy overhead. Swirling mist blanketed the ground. Inky shadows filled the gaps between the encroaching trees and underbrush. The trail winded through a maze of naked oaks and beeches. Grayish lichen clung to the mottled bark.

Sonja's eyes searched the sylvan shadows, fearful of what they might hide. Polished black armor, hand-crafted to fit her svelte figure, gleamed in the moonlight. Intricate runes and rosettes were embossed upon her ebony cuirass and gorget, which she wore over a chain mail gusset, skirt, and leggings. Forged metal plates guarded her shoulders and knees. A menacing steel helmet concealed her features. A matching shaffron and crinet shielded her horse's head and neck. Steam jetted from the steed's flaring nostrils. Lather dripped from its sides.

"Easy, Hecate," Sonja whispered to her mount. She drew back on the reins and the horse skidded to a halt. Trees lined like the narrow road like the columns of some forgotten temple. The crisp night air smelled of damp wood and loam. Every sense alert to danger, she looked about her in all directions. She listened tensely to the nocturnal murmurs of the forest. Unseen animals rustled through the bush and bracken. An owl hooted in the branches above her. Bats flapped in the darkness. A cold wind shuffled the fallen leaves hidden beneath the fog. Sonja held her breath, every muscle in her lithe body primed for action. Her tongue traced the smooth contours of her fangs.

No obvious threat presented itself, and yet . . .

A savage howl tore through the night, sending a thrill of terror down her spine. Glancing back over her shoulder, she glimpsed large dark shapes skittering through the canopy behind her, bounding from tree to tree. Flocks of crows, abruptly roused from slumber, flapped noisily as they took to the sky in panic. Hecate reared up onto her hind legs, almost throwing Sonja from the saddle. The horse's eyes rolled wildly. It whinnied in fright.

Hellfire! Sonja cursed herself for her recklessness as she struggled to bring the agitated mount under control. Her father had often warned her against riding alone at night, yet the desire to escape the claustrophobic confines of the castle, as well as the stifling proprieties and expectations that came with being an Elder's daughter, had driven her to ignore his advice on more than one occasion. Tonight, it seemed, she had tempted fate once too often. *I'll not hear the end of this . . . should I be lucky enough to survive.*

Drawing her sword from its scabbard, she dug her spurs into Hecate's flanks. The horse sprung forward without hesitation, no doubt as eager to flee as Sonja was. She held on tightly to the reins with one hand as they galloped swiftly through the foggy woods. The silver-plated blade caught the moonlight. Silver stars glinted upon its ornately crafted hilt. Greedy branches grabbed at Sonja, making her grateful for the helm protecting her face. She ducked beneath an overhanging branch only seconds before it took her head off. A fallen log blocked their path, but Hecate vaulted over the obstacle with ease. Sonja's heart pounded beneath her burnished steel breastplate. Cold vampiric blood raced through her veins.

A chorus of blood-chilling howls erupted behind her as an entire pack of werewolves dropped from the trees and bounded after her on all fours. Fierce growls echoed through the lonely wilderness. Glancing back again, Sonja was alarmed to see the wolves gaining on her. They tore up the trail at such frightening speed that she doubted that her exhausted steed could long outpace them. Tearing her eyes away from her rabid pursuers, she peered desperately through the fog before her, hoping to catch sight of sanctuary.

If she could just make it back to the castle!

They burst from the woods into a rocky canyon. Gravel was heaped at the bottom of steep granite banks that rose sharply from both sides of the road. Sonja braced herself for an ambush, which came upon her almost at once. A snarling werewolf lunged at her from the right, its dagger-sized fangs and claws extended toward her throat. Foam sprayed from the monster's lips. Its cobalt eyes blazed with carnivorous fury.

Not so fast! she thought defiantly. Her own eyes shifted from brown to azure. She slashed out at the beast with her sword, the silver blade cutting a bloody gash across the werewolf's chest. Roaring in pain, it somersaulted backward, landing hard upon the floor of the canyon. Sonja smiled grimly behind her helmet, but there was little time to savor her victory as a second werewolf leapt at her from the left.

The creature's powerful forequarters slammed into Hecate's side, knocking both horse and rider into the canyon wall. The impact jarred Sonja to her bone and threw Hecate off her stride, but, to her vast relief, the horse recovered from its stumble and kept on running, even as the determined werewolf climbed up its side toward Sonja. Its frothing jaws snapped at her back— until she buried her steel-shod elbow into the beast's mouth, breaking several of its teeth. The move bought her a precious moment, which was all she needed to flip her sword into a backhanded grip. She drove the blade through the wolf's skull with all her strength, then yanked it back out again. The slain beast tumbled to the ground, throwing up a plume of pulverized dust and rock. Hot blood streamed from the claw marks upon Hecate's flanks.

Sonja didn't look back. Instead she squinted through the fog to see yet another werewolf racing to intercept her. The monster was several yards away from her but closing fast. It seemed to grow before her eyes as it charged at her like a shaggy black thunderbolt. Sonja realized she had to move fast if she wanted to avoid another battle at close quarters. Despite her thick metal gauntlets, her nimble fingers found a concealed latch on the guard of her sword. She released the latch, freeing the two shining silver stars cradled in the hilt. Steel points radiated from the miniature pentagrams.

In a practiced motion, she swung the sword at the oncoming werewolf. The stars spun along the edge of the blade before flying past the sword point as though propelled by a slingshot. They whistled through the air to strike the werewolf in its head and shoulders. Their keen edges, which had been honed to razor sharpness, sank deep into the monster's hide and the beast yelped in agony. Acrid white fumes rose where the toxic silver burned the wolf's flesh. It crashed to the ground directly in the path of the speeding horse.

Thank you, Tanis, Sonja thought. Although she had little respect for the sniveling scribe, whom she regarded as both a toady and a lecher, she had to concede that his ingenuity had it uses. The built-in throwing stars had been his idea.

Proving her valor, Hecate vaulted over the convulsing werewolf, who clutched frantically at the poisonous missiles with its clumsy paws. Sonja left the writing monster in the dust as the horse's hooves thundered against the ground. The opaque fog swallowed up the downed creature.

But not, alas, the rest of the pack, who were in no way ready to abandon the hunt. . . .

The shadowy crypt was the slowly beating heart of the coven. The cavernous stone mausoleum was built into one side of the castle, buried halfway beneath the ground. Granite ribs supported the high domed ceiling. Flickering torches sputtered in their sconces. Green stained-glass windows occupied recessed niches in the upper tiers of the walls. Granite steps led down to the sunken lower level, where three burnished bronze disks were embedded in the marble floor. A concentric pattern of overlapping Celtic runes surrounded the circular hatches, each of which was engraved with a single letter: *A* for *Amelia*, *M* for *Marcus*, and *V* for *Viktor*.

Viktor wondered what his fellow Elders were dreaming of as they took their turns hibernating beneath the earth. Hallowed tradition dictated that only one Elder ruled over the coven each century, the better to avoid the internecine power struggles that had threatened to tear them apart in the early history of the vampire kind. At times Viktor envied Marcus and Amelia as they slumbered peacefully in their respective sarcophagi, cut off from the petty annoyances that plagued him these days. He often visited the crypt to be alone with his thoughts.

But sometime his troubles found him anyway.

"The nobles are upset, milord," Coloman insisted. A

member of the high council, the undead boyar had intruded upon the Elder's meditations with yet another dreary litany of grievances. The man's lean face bore a habitually disapproving expression. His dark brown hair was gray at the temples. He wore a crisp black leather doublet over a high-necked black satin robe. Bronze medallions reflected his rank. "Although William himself is locked away for all eternity, his pestilence has not been checked. Marauding packs of werewolves have killed our vassals' slaves. . . ."

"Humans upset," Viktor said archly. Smirking, he placed a hand over his heart. "Tanis, please take note of the pain that brings me."

The scribe dutifully scribbled the Elder's remark onto a piece of parchment. He stood attentively at Viktor's side, the better to preserve his master's thoughts for eternity. So ubiquitous was the scholarly vampire that Viktor often forgot he was there.

Coloman ignored Viktor's sarcastic tone. "Perhaps, milord. Yet their lost slaves mean our lost silver."

"Enough!" Viktor barked. The man's effrontery bordered on insolence. One of Marcus's favorites, Coloman had long been a thorn in Viktor's side. He would have banished the man centuries ago had Coloman not enjoyed the other Elder's protection. "Have I not increased our holdings tenfold since Marcus and Amelia took their sleep?" He sat down upon an imposing stone throne overlooking the crypt. "We will deal with the wolves as we always have."

But his confident assertion was belied by a sudden howl that penetrated even the gloomy recesses of the crypt. Viktor and his minions looked up in alarm. A warning horn sounded from the ramparts many stories above them. A second howl, even louder than the first, added to the clamor.

The baying seemed to come from right outside the castle walls.

Sparks flew from the anvil as Lucian hammered out the dents in a damaged iron breastplate. The white-hot metal, which he had heated to incandescence in the nearby forge, was molded by his skillful blows. A pair of long metal tongs held the molten armor in place. Bell-like tones pealed whenever the hammer tapped the thin steel plate welded to the face of a large wrought-iron anvil, which sat atop the stump of a hewn elm tree. Lucian held the metal firmly against the anvil's horn in order to curve it just so. Singed leather hides enclosed his smithy, the better to shield the rest of the castle from the sparks thrown off by his work. A large barrel of brine waited to cool and temper the metal once he was through pounding it back into shape. Horseshoes were draped over the rim of the tub. The smell of burning charcoal rose from the glowing forge. Pokers, rakes, shears, and other tools were scattered haphazardly about the shop. Droplets of molten slag cooled upon the rough stone floor. Racks of swords, pikes, halberds, and battle-axes lined the walls. Smoke from the forge escaped through a gap in the smithy's cracked stone roof. A thin layer of soot and ash covered both shop and blacksmith alike.

He paused to wipe the perspiration from his brow. No longer a youth, Lucian had grown into a strapping adult whose sooty face now sported a scruffy mustache and beard. Disorderly brown hair fell past his shoulders. A leather vest bared his muscular chest and arms. Sweat glistened upon his sinewy thews, which had been strengthened by years of toil as a blacksmith. A moon shackle fit uncomfortably around his neck, but he had worn the collar for so long that he barely noticed the vicious silver barbs pricking his throat. Viktor's brand remained seared onto his right biceps. Leather trousers protected his lower body from sparks and slag. A crude copper knife was tucked into his belt.

A tankard of lukewarm water slaked his thirst before he turned back to his labors. The work of a blacksmith was never done. Just keeping Viktor and his Death Dealers armed and armored was a never-ending task in its own right; add to that the necessity of maintaining the castle's stock of horseshoes, hinges, barrel hoops, stirrups, nails, thimbles, and the like and there were scarcely enough hours in the day to keep up with his work. Still, he couldn't complain. As a skilled artisan, he enjoyed more freedom than any other lycan servant, most of whom were confined to guard duty or back-breaking manual labor. Given his barbaric origins, he was fortunate to have climbed so high.

Not that Viktor can't revoke my privileges at the slightest whim. . . .

The heated metal was already cooling from white to sunrise red. It was still workable, but he needed to get back to work before it became too brittle to shape. Before he could hammer another blow, however, the unmistakable howl of a werewolf invaded his smithy. Despite himself, the call of the wild stirred something deep and primal within him. Moments later, the clarion call of a blast horn competed with the baying of the wolves. Shouted exclamations and curses sounded from the courtyard outside the smithy. Racing footsteps pounded on weathered brick paving-stones.

Lucian froze in place, momentarily riveted by the howls and commotion. Was the castle truly under attack? This was not the first time in recent memory that werewolves had come within sight of the fortress's walls, yet it struck Lucian as extremely unlikely that they actually intended to brave the castle's defenses; no mere wolf pack, no matter how ferocious, could mount a coordinated assault on so formidable a stronghold. They were nothing but unreasoning animals, after all, who preferred to prey on peasant villages and stray travelers instead. Surely, they posed no threat to anyone safely inside the castle's walls?

Then he remembered who was riding abroad this night.

Lady Sonja!

His hammer and tongs clattered to the pavement as he tossed them aside. Moving quickly, he snatched a freshly repaired crossbow from the racks. The cunning weapon boasted three separate bow arms, stacked atop each other, so that it could fire thrice without reloading. He hastily loaded three bolts into the grooves and raced out of the covered smithy into the courtyard beyond.

The inner bailey lay between the outer walls and the looming keep, which had been carved from the very face of the mountain, with many ledges, balconies, and levels hewn from solid granite and limestone. To lessen the risk of a catastrophic fire, Lucian's smithy abutted the eastern wall of the castle, safely distant from the keep and stables. A nearby well offered him ready access to fresh water. Pigs squealed loudly in their pens. Glancing quickly at the gatehouse, Lucian saw that the huge oak doors defending the gate were securely closed and bolted. Torches flared atop the watchtowers.

Scores of Death Dealers rushed to the castle's defense, while courtiers, craftsmen, grooms, laundresses, and scullions retreated to the safety of the keep. Shouts and screams added to the chaos. A vampire lady-in-waiting sought reassurance from a rushing Death Dealer, who impatiently brushed her aside. Lycan slaves cowered in the corners of the courtyard, lest they attract the vindictive attention of the intemperate Death Dealers; two hundred years of bondage had not freed the castle's lycan servitors from guilty associations with their more savage brethren. More soldiers poured from the gatehouse atop the outer wall of the fortress. Caught unawares by the emergency, many of them scrambled to don their armor and helmets as they took their positions upon the palisade. Frantic chickens flapped and clucked underfoot. A clamor arose from the stables as agitated horses whinnied and stomped their hooves. Captain Sandor barked commands at his troops.

Frustrated by the disorder blocking his path, Lucian sprang over the heads of startled knights and civilians. Lycan strength and agility propelled him from ledge to ledge as he traversed the crowded courtyard in a matter of moments. A single bound carried him from the floor of the bailey to the roof of the dovecote. A final leap catapulted him onto the ramparts overlooking the rocky plain at the base of the mountain. Unnoticed amidst the tumult, he slid into place at an archer's port between two dense stone merlons. All around him, zealous Death Dealers manned the massive ballistas deployed atop the battlements. Each siege bow required two soldiers to operate and was mounted upon a swiveling base that could be rotated in any direction. Bolts the size of lances waited to be launched at an enemy to devastating effect. Large mechanical windlasses were employed to draw back the taut cables attached to the bow arms. In times of war, the ballistas could impale dozens of attacking soldiers at once, or perhaps bring down a catapult or siege tower. They'd killed more than a few werewolves, as well.

Lucian hefted his own crossbow. Although only a fraction of the size of the enormous siege weapons, it might suffice if his aim was true. He held his breath as his keen senses probed the fog-shrouded darkness stretching before him. Was that the thunder of hooves he heard in the distance, above the cacophonous baying of the wolves? He prayed that the racing steed still bore its illustrious rider toward safety. Fighting an urge to leap from the parapet to see for himself, he focused intently on the sound of the oncoming hooves. His finger tightened on the trigger of the crossbow.

Where are you, milady?

An endless moment later, his patience was rewarded by the sight of a solitary horsewoman galloping out of the mist. A gasp of relief escaped his lips as he saw that she seemed to be in one piece, at least for the moment. Her steed was obviously straining, though. Lather soaked its quivering flanks and he could hear the horse's labored breathing even from half a mile away. Steam jetted from the charger's nostrils. Lucian had shod Hecate himself and he could only hope that the panting horse would not throw a shoe before it reached the castle's looming gates.

If it even got that far. Horrified cries came from the knights upon the walls as three snarling werewolves burst from the fog in pursuit of the horsewoman and her faltering steed. Bounding across the plain, their blazing eyes burning through the fog, the hungry beasts quickly ate up the distance separating them from their intended prey. It was obvious to all who watched that they would surely bring down the fleeing rider at any moment. Sonja brandished a crimson sword above her head, suggesting that she had already drawn blood from her voracious foes, but could she stand alone against the entire pack?

Lucian doubted it.

Careful, he cautioned himself as he took aim with the crossbow. The rear of the stock pressed against his cheek. He squinted down the length of the weapon as he tried to catch a wolf in his sights. The last thing he wanted to do was hit Sonja by mistake; Viktor would not be amused if someone slew his daughter while trying to save her. There was little room for error here. . . .

He clicked the trigger twice and the top two bolts shot from the crossbow. The missiles whistled past

Sonja, barely missing her head, to strike the first two werewolves in the throats even as they sprang at the imperiled noblewoman. They tumbled head over heels across the rocky soil while Sonja raced her gasping steed up the steep path leading to the castle's front gate.

She was almost there, but there was still one more werewolf hot on her heels.

"The gates!" an imperious voice cried out. Lucian glanced behind him to see Viktor standing upon a balcony overlooking the castle's walls. Tanis, his ubiquitous scribe, lurked behind him, clinging to the shelter of a carved stone archway. The Elder's voice held equal quantities of fear and anger. "Open the gates, you fools!"

Lucian silently cursed the idiots who had not yet hastened to clear the way for Sonja. Had they been willing to risk the Elder's only heir just to keep the doors barred against the werewolves without? Chains clanked loudly as the drawbridge began to be hastily lowered into place. Creaking gears inside the gatehouse turned to raise the iron-studded portcullis guarding the gate. Tardy Death Dealers rushed to draw back the large steel bolt securing the final pair of heavy oaken portals. Mist infiltrated the courtyard as a narrow crack opened between the ponderous doors.

Finally! Lucian thought.

But could Sonja make it to the gateway before the final werewolf ripped her to shreds?

Lucian strained to get the remaining beast in his sights, but the crafty wolf zigzagged back and forth behind Hecate, making a clean shot difficult. Lucian's mouth went dry as he waited anxiously for his shot. He had only one bolt left. If he missed, there would no time to reload. And if he hit Sonja or her horse by accident . . .

He didn't even want to think about that.

Light spilled from the open gate onto the drawbridge. Hecate's hooves tore up the gravelly road, spewing a cloud of dust in her wake. Her face hidden behind her crested metal helmet, Sonja spurred the horse toward sanctuary. Her midnight cloak hung in shreds from her steel-plated shoulders. The bloody sword was poised and ready. Sensing that its prey was on the verge of escape, the final werewolf let out a deafening roar and leapt through the air at the endangered horse-woman. Serrated fangs gleamed within its gaping jaws.

Lucian squeezed the trigger.

Cheers erupted from the ramparts and balconies as Sonja galloped through the half-open gates. Right behind her, the airborne wolf took a silver bolt to the skull. It slammed headfirst into drawbridge and skidded through the gate before coming to a rest inside the courtyard. Alarmed Death Dealers charged toward the felled beast, their swords and battle-axes raised high, but there was no need. Canine fur and muscle melted away as the lifeless carcass reverted to human form.

Yes! Lucian rejoiced. *I killed the monster just in time!*

His crude leather boots touched down onto the courtyard as he dropped fifty feet to land before the open gate. He looked quickly to see if any more beasts were coming, but it appeared that he had indeed slain the last of the pack. Guards hurried to close the doors and bolt them securely once more. He heard the portcullis being lowered back into place. A horn informed all within earshot that Castle Corvinus was secure once more.

The crisis was over.

Sonja pulled back on her reins, bringing Hecate to a halt only a few feet away from Lucian. He stared up at the imposing armored warrior upon the black steed. Her blade and plate armor were splattered with crimson, but she appeared personally unharmed. A molded steel breastplate fit her shapely torso to perfection. A diagonal sash stretched across her chest, holding onto the tattered remains of her cloak. Fierce azure eyes peered out from behind her masklike helmet. He heard her breathing hard.

She reached up and removed the helmet, exposing a face of exquisite beauty. Lustrous dark brown hair, the color of stained walnut, framed her elegant features. Her pale white skin was as smooth and flawless as polished alabaster. Her fiery eyes burned like sapphires. The delicate points of her incisors peeked out from beneath her ruby lips. The excitement of her close brush with death added a rosy flush to her cheeks as she gazed down at Lucian with icy disdain. A crowd of soldiers, servants, and courtiers gathered around them, murmuring excitedly amongst themselves.

"Have you nothing better to do, blacksmith," she asked coolly, "than play with weapons of war?" She casually lobbed the gore-smeared sword at him, much to the amusement of the vampires in the vicinity, who chuckled at her quip. Her azure eyes gradually faded back to their customary shade of chestnut brown. "At least make yourself useful."

He plucked the blade from the air, holding her look as long as he dared. The hubbub of voices muted as the crowd parted to admit Viktor and his retinue. A phalanx of Death Dealers followed after the lord of the castle. Lucian was careful to stay out of their way.

"A little gratitude," Viktor chided his daughter, "to the one who saved your life."

She burned him with a look. "I needed no saving."

Viktor took her defiance in stride, perhaps attributing her attitude to wounded pride. He was known to be indulgent of his headstrong daughter, at least to a degree. Letting the matter drop, he turned his attention to the slain werewolf instead. Striding over to the corpse, he yanked the crossbow bolt from its deceptively human-looking skull. Bits of bloody brain tissue clung to the quarrel's silver point. He toyed with the missile as he turned toward Lucian. His face bore a quizzical expression.

"Tell me, Lucian," he asked benignly. "Does it burden your heart to kill your own kind?"

"Not at all," the blacksmith insisted. In truth, he resented being compared to such a creature, but, in deference to the Elder's rank, he kept his tone suitably respectful. "They're mindless beasts, milord. No brethren of mine."

He spoke sincerely and from the heart. As a blacksmith, rather than a warrior, he had never had occasion to slay a werewolf before, but now that he had done so, he felt not a twinge of remorse. Indeed, he had spent his entire life trying to kill the wolf inside him—and to put his shameful ancestry behind him. That he had now literally taken arms against his loathsome cousins struck him as both fitting and something to be proud of, especially under the circumstances. As far as Lucian was concerned, Sonja's life was immeasurably more valuable than that of any mangy animal.

"Really?" Viktor stepped closer. He sounded intrigued by Lucian's answer—and perhaps a trifle suspicious. Narrow eyes searched the lycan's face for any hint of deception, but Lucian stood his ground. His bearded face gave nothing away.

Sonja observed the exchange for a moment, then seemed to lose interest. "Father," she addressed her sire, before spurring her weary mount toward the stables at the rear of the bailey. Lucian watched her regal form depart, with perhaps more appreciation than was prudent for one of his station. Belatedly realizing his mistake, he looked away from the retreating noblewoman, only to find Viktor scowling at him. Clearly, the blacksmith's attentions had not escaped the Elder's notice.

Fool! Lucian castigated himself. *What were you thinking?*

"You are a credit to your race," Viktor said frostily. "Do you know how to remain so? Keep your eyes to the ground." He gestured at the dead werewolf with the bloody arrow. "Get rid of this carrion."

Lowering his eyes, Lucian knelt to carry out the Elder's command. The lifeless carcass did not feel half as heavy as the terrible weight of Viktor's eyes upon him. Lucian prayed that he had not placed his very position in the castle in jeopardy. As every lycan knew, a vampire's memory could be both long and unforgiving.

I must be more careful in the future, he vowed. *Or risk losing everything.*

Chapter Three

*T*he great hall of the keep dwarfed any other chamber in the castle. Ponderous granite pillars supported the high vaulted ceiling, while arched doorways led off to murky passageways lit by racks of torches. Dried rushes carpeted the floor. Iron chandeliers hung from the ceiling, holding arrays of beeswax candles. Rusty chains and manacles dangled from the pillars, as a reminder that all who prospered within the keep did so only by the sufferance of the Elders. The somber stone walls had witnessed bloody executions as well as courtly celebrations.

Sonja paid little attention to the familiar surroundings, which had been her only home for more than two centuries now. She strode briskly through the hall after leaving Hecate in the care of her grooms; to her relief, the horse's wounds did not appear life-threatening. Still encased in her gore-splattered armor, Sonja hoped to make it to the privacy of her own chambers without further incident. She wanted nothing more than to shed her metal carapace and perhaps indulge in a soothing tub. Alas, her father intercepted her before she reached the spiral staircase leading up to her bed-chamber on the topmost floor of the keep.

"You were sorely missed at Council," he reproached her.

She was in no mood for another one of his lectures. "There are other demands on my time, you know."

"Yes, I see." He swept a withering gaze over her battle gear. He had never approved of her dressing like a Death Dealer. "I do hope then that you enjoyed your little moonlight ride."

"I was *patrolling*," she said indignantly. As always, she chafed at her father's overprotective ways. Why shouldn't she be a warrior like Amelia or her mother? Other female vampires served among the Death Dealers. Why was her father so determined to mold her into some pampered aristocratic lady instead? She couldn't imagine spending a lifetime as a dainty creature of the court, let alone eternity.

"You were *disobeying*," he shot back. He came up beside her. "Time and again, I've told you to stay within these walls. You risk too much for a father to ignore. You will leave the wolves to the Death Dealers."

She turned to confront him. "Why should my risk be less than theirs?"

"They are not my daughters!" His voice quaked with

emotion, betraying the deep love he felt for her. The outburst caught them both by surprise, and he needed a moment to compose himself. "And they are not council members. You are. And one night you will become an Elder, your birthright should you endure long enough." He leaned toward her, intent on making her understand. "Sonja, you are well thought of at Council, but that is a precarious thing. They grow tired of your games, your perpetual absences. The dangers of the forest are no greater than those of the council chamber. You must learn the dance of politics, to be ruthless and cunning. And, above all else, you must be loyal to your family. To me."

Sonja held her tongue. She had not been unmoved by her father's spontaneous display of emotion; despite their frequent quarrels, she never doubted that he cared for her profoundly. And yet his talk of duty and politics bored her to tears, and sometimes made her feel like one of the caged werewolves in the dungeon. Palace intrigues and diplomatic maneuvers held no attraction for her. Where was the life, the passion, in such bloodless games? The prospect of wasting her precious immortality thus filled her soul with dread. She'd sooner be chased through the forest by a dozen werewolves than suffer through another interminable council meeting. . . .

Why couldn't her father understand that?

Instead he stepped forward and cupped her chin in his hand. A little more warmth crept into his stern voice and gaze.

"After all," he reminded her, "without the bonds between us, we are no better than the beasts at our door."

Viktor's ominous warning echoed in Lucian's mind as he returned to his smithy. The naked body of the dead werewolf was slung over his shoulder. He was anxious to dispose of the corpse, if only to remove any reminders of the incident from the Elder's sight. Lucian continued to lament his own stupidity; whatever goodwill he had incurred by coming to Sonja's rescue had been lost by his careless behavior in the aftermath of that event. He wondered whether Viktor would ever truly trust him again.

I might as well as have shot that silver quarrel through my own brow.

He flung the carcass into the smoldering bed of his forge, then pumped the bellows to stoke the flames to a roaring blaze. As he somberly watched the bright orange fire consume the corpse, he had to admit that the burning body looked disturbingly human. Was it possible that some trace of a soul still lurked within the savage hearts of the werewolves? Lucian didn't want to think so and yet . . . where did his own mind and spirit come from if not from the blood and loins of a creature such as this?

The stench of charred flesh, as well as his own unwanted doubts, drove him to seek the fresher air of the courtyard outside his smithy. Glancing around, he saw that, despite the excitement earlier, the castle had fallen back into its usual nightly routines. Lycan slaves labored to rebuild a watchtower that had fallen into grievous disrepair. Their dirty bodies drenched in sweat, the men dragged and pushed massive slabs of granite up steep wooden ramps and ladders. Other slaves mixed enormous quantities of mortar, which were hauled up onto the scaffolding. Cranes and pulleys lifted the larger blocks, which dangled ominously over the courtyard below. Grunting workers manned the ropes and tread wheels.

Studded leather harnesses were strapped to the slaves' hairy chests, while fraying wool trousers satisfied the demands of decency. Moon shackles pricked their necks, keeping their inner wolves safely caged. The brands upon their arms bore the initials of one of the three vampire Elders; Marcus and Amelia had embraced with enthusiasm Viktor's idea of turning the lycans into slaves, so that each of them now claimed equal portions of the breed as their personal property. The slaves' eyes bore the numbed, hopeless look of men whose futures held nothing but an eternity of endless toil. Immortality for such as these was not a blessing but a curse.

A shaggy blue-eyed laborer, who had been christened Xristo by his masters, looked near the limits of his endurance. Gasping in exhaustion, he chipped away at a crumbling wall with a pickax in order to clear a space for the replacement stones. Perspiration dripped from his light brown bangs and he lowered his pick long enough to wipe the sweat from his eyes. He leaned his muscular frame up against a wooden ramp as he paused to catch his breath.

This did not sit well with Kosta, the sadistic overseer in charge of the project. Unforgiving gray eyes glared at Xristo from beneath heavy black brows. A long white scar, left over from his mortal days, ran down one side of his grizzled face, which gave him the look of a mortal in his late fifties. His stiff gray hair was cropped close to his skull. Jet-black plate armor added to his intimidating aspect. Frown lines were etched deeply into his saturnine countenance. The sneer on his lips made it clear that he despised his lycan charges nearly as much as they hated and feared him.

His fist tightened on the grip of a thick leather whip. Silver glinted at the tip of the whip as he cracked it loudly against Xristo's face. The lash opened a deep cut in the lycan's cheek. The pickax crashed against the rubble as Xristo cried out in pain and clutched his face. Blood seeped through his dirty fingers.

Lucian winced in sympathy. He knew Xristo casually, as he knew most of the lycans in the castle. *He didn't deserve that,* he thought angrily.

The other lycans backed away from their bleeding comrade, averting their eyes from the ugly spectacle. Kosta was infamous for his harsh ways and short temper; rumor had it his only son had been killed by a werewolf centuries ago and he had been taking out his grief and bitterness on the lycans ever since. None wanted to share Xristo's punishment.

Lucian couldn't blame the other slaves. If he was smart, he would follow their example. *Stay out of this,* he cautioned himself. *It's none of your affair.*

"Lazy mongrel!" Kosta snarled. "You'll rest when I tell you to . . . and not before!"

He raised the lash to administer another vicious blow. Before he could crack the whip again, however, a strong arm seized hold of his wrist.

"That's enough," Lucian said.

Kosta erupted in fury. Spittle sprayed from his lips as he yanked his hand free from Lucian's grip. "You dare raise your hand to me?"

He drew his sword.

Lucian refused to back down. He realized he was taking his life in his hands, but he wasn't about to let this brute flay Xristo to the bone for no reason. His dark eyes burned as hot as his forge. "I said, that's enough."

Kosta swung his sword at Lucian's neck, and for an instant, the blacksmith expected his head to go flying across the courtyard. He had heard tales of severed heads that had lived for a heartbeat or two after being chopped off. Would he survive long enough to see his own decapitated body crumple to the ground?

The sword halted at the last moment, coming to rest against Lucian's jugular. The edge of the blade pressed against his skin, just above his leather collar. The touch of the sword reminded him of the silver spikes forever pressing against his throat, but the threat it posed was far more immediate. Lucian was only too aware that Kosta could end his life with just a flick of his wrist. He thought briefly of the knife in his belt but knew better than to draw it. Pulling a knife on a vampire was a sure invitation to death by torture.

The sneering vampire searched Lucian's face for the fear he expected, but the blacksmith refused to give him the satisfaction. He didn't even flinch. Groveling for mercy would do nothing to soften the heart of a heartless bastard like Kosta, so why bother? If he was to die this night, Lucian resolved, he would at least do so with some vestige of his pride intact.

Like a man, not an animal.

Disappointment flickered across Kosta's face. Snorting in disgust, he drew the sword away and returned it to his hip. "The master's dog," he growled at Lucian.

Apparently, he didn't think killing Lucian was worth risking Viktor's displeasure. Lucian wasn't quite sure that Viktor would truly be that unhappy if he perished, especially after what had happened earlier this evening, but he chose not to contradict Kosta.

"You will not always be his favorite," the overseer warned. "And when you fall, I will be there."

"Let us hope so," Lucian murmured under his breath. Peering past Kosta, he was glad to see that Xristo had made himself scarce. With luck, the overseer's ire was now directed at Lucian alone, so that the other lycan would not receive any more lashings tonight. Lucian could only hope that his foolish bravado had done one poor soul some good, even as he suspected that he had just made a lasting enemy of the brutal slavemaster.

At this rate, I'll have offended the entire coven before the sun rises.

Kosta glared at Lucian, trying to read some hidden message of defiance in the lycan's words, then wheeled about and stormed away in high dudgeon. He barked furiously at the milling slaves, who were doing their best to keep to the shadows. Lucian wasn't sure, but he thought he caught a few furtive looks of admiration from his fellow lycans.

"What are you looking at, you worthless curs!" Kosta raged. He cracked his whip above their heads. "Back to work!"

Chapter Four

As was tradition, the High Council had convened in the crypt of the Elders, above the buried tombs of Marcus and Amelia. Viktor presided over the session from an imposing granite throne. An ornate capital V was inscribed on the high stone back of the throne. Stone-faced Death Dealers, as well as lycan sentries in leather armor, stood stiffly around the perimeter of the mausoleum, as immobile as the marble columns supporting the domed ceiling. The highborn lords and ladies of the Council were seated facing the throne in two rows of six chairs each. Embroidered pillows cushioned their high-backed seats. Burning torches and braziers cast dancing shadows upon the somber gray walls. Mosaic tiles, running around the base of the dome, depicted the history of the coven. Capering skeletons symbolized the fearsome plague that had given birth to the immortals, while subsequent panels celebrated the rise of the vampires, the capture of William, and the ongoing war against the werewolves. Tanis stood beside Viktor, transcribing the proceedings for posterity. His quill pen scratched against an unrolled parchment. Looking out over the crypt, Viktor was irked to see that one of the council members' seats was conspicuously empty.

Damn that girl, he thought impatiently. *Where in perdition is she now?*

To add to his displeasure, Coloman had the floor:

"The matter before the Council is simple," the troublesome boyar declared from the center of the mausoleum. "We are under attack. Six times in half as many weeks, William's kind have reached our very walls." He paused to let that ominous figure sink into the minds of his peers. "What mayhem would follow if just one of them got past our defenses?"

Hushed gasps and murmurs emerged from the Council as they envisioned that appalling prospect. Not all of the castle's diverse inhabitants were seasoned warriors, after all; many of the more refined council members and their families would stand no chance against an invading werewolf. Coloman smirked in satisfaction at the audience's response. He clearly felt that he had made his point.

Viktor was not amused.

"Your . . . *fear* . . . is misplaced." His acerbic tone called Coloman's courage into question. Viktor gestured at the lycan guards posted around the chamber. Handpicked for their loyalty and intimidating stature, the sentries had been armed with swords and lances. "Are we not protected, even during the daylight hours, by an army of immortals?"

Coloman bristled at the implication that he was a coward. "Superbly, milord. However, the nobles of this region are not. And, as I have often pointed out, they are the grass on which we graze."

A well-preserved vampire lady, Orsova by name, rose from her seat to join Coloman before the throne. Her silver hair was bound up in a bun. A black satin corset cinched her waist. A diamond choker adorned her swanlike neck, while her jeweled bracelets were fashioned in the shape of glittering cobwebs. "If we cannot protect our human vassals, it makes us look weak."

Viktor's eyes flared dangerously. Orsova was also one of Marcus's creatures, so there was little love lost between her and Viktor. Rumor had it that, perversely, she enjoyed the taste of her own blood as it circulated through the veins of her various nubile maidservants. Viktor's sharpened nails scraped against the carved stone armrests of his throne. "And how exactly would you project strength?"

"As our Death Dealers patrol the countryside by night," Coloman proposed, having plainly anticipated Viktor's challenge, "so our lycan guards can patrol by day."

Viktor could not believe his ears. Incensed, he lurched to his feet. "Lycans patrol beyond the walls of this castle? Unsupervised by their vampire masters? Have you lost your mind?" He found it difficult to grasp how even Coloman could not see the manifest insanity of such a proposal. "They are mere beasts, and the savagery of this despicable fact cannot be bred away."

As useful as their lycan slaves had proved to be, Viktor had no doubt that even the most docile lycan would revert to barbarism if given half a chance. Only strict control and constant discipline kept them in line. Coloman was a naive fool if he thought otherwise.

"I think your *fear* of this idea is misplaced," the boyar insisted. "We can create a privileged class of lycans—greater rations, finer quarters, better mating opportunities—and put them under the hand of a lycan we know we can trust. Perhaps your pet, Lucian, the one who saved your daughter's life earlier tonight." A sly smile lifted the corners of his thin lips. "In fact, I think we should hear her thoughts in this matter."

He made a production of turning dramatically toward Sonja's empty seat. As usual, the impetuous heir was nowhere to be seen.

Fuming, Viktor leaned over to whisper to Tanis. *"Find her."*

Coloman feigned surprise at Sonja's absence. "Mmm. She seems to be needed elsewhere."

"I will . . . take your suggestion under advisement," Viktor said icily. He considered explaining away Sonja's lack of attendance by citing her narrow escape earlier that evening, but decided against it. That would simply provide Coloman and his lackeys with an opportunity to remind the Council of Sonja's many previous absences. Better to offer no excuse or apology, lest that be taken as a sign of weakness. Viktor maintained a stoic façade as Tanis quietly exited the crypt in search of the missing heir. The Elder wondered what exactly his errant daughter was doing right now. *She had best have a very good reason for embarrassing me like this!*

"Thank you, milord," Coloman said, enjoying his victory. "It would be gratifying to be able to reassure the nobles when they arrive tomorrow that we have their best interests at heart."

Viktor recalled that a delegation of wealthy human vassals was expected at the castle one night hence, to pay tribute to their lords and masters. Frankly, the best interests of insignificant mortals were of little concern to him, but he conceded reluctantly that such rituals helped preserve the social order. He would have to make certain that Sonja was on hand to welcome their guests—even if he had to drag her physically from her room.

Dawn was only a few hours away when Lucian put down his hammer and tongs. Steam rose from the slack tub as the brine cooled a red-hot sword blade that he had just pounded into shape. The night was winding down and the castle was already settling in to sleep the day away. Silence fell over the courtyard outside as the construction efforts ceased for the evening; without any vampires to oversee their labors, the exhausted lycan slaves were allowed a brief respite until sunset the next day. Heavy drapes and shutters were drawn over the castle's windows, to protect the slumbering vampires from the burning rays of the sun. Lycan sentries, often referred to as "daylight guardians," would soon replace the Death Dealers stationed upon the castle's outer walls and watchtowers. If past history was any guide, most of the vampire lords and ladies were even now retiring for the evening.

Finally! Lucian thought. He wiped the soot and sweat from his face with a tattered rag. The last few hours had dragged on interminably while he had waited impatiently for this very moment. Drawing aside one of the heavy leather curtains enclosing his smithy, he peeked out into the courtyard to see if anyone was coming. He nodded in satisfaction as he saw that the courtyard was just as quiet and deserted as he had hoped. The only sign of life was a scrawny kitchen scullion darting back from the well with a fresh bucket of water. Lucian watched as the boy disappeared back into the keep, leaving the inner bailey all but deserted. No one would be coming in search of a blacksmith anytime soon.

Or so he prayed.

He looked about one last time, just to be certain that no one was watching, then retreated to the rear of the smithy. The fire was dying in his furnace as he crept around the back of the forge to where a scorched hide hung against the eastern wall of the castle. A rusty metal grate was embedded in the floor. Taking no chances, Lucian glanced back over his shoulder before kneeling beside the grate. His fingers dug into the edge of the grille and pried it from the floor, revealing the open mouth of a narrow drain. The malodorous reek of a cesspit wafted up from below. He placed the grate aside, taking care not to bang it against the wall or floor.

Lucian recalled an Arabian folk tale he had once heard from a Saracen trader.

Open sesame, he thought.

The drain was intended to carry away the water Lucian used to douse his forge at the end of the night, but Lucian had furtively worked the metal grate loose some time ago. The chute beneath was barely wide enough to accommodate a grown man, yet he managed to squeeze through the gap and slide down the sloping passageway, which led to a maze of fetid drainage tunnels winding far beneath the castle. Slime coated the clammy stone walls, which hemmed Lucian in as he navigated the tight, constricting sewers. His lycan eyes needed a moment or two to adjust to the near-total darkness, yet he did not hesitate. It would be easy to get lost in this subterranean labyrinth, perhaps never to taste the open air again, but Lucian had groped his way through these tunnels before; by now he knew the route by heart. He waded confidently through the raw sewage, which lapped sickeningly at his ankles. Algae floated atop the stagnant waters, whose polluted contents did not bear thinking about. Heaps of human skulls and scattered bones, tucked away in carved stone niches, revealed that these catacombs had once been used to bury the castle's dead; now that the immortals resided within its walls, however, such funereal practices had long since been discarded. Lucian suspected that he was the first person to explore these depths in countless generations.

Rats scurried away from his approach. Something slithered past his leg. Lucian kept his jaws tightly clenched, to try to keep from inhaling too much of the foul miasma filling the air, but the reek of the sewers was inescapable. Not for the first time, he wished there was a cleaner, less revolting way to get where he wished to go; no civilized being would take this path unless he or she had a very compelling reason to do so—which is exactly what Lucian had. His pace quickened at the thought of what lay ahead. He would have gladly walked through hell itself if need be.

Certain things were worth any risk.

Starlight filtered through a vertical crack in the wall ahead. The narrow gap was barely wide enough to squeeze through sideways, and the rugged masonry scraped across his back as he did so, but Lucian emerged from the drains to find himself outside the castle walls. Peering upward, he saw the forbidding exterior of the fortress looming above him. A cold winter breeze came as blissful relief after the suffocating stench of the sewers. He filled his lungs with the crisp mountain air. His hot breath frosted before his lips.

He was free—at least for the moment.

The open spaces, as well as the sight of the moonlit forest in the distance, stirred something deep in his soul. His fingers tugged at the stinging collar around his neck, which he had worn for two centuries now. Part of him was sorely tempted to turn his back on the castle forever and seek out a new life in the great wide world, far from the capricious whims of Viktor and his ilk. He could be the captain of his own destiny. The master of his fate.

But, no, that was not the purpose of tonight's outing. Instead he looked to the west where an abandoned watchtower clung to a sheer cliff more than a hundred feet above the castle. The ruins dated back centuries, to when the castle's own walls and spires had not yet risen to their present heights. A fire several generations later had gutted much of the tower's interior, and the Elders, by then securely ensconced in their newly fortified stronghold, had not seen fit to repair it. No light shown from the tower's thin loop windows, or "murder holes." The worm-eaten remnants of a rickety wooden stairway led up a steep incline to the base of the tower. Like the drainage tunnels, the stairway showed no sign of having been used in ages.

At least not by the vampires . . .

Lucian advanced cautiously toward the stairs. He hugged the walls, keeping to the shadows to avoid being spotted by the lookouts upon the ramparts. Neither he nor any other lycan could expect any mercy should he be caught venturing outside the castle walls; he would be lucky to avoid being skewered on the spot by a harpoon fired by one of the siege crossbows above him. He knew that he was taking a tremendous risk with every step he took.

But no power on earth could make him turn back now.

A wolf howled in the distance. Lucian froze. He swallowed hard. His hand went to the knife at his belt. Had he worshipped the Nailed God, as the mortals did, he would have been tempted to cross himself, but the denizens of Castle Corvinus had long ago shed their faith along with their mortality. More wolves joined in the howl. The atavistic baying reminded him that the Death Dealers were not the only the danger he tempted tonight. Should he be caught outdoors by a pack of hungry werewolves, he doubted that the castle's guards would come to his rescue. In fact, they would be happy to see him torn apart.

Thankfully, the howling sounded as though it was coming from many miles away. Still, he remained frozen in place, barely breathing, until the baying finally faded away. Only then did he venture up the trail leading to the old tower. Shunning the dilapidated stairway, with its rotting wooden planks, he silently scaled the rocky cliff face. His hands and feet found purchase in minute cracks and outcroppings in a way that few mortals could have emulated. Gravity held no terror for him, yet he lived in fear that at any moment a castle guard would notice his ascent. Cold sweat glued his vest to his back. His ears waited anxiously for an angry shout of alarm.

The climb lasted only moments but felt like an eternity. He bit back a sigh of relief as he spied the entrance to the tower only a few yards away. A moldering oaken door hung ajar, supported by only a single rusty hinge. Just then, alas, a gust of wind blew away the clouds overhead. Moonlight flooded the weathered stretch of cliff lying between him and the doorway, exposing it to the clear view of the castle guards.

Lucian's heart sank. He looked about anxiously for an alternative route into the tower, but none presented itself. His eyes searched the skies for another cloud, only to see nothing but the unforgiving glare of the moon. His fingers ached from clinging to a shallow depression in the cliff as he realized he had only two choices. He would have to abandon the shadows or turn back for the night.

Never! he thought vehemently. *Not when I'm so close!*

Mustering up his courage, he grabbed for the next handhold and scrambled across the light as fast as inhumanly possible. If he moved quickly, perhaps none of the sentries would notice him. The silvery lunar radiance seemed impossibly bright. His mouth felt as dry as a desiccated corpse. In his haste, he missed a hold and slid several inches down the face of the cliff before grabbing onto a jutting stone bulge. For the moment, he dangled precariously over the barren plain hundreds of feet blow, hanging onto the cliff by naught but a finger or two, but he quickly regained his footing and scampered up the side of the precipice until he finally reached the inviting black shadows of the breached archway. He heaved himself past the askew door into the murky confines of the gutted tower. Only once he was safely out of sight of the soldiers did he breathe again. He panted in relief.

I made it!

The Lady Sonja's personal quarters were located on the top floor of the keep, only a few doors away from her father's chambers. Tanis hurried down a drafty corridor until he reached the thick oak door defending Sonja's privacy. Faded tapestries hung upon the hallway walls in hopes of keeping out the chill of the night. Decorative suits of armors stood silent vigil. Mounted torches were sputtering out as dawn approached.

He knocked hesitantly upon Sonja's door, wishing

Viktor had chosen someone else—anyone else—for this particular errand. The nervous scribe had no illusions concerning Sonja's opinion of him; he was well aware that Viktor's adventurous daughter regarded him with contempt. A warrior woman like her late mother, she valued strength and courage, not guile and erudition. Tanis had no wish to fall even further out of her favor by disturbing her thus, especially since she was destined to become an Elder someday. Still, her father's wishes could not be denied.

His knock received no answer.

"Milady?"

He flirted with the idea of reporting back to Viktor empty-handed, yet that prospect held little appeal. The ruthless Elder was not known for his patience when it came to the bearers of bad news. Even as a mortal warlord, Viktor had been infamous for his harsh treatment of those whom had displeased him; the scribe had seen ancient woodcuts of Viktor dining amidst a field of gallows and impaled prisoners. Tanis pressed his ear to the door, but heard nothing stirring inside. A second knock was also greeted with silence.

"Lady Sonja?"

He tentatively tried the door and found it unlocked. Curiosity won over caution and he gently pushed the door open, ready to retreat at the first indignant protest from the Elder's daughter. But no objection came from the opulent suite beyond the door. A canopied four-poster bed, much grander than the scribe's own modest pallet, was piled high with pillows and fine linens. A hand basin, jewelry box, and other feminine trinkets littered the top of a mahogany dressing table. Moonlight filtered through stained-glass windows. Lavender and tansy freshened the air. A large framed mirror, mounted on the wall above the vanity, gave lie to the myth that vampires cast no reflections. A discarded suit of armor was mounted upon a rack. Unlit kindling was piled in the fireplace. A Persian carpet, imported from the Holy Land, covered the cold stone floor. An antique wooden armoire doubtless held Sonja's extensive wardrobe. Standing in the doorway, Tanis's crafty eyes meticulously scoured Sonja's private domain.

Only one thing was missing.

The lady herself.

Now nothing stood between Lucian and his goal but a winding spiral staircase leading up to the top of the tower. Throwing caution to the wind, he raced up the crumbling stone steps, taking them two at a time. Cobwebs hung like filmy curtains in his path and he tore through them without hesitation. The sticky strands adhered to his skin, but he paid them no heed. He had more important things on his mind at the moment. He couldn't climb the stairs fast enough.

At last he arrived at the top of the steps. The upper turret of the tower was cloaked in darkness. Only a sliver of moonlight entered through the arrow loops, which were narrow enough to shield the tower's bygone defenders from flaming arrows and other missiles from below. Cramped embrasures offered archers further shelter from their foes without. Decades of dust and grit coated the charred remains of a ruined wooden bench. A moldy leather tankard, which looked as though it had been partially devoured by rats, had been left behind on the floor, along with the broken shards of a shattered chamber pot. A spider scuttled across the floor. Bats hung from the rafters.

Lucian looked around anxiously. He had come here for a reason, yet there was always the possibility that, despite his stealth, his plans had been discovered and vengeful enemies waited to catch him in the act. What if Viktor or his Death Dealers were lurking in the shadows? Or a stray werewolf had chosen to make the tower his lair?

He heard something brush softly across the floor behind him. Spinning around, he reached again for the knife at his belt. A silent figure emerged from an embrasure. His eyes widened as she stepped into the moonlight.

"Blacksmith," Sonja said.

The beautiful immortal had changed out of her armor into a shimmering gown of scarlet samite. A crescent-shaped pendant, which she had worn since childhood, rested upon the ivory slopes of her bosom. Moonbeams accented her regal cheekbones and elegant features. Her white skin gleamed like fine china. Lustrous dark brown hair framed a face worthy of some pagan goddess. Chestnut eyes gazed boldly into his. Her voice was deep and husky.

"Milady," Lucian replied. All thought of hidden ruses and ambushes fled his mind. He could see only the highborn vampire before him. His pulse quickened.

"This is madness," she declared.

"Yes."

Unable to hold back any longer, he crossed the floor in an instant. He crushed her against him in a passionate embrace. Their mouths met hungrily, her ardor fully the equal of his own. His senses swam as he lost himself in the unimaginable rapture of her kiss. The intoxicating scent of her lavender perfume went straight to his head. Honey and coriander sweetened her breath. He caressed the graceful contours of her back through the thin fabric. Her mere presence, wrapped tightly in his arms, affected him as powerfully as the full moon, unleashing emotions and impulses beyond his control. His manhood instantly grew as hard as tempered steel. She buried her hands in his hair, pulling his head ever closer.

Sonja, he thought. *My love.*

His eager fingers fumbled with the solitary strap over her shoulder, then impatiently tore it apart. Succumbing to gravity, the loose gown slithered to the floor with agonizing slowness, revealing that she wore nothing underneath but her own flawless white skin. Only the golden pendent about her neck adorned the naked splendor of her body. Her breasts were full and inviting. Blood-red nipples aimed like spear points at his heart. Smooth legs parted beneath his touch.

Lucian wondered what he had ever done to deserve such a treasure.

Tanis prowled the battlements in search of Sonja. A thorough inspection of her bedchamber, although mildly stimulating, had yielded no hint as to her present whereabouts. He had scoured the castle from the scullery to the belfry, yet found no sign of her. Now the dawn was nigh and he was no closer to carrying out Viktor's command to locate his missing daughter. Tanis did not relish the idea of reporting his failure back to the short-tempered Elder.

Irresponsible bitch! he cursed Sonja spitefully. How dare she put him in such an untenable position? *I have better things to do with my immortality than play nurse-maid to a spoiled brat less than half my age!*

He glanced nervously to the east, where the horizon was already starting to lighten ominously. The sun would be rising soon and he was eager to retire to his own modest chambers, where he had arranged an assignation with a pair of bawdy scullery maids, only lately inducted into the coven. The sybaritic scribe preferred to double his private pleasures whenever possible, and his mouth watered at the prospect of sampling both trollops simultaneously. He sorely resented being kept from his frolics by this burdensome chore.

Yet more one reason, aside from her haughty attitude toward him, for him to bear the Lady Sonja considerable ill will. *She would do better to curry the favor of those who might assist her in the future.* He knew he was not the only member of the coven who looked askance at her impolitic behavior, which might come back to haunt her down the road. After all, even an Elder could suffer reversals of fortune on occasion, as Marcus had learned when Viktor usurped control of the Death Dealers back during the final battle against William. Sonja's exalted bloodline could only protect her so far. . . .

A bell tolled from atop the keep, warning of the dawn, leaving the vexed scribe at his wit's end. Restlessly pacing the palisade, he found himself running out of options. He had tried everything he could think to track down his elusive quarry, but to no avail. Sonja's lady-in-waiting, a lissome blond vampiress named Luka, had maintained total ignorance of her mistress's whereabouts, while none of the castle's other servants and retainers had reported seeing her anytime in the last few hours. He had even checked the stables, where he had been relieved to discover Sonja's favorite courser, Hecate, sleeping safely in its stall. At least the reckless woman was not out riding again. She had to be somewhere within the castle.

Didn't she?

Their lovemaking was wild and abandoned. Sonja's nails raked deep furrows down his naked back as they rutted furiously against the quaking wall of the tower. Her limber legs were wrapped tightly about his waist while he supported her succulent rump with both hands. Her bare breasts pressed insistently against his hairy chest. The golden pendant bounced between them. His own filthy garments lay in a heap upon the floor alongside the discarded gown, so that he wore only the slave collar around his throat. Delicate fangs teased his neck, never quite breaking the skin. Sweat glistened on their colliding bodies. Wordless groans and growls punctuated every feverish thrust.

Lucian arched his back in both agony and ecstasy as her claws drew blood. He rammed his engorged member into her, slamming her backward into the wall so hard that dust rained down on them from the ceiling. Sonja gasped out loud and her eyes glowed like sapphires. Her lips claimed his in a fierce kiss that literally took his breath away. He tasted blood upon his lips.

Matching his lycan strength with her own preternatural stamina, she pushed off from the wall and shoved him down onto the floor of the turret, where their strewn clothing cushioned their conjoined bodies. Their busy hands and mouths explored each other without reservation. Sonja's alabaster skin felt as cold and refreshing as a mountain stream, while Lucian's own flesh was as hot as his forge. He plunged into her like a bar of red-hot iron thrust into cooling brine. His eyes flashed cobalt blue. Even with the collar still in place around his neck, he had never felt so free, so wild, so like a wolf.

He knew that what they were doing was forbidden. That Viktor would surely have him flayed alive or worse if he knew. But Lucian didn't care. All that mattered at this moment was making love to Sonja with every fiber of his being—until they collapsed, spent and exhausted, into each other's arms.

Chapter Five

Sonja nestled in Lucian's embrace upon the floor of the turret. Her weary head rested upon his shoulder while her bare arm and leg were draped over his supine form. His sinewy body felt as warm and comforting as a blazing hearth compared to her cool undead flesh. Her fingers toyed with the wiry hairs upon his chest. Both exhausted and sated by their vigorous lovemaking, she was content to snuggle against him for what little time remained to them. Part of her still couldn't believe that this was really happening, that she had actually taken a lycan as a lover, but right now, at this very moment, there was nowhere else she would rather be than wrapped securely in his strong arms. She wished they could stay like this forever.

This must be what the mortals imagine heaven to be like.

Their clandestine affair had caught them both by surprise. Furtive looks exchanged in the castle corridors, as they "accidentally" brushed against each other in passing, had led to stolen moments in the smithy, and whispered confessions of mutual ardor. It was she who had first divulged the true depths of her feelings, but not until Lucian trusted her with the secret route to the deserted watchtower had they dared to consummate the forbidden passion between them. Fearing exposure, she had told no one of their trysts, not even Luka, her faithful lady-in-waiting.

If my father knew of this!

"So," he murmured softly into her ear, "did I make myself useful, milady?"

"Indeed." Her nude body quivered at the memory of their strenuous exertions. Lifting her head, she contemplated her lover thoughtfully. The dashing blacksmith was like no man she had ever known, and a marked improvement over the arrogant aristocrats who courted her relentlessly. Loving, courageous, and intelligent, Lucian was twice the man of any vampire in her father's court. She found it hard to accept that he was truly a lycan. "Is it true what you told my father, that you feel nothing when you kill them?"

He realized she was referring to the werewolf he had slain earlier tonight. "They are just animals," he said bluntly. "Incapable of thought or feeling. Why should I care anything for them?"

Sonja nodded, accepting his answer. She did not question the sincerity of his response. There were no secrets between them. *I always thought the same of were-wolves,* she mused, *until I came to know you with all my heart. . . .*

Now she wasn't so sure.

He rolled over onto his side so that he could look her in the eyes. A serious expression came over his face, which was only inches away from hers. His dark brown eyes looked more human than lycan.

"If I were to leave from here, would you come with me?"

She sat up in alarm. "Do not say that! Do not even think it." She clutched his arm. "They would hunt you down like all the others. You would be marked for death!"

Lycan slaves had on occasion attempted to escape to freedom. A few had even managed to slip past the castle walls. But her father's Death Dealers had always succeeded in tracking down the fugitives, most of whom had no idea how to cope in the wild on their own. Those captured alive were dragged back to castle in chains, then tortured to death in the courtyard as an example to any other lycans who might be contemplating going on the run. Sonja shuddered at the thought of Lucian facing such a dreadful fate.

I could not bear to see him suffer so!

To her dismay, he appeared undaunted by the danger. He fingered the moon shackle around his throat. "Not if I can remove this."

But that's impossible, she thought. The spiked collars were locked onto the slaves for life—to prevent them from transforming into monstrous werewolves. *Why speak of things that cannot be?*

He rifled through the strewn garments beneath them, retrieving a small woolen pouch from his discarded belt. He reached inside the pouch, then held out his hand. His fingers opened to reveal a small pewter key lying in his palm.

"I made it myself," he explained. His eyes shone with pride and determination. "This will be my freedom."

She stared at the key as if it were a venomous spider, poised to destroy their happiness forever. "Lucian," she pleaded, desperate to dissuade him from this rash course. "Promise me you will not use it. Please!"

He frowned, clearly disappointed by her response. "Is that your answer, then? You will not come with me, so you want me to stay here for you?" He tugged bitterly on the moon shackle. "Like this? Like an animal?"

"Lucian!" She had never realized he felt this way. *Perhaps I do not truly know him as well as I believed?* She sympathized with his frustration, but was horrified by the drastic measures he seemed willing to take. *No,* she thought fearfully. Images of Lucian being flayed alive in the courtyard rushed before her mind's eye. *The risk is too great!*

"Vampire and lycan," he brooded darkly. He placed a hand against her cheek; his hot, callused palm felt rough compared to her own smooth white skin. He stared soulfully into her anguished chestnut eyes. "We are both the children of Corvinus. Yet my kind are slaves."

He held the key up before her eyes. "I will use this one day. And I will leave this place."

By the fates, he means it! There was no doubting the

passionate intensity of his words, which struck her like a wooden stake through the heart. Her ivory complexion went paler still. A gasp that was almost a sob escaped her lips.

No good can come of this.

Her obvious distress was not lost on him. Anger gave way to tenderness on his handsome face. His voice softened and he reluctantly returned the key to its pouch before taking her into his arms once more. Sonja clung to him fiercely, as though she could keep him safely at her side for all eternity. Her nails dug deeply into his naked back. She inhaled deeply of his musky aroma. She never wanted to let him go.

"But I can never be without you," he promised.

Nor I you, she thought.

Tanis reached the far end of the palisade, where the rough-hewn walkway merged with the rocky slope of the mountain. To the east, a frightening rosy glow was rising on the horizon. A warning bell once again foretold the dawn. Although he had not yet located Sonja, he would soon be forced to retreat to the safety of the keep's impenetrable walls, and to take his chances by abandoning his futile quest. Perhaps Viktor had already retired for the night?

That would be fortunate indeed. . . .

A wolf howled from the distant wilderness, eliciting a shudder from the faint-hearted scribe, who pulled his fur-lined robe tightly about his slight frame. A scholar, not a warrior, he preferred to read about werewolves in his dusty tomes, not to hear them baying only a few leagues away. He looked forward to the day when Viktor and his Death Dealers exterminated the wretched breed once and for all.

Save for our domesticated lycan slaves, of course.

Sighing, he turned away from the parapet and gazed out over the courtyard one last time. A shimmer of motion caught his eye and he leaned out over a guardrail to get a better look. Crafty blue eyes widened in surprise as he spotted Lucian emerging from his smithy, accompanied by Sonja herself!

What the devil?

A heavy gray cloak was draped over Sonja's rumpled scarlet gown. Her streaming walnut tresses were loose and disordered. She glanced about furtively as she stepped out from behind one of the crude hides enclosing the blacksmith's forge. If Tanis didn't know better, he would have sworn that she had just tumbled guiltily out of a lover's bed.

But with a lycan? That was inconceivable. . . .

Or was it?

Despite the imminent arrival of the sunrise, which Sonja could no more survive than any other vampire, she and Lucian lingered outside the smithy as though reluctant to part. His hand brushed her hip, a tiny gesture that might well have escaped the notice of anyone less observant than Tanis. They shared a long, poignant look before the lightening sky mercilessly drove them apart. They reached out to each other, their outstretched fingers grazing one final time before Sonja finally tore herself away from the imprudent blacksmith and scampered for the keep, leaving Lucian alone in the courtyard. Reaching the shelter of the portico, she glanced back over her shoulder in manner that could only be described as longing. Welcoming shadows swallowed her up as she disappeared into the keep. A heavy oak door swung shut behind her.

Up on the rampart, Tanis could scarcely believe his eyes. The Elder's daughter—and a *lycan*? Such a thing had never been heard of, and moreover was expressly forbidden by the Covenant on pain of death. Not even the most wanton vampire serving-wench would ever dream of sullying herself by consorting with an animal, yet Tanis could not deny the evidence of his own eyes. There could be no other explanation for the intimate drama he had just spied upon. A muscle tightened on the scribe's cheek.

Who knew the Elder's daughter was so . . . *perverse*?

Not until Sonja had completely vanished from sight did Lucian look away from the doorway. He glanced up at the palisade and Tanis hastily ducked behind a ballista to avoid being seen. For an instant, he feared that Lucian might spot him upon the ramparts, but then another wolfen howl captured the blacksmith's attention instead. More voices joined the bestial chorus until it sounded like an entire pack was serenading the moon. Lucian listened intently, seemingly transfixed by the ghastly din, before shaking off its spell and retreating back into his smithy.

What do you hear in the wolf's song? Tanis pondered. *A reminder that, deep down inside, you're still just an animal after all?*

A beast that had apparently claimed the affections of a noblewoman.

Interesting, Tanis thought. Overcoming his initial shock at so unnatural a pairing, the calculating scribe realized that he had come into possession of knowledge both valuable and highly dangerous. There was surely some way to turn Sonja's scandalous secret to his advantage, but he would have to be careful. The untimely exposure of such an explosive revelation could have a cataclysmic effect upon the entire coven, with little guarantee of who might end up on top when the ashes settled. Innocent bystanders, such as himself, might well find themselves caught in the crossfire. *I need to give this matter much serious thought.*

Once he got safely indoors, that is.

He returned to the keep himself, by means of an inconspicuous side entrance, where he was dismayed to find Viktor waiting for him in the great hall. The Elder sat upon a regal throne at the far end of the chamber, while lesser gentlemen and their ladies lounged on richly upholstered chair and divans. Elegant courtesans displayed their charms in filmy black gowns. A blazing fire roared in the hearth. Apparently the coven was making a late night of it, perhaps in anticipation of tomorrow's delegation from the neighboring lands. Flutes of chilled steer's blood clinked lightly; as the Covenant forbade preying upon their mortal serfs, the coven subsisted on the blood of cattle instead. A cunning potion, extracted from eels, kept their liquid refreshment from congealing. Light conversation and gossip echoed off the cold stone walls. Incense flavored the air. A lute played softly in the background.

Any hopes Tanis had of evading Viktor's notice were swiftly crushed. He summoned the scribe to his side with a peremptory gesture. Viktor spoke in a low tone so that they would not be overheard by the rest of the coven.

"What news of my daughter?" he demanded.

Tanis weighed his options carefully. *No*, he concluded, *this was neither the time nor the place. . . .*

"She is most defiant," he lied shamelessly. "She refused to see me. Would not even open her door."

Viktor scowled. "Why are the young so shortsighted?" he lamented. "She risks her seat on the Council. And for what?"

Better you should not know that, Tanis mused. *At least for the present.* It required an effort not to smile slyly as he replied. "I cannot imagine, my lord." He moved quickly to change the subject. "Now we must prepare. The human nobles will begin arriving as soon as the sun goes down again."

With any luck, the upcoming festivities would distract Viktor from his daughter's alarming doings long enough for Tanis to figure out how best to exploit his newfound knowledge. *Patience*, he counseled himself. If immortality had taught him one thing, it was that all things came to those who wait. For now, it was enough to know that he held the haughty Sonja's reputation in his hands.

A pity she never chose to smile upon me before. . . .

Chapter Six

*W*agon wheels dug deep trenches in the bumpy dirt road as the armored carriage rattled through the forest. Blue-gray steel plates were riveted to the sides of the coach, which was drawn by a pair of large black horses. Two glowing lanterns, mounted on either side of the driver's seat, did little to illuminate the dense wilderness through which the carriage traveled. Moonlight leaked through the barren tree branches overhead, casting eerie shadows in the coach's path. The swirling fog was so thick that the driver could barely see more than a few yards ahead of him. He cracked his whip above the horses, anxious to leave the gloomy forest behind. A pair of Death Dealers rode ahead of the carriage, offering a measure of protection. Crested Corinthian-style helmets concealed their faces. Watchful eyes searched the surrounding woods.

Denied that luxury were the half-score human slaves chained behind the carriage. Coarse burlap hoods covered their heads so that they were forced to stumble blindly after the rushing coach, fighting to keep their balance lest they fall and be dragged to their death. The prisoners were shackled together in two columns of five slaves each. Their ragged garments were soiled and drenched in sweat. Fresh scars and bruises chronicled their ordeal. They panted hoarsely beneath their hoods as they struggled to keep up with the carriage's exhausting pace. Iron rings, clamped tightly around their necks, chafed against their flesh. Manacles bound their wrists. Fifteen prisoners had actually set out on this hellish trek, but five had already fallen by the wayside. Their lifeless bodies had been tossed into ditches alongside the road, to be consumed as carrion by whatever beasts chanced upon their remains. The poor souls had been denied even the dignity of a decent burial.

Now only ten prisoners remained. Raze wondered whether any of them would reach the castle alive.

A powerfully built man whose dark skin announced that he had been born far from these cold Carpathian Mountains, he towered over the other prisoners like a veritable Goliath. His true name was Razahir, but most called him Raze. A brown leather vest strained to contain his impressive build. Crude boots defended his aching feet from the rocky road. A taut chain tugged mercilessly at his neck, compelling him forward against his will, while a second chain was affixed to his manacles. The suffocating hood made it hard to breathe. His own ragged panting echoed in his ears.

Will this hellish journey never end? he thought darkly. *How much farther must we travel so?*

Raze cursed the malicious fates that had brought him to this sorry pass. Once the son of a mighty sultan in his native Sudan, he had lost his family and his heritage when his land was overrun by Saracen invaders. Only his formidable strength had kept him alive to wander the world as an outcast before ending up a prisoner here in Europe, far from his distant homeland, which he feared he would never see again. Only the gods knew what miserable fate awaited him at Castle Corvinus, which was said to be the domain of ageless demons who fed on the blood of the living. Although their masters denied it, insisting that the castle was merely the home of a powerful warlord and his court, tales were told in the slave quarters of the living dead, *vampires*. What the shamans back home would have called an *obayifo*.

Although brave enough when facing mortal foes, Raze shuddered at the prospect of falling into the hands of unclean spirits. Had he not already suffered enough?

Inside the carriage, Natalya tried not to let her parents see her fear. Only sixteen years old, she had pleaded with them to let her accompany them to Lord Viktor's castle for the first time; she didn't want them to think that she was a timid child, afraid to travel through a scary forest at night. Even if that forest was rumored to be haunted by werewolves. . . .

She didn't know whether to be worried or comforted by the fact that her parents seemed equally ill at ease. Although they were also striving to conceal their nerves, Natalya could tell that both her mother and father were obviously concerned for their safety. Seated across from Natalya in an overstuffed padded seat, her father busied himself with a stack of documents, while her mother sat beside her, pretending to concentrate on her embroidery. A pale green wimple, held in place by a brooch beneath her chin, covered Mother's hair, as was only fitting for a married woman. Her plump cheeks and round face were proof of their prosperity. Father wore a heavy wool cloak over his stocky frame. His bushy brown beard had lately been infiltrated by strands of gray. Natalya's own flaxen curls hung in ringlets past her ears. Her simple blue kirtle suited the rigors of travel; a more elegant and expensive gown was packed away for her debut at court.

Assuming they ever made it to the castle alive. . . .

A locked wooden chest, reinforced with iron straps, rested on the floor between them. Crammed with tribute for Lord Viktor, Father had not allowed the treasure chest out of his sight. It bounced noisily with every bump and rut in the road. A candle flickered inside a mounted iron lantern. Natalya prayed that the candle would not burn out before they reached their destination. The idea of making the rest of the perilous journey in darkness was too dreadful to contemplate.

She placed a hand to her face, which felt cold to her touch. Did she look as pale and frightened as she felt? She trembled and wrung her hands together, listening in terror to every creak and thump from outside as though they might be the last things she ever heard in this life. The door of the carriage was made of sturdy oak and bolted with iron, but would that be enough to spare them from the monsters stalking the woods?

Would anything?

She closed her eyes and tried to pretend that she was back in her own room in her father's mansion, safely tucked under the covers. But the rough jolts shaking the carriage made the fantasy impossible to sustain. There was no escaping the fact that she was trapped inside an uncomfortable moving box far from the security of home. That she couldn't see what was going on outside only made it worse; she felt as helpless as one of the hooded prisoners being dragged behind the carriage. For all she knew, an entire pack of werewolves was running alongside the carriage at this very minute, their feral eyes glowing demonically in the dark.

A closed metal slit was built into the side of the carriage. Natalya eyed the slit for several moments while she wrestled with the temptation to take just a tiny peek outside. What if she saw something terrible, like a hungry werewolf pouncing right at her? The thought gave her pause, but in the end, her curiosity could not be denied. Over her mother's protests, she reached over and slid open the seal. . . .

To her relief, she saw only one of their armored escorts riding beside them. The gallant Death Dealer paid her no heed as he lit a flaming arrow and loaded it into his crossbow. A second later, he fired the burning bolt high into the sky, where it blazed brightly for a moment or two before crashing to earth like a fallen star.

Natalya realized that the horseman was surely signaling Castle Corvinus of their approach.

Praise the saints! she thought. *We're almost there!*

Lucian was sorting weapons in his smithy when Sonja entered in full armor. Only her lovely face was bared as she cradled her helmet in the crook of her elbow. Her martial garb made it clear that she was not here for another amorous interlude. Indeed, he had anticipated her arrival upon spotting the signal arrow in the sky a few moments past.

The first of her father's guests will be arriving soon.

Although the mere sight of her made him yearn to kiss those ruby lips, he handed her a freshly polished sword. He had labored all day to repair the damage done to the blade by her battle with the werewolves yesterday. Its keen edge reflected the glow of his forge. The silvery glint hurt his eyes.

"It is sharp," he promised her. "No wolf will stand against it."

She nodded, artfully concealing her emotions, and turned to her men, who were waiting just outside the smithy. Like her, they were decked out in gleaming black armor, most of which had been forged by Lucian himself. A lycan groom stood by in the courtyard, holding onto Hecate's reins. "Ready the horses," she commanded.

The Death Dealers dispersed, momentarily leaving Lucian and Sonja alone. Their eyes met and a soft, almost inaudible sigh escaped her lips. He could tell that she was just as frustrated by hopeless longing as he was. They desperately wanted to make the most of this moment together, to share a touch, a kiss, but the smithy was too exposed, her men too near. They couldn't risk it.

"Let someone else go," he pleaded.

She shook her head, tossing back her sleek dark hair. "Why?"

Need I explain? He did not like the idea of Sonja venturing out into the night once more, so soon after her narrow escape from the wolves the night before. He still recalled the agony of suspense he had endured when it had seemed as though he might lose her forever. Plus, there was one thing more.

"Last night. After we parted . . . I do not know. Something . . ." He found it hard to put his apprehensions into words, and yet there had been a moment when, alone in the courtyard after he had watched her disappear into the keep, he'd felt a peculiar chill run down his spine, as though unseen eyes had been spying upon them with malign intent. And then the howling had commenced, sounding far too close to the castle for comfort. "Just let someone else go."

Sonja frowned. "In case it has escaped your notice, blacksmith, I can look after myself."

I know, he thought. He also knew from experience that few things vexed her more than being treated like a helpless damsel. Nevertheless, he had felt compelled to voice his fears even at the risk of provoking her ire. *I would sooner quarrel with you than lose you to some nebulous danger. . . .*

Seeing his chagrin, her voice softened. "And besides, you can always watch over me from the walls."

He saw there was no point in attempting to dissuade

91

her. Sonja was nothing if not fearless. When she set her mind to do something, like dare to love a lycan, no power on earth could turn her from her chosen course of action. It was one of the things he loved most about her.

"But of course," he said.

Tanis lurked in the shadow of the gatehouse until he saw Sonja approaching on horseback. Two Death Dealers rode behind her. Together, the trio of mounted warriors presented an intimidating aspect, so it required no little courage to step out in front of them and block their path. He threw up his hands to get their attention.

"Lady Sonja! Your father has ordered you to stay behind."

Irritation flashed across her face as she pulled back on Hecate's reins. The horse snorted indignantly in the scribe's face.

"I intend to see our guests safely through the gates," Sonja declared. She lowered her helmet over her head, so that its masklike visor concealed all but her eyes. A mane of horsehair crested the helm.

Tanis stood his ground. "This is not a request. Your father is ruler of this coven."

"Yes, he keeps reminding me of that." She drew her sword from its scabbard and pointed its tip directly at the scribe's heart. Her cold brown eyes dared him to defy her. Hecate's hooves pawed impatiently at the paving-stones. "You are in my way."

Tanis looked anxiously to the other Death Dealers

for support, only to see the armored warriors draw their own swords, as well. Despite her strained relations with Viktor and the High Council, she clearly enjoyed the loyalty of her men. His eyes searched Sonja's grim, implacable expression, and he came to the unmistakable conclusion that she was not bluffing.

He got out of the way.

Dismissing him without another word, Sonja locked eyes with the master of the gate, a burly lycan slave whose bare chest was liberally adorned with battle scars. His valiancy in holding back the werewolf hordes had earned him a privileged status second only to Lucian's. He stood to one side of a massive steel bolt, shrewdly keeping his silence while his superiors quarreled. He lowered his head before Sonja's gaze.

"Gatemaster!" she commanded. "Do your duty!"

The obedient slave drew back the bolt and pulled open the ponderous double doors that served as the castle's last line of defense. The portcullis beyond rose slowly until nothing lay between Sonja and the lowered drawbridge beyond. Thick fog hid the winding road leading down the side of the mountain. The untamed wilderness rose to meet the lower slopes of the hill.

Her sword at the ready, she spurred Hecate onward. The horse's hooves thundered across the drawbridge, followed by the other two Death Dealers on their steeds. Tanis sullenly watched them depart, his ego still smarting from Sonja's brusque and insulting treatment.

She might not be so arrogant, he thought sourly, *if she*

knew that her sordid little secret *is mine to expose.* He looked forward to flaunting that knowledge in her face someday soon. *When the time is right.*

Turning away from the gate, he found Lucian standing only a few feet away. A loaded crossbow, perhaps the same one he had employed to save Sonja the night before, resided in the lycan's grip. He stared after the galloping horsemen with a look of obvious concern.

Tanis remembered an old adage. *Speak of the wolf and you will see his teeth.*

He could not resist taunting the foolhardy slave a bit. "Careful, blacksmith," he whispered in an insinuating tone. "Lest your eyes betray your secret."

Lucian's startled expression was a thing of beauty. Tanis savored the worried look that came over the other man's face as the scribe casually turned his back on Lucian and strolled back toward the keep. *Let him wonder what I could possibly know, and whom I might tell.* No doubt such questions would prey cruelly on Lucian's mind. *As well they should.*

It was the least the filthy lycan deserved for presuming to dally with one of his betters.

Sonja heard the carriage trundling through the fog before she caught sight of it. She and her men met the envoy at a crossroads along a lonely forest trail that reminded her of her thrilling adventure the night before. The driver of the coach started in alarm at the sound of their hooves, then relaxed at the sight of the armored trio. He slowed the carriage to a halt, giving his weary horses a much-needed rest. Sonja did not envy the poor animals the task of having to pull the heavy, steel-plated carriage over these bumpy roads.

She pulled up to the coach and greeted the two Death Dealers escorting the delegation. The was just the first of several caravans expected this evening. "I thought you could use some company."

The knights looked grateful for the reinforcements. These woods could be perilous at night, as she knew better than most. A pair of wide green eyes peered from a narrow slit in the side of the carriage; from the look of them, the eyes belonged to a frightened young girl on the cusp of womanhood. Sonja removed her helmet and smiled tightly at the girl, hoping to reassure her, before circling the caravan. The sight of the hooded prisoners chained to the rear of the carriage brought a scowl to her face. The mortals were doubtless intended as gifts for her father, but that hardly excused such reprehensible treatment. Her love for Lucian had opened her eyes to the often cruel inequities of the world they lived in. For all she knew, these unfortunate slaves no more deserved such abuse than Lucian himself.

When I become an Elder, she resolved, *such injustices will not be permitted.*

For now, however, the best she could do was see to it that they reached the castle in one piece. Her eyes scanned the shadowy wilderness surrounding them. A thick gray mist drifted through the underbrush, obscuring her vision. A wind rustled the shrubs and branches. Nothing stirred in the brush. Clouds drifted past the moon and stars. All seemed in order, and yet . . .

One of the Death Dealers, a grizzled veteran named Ivan, sat up straight up in his saddle. His head swiveled to the right, as though he had heard something from the encroaching woods. His hand went to the hilt of his sword. A note of alarm crept into his voice.

"Milady?"

Sonja peered into the darkness. Lucian's ominous warning echoed in her memory. Perhaps she should not have dismissed his fears so readily? The shackled slaves grew restive, perhaps sensing a change in the atmosphere. Muffled cries and whimpers escaped their hoods. Fear showed in the bulging eyes of the girl in the carriage. Ardent prayers issued from inside the armored coach.

I don't like this, Sonja thought. Her eyes had yet to detect any obvious threat, but she felt a distinct presentiment of impending doom. The sooner they left these accursed woods, the better she would feel. "Get it moving."

Before the procession could start rolling again, however, a blood-chilling howl shattered the tranquil stillness of the night. Adrenaline rushed through her veins. Her eyes widened. *Hellfire,* she cursed, experiencing an unwanted sense of what the Franks called *déjà vu.* Her voice rang out urgently.

"FORM UP!"

All five Death Dealers spread out to establish a defensive ring around the carriage, with Sonja taking up a position near the head of the wagon. Hecate whinnied in alarm and Sonja took a moment to try to calm the worried destrier. Inspecting their meager forces, she wished that she had brought a larger complement of soldiers.

Forgive me, Lucian, she thought. *I should have paid more heed to your warnings.*

She wondered if she would see her lover again.

Lucian paced restlessly in the courtyard. His eyes probed the fog beyond the gate for any sign of Sonja's return. He listened anxiously for the sound of hoof-beats or the clatter of a rolling carriage. Assorted Death Dealers and courtiers milled about by the gateway, waiting to welcome the mortal delegation upon their arrival. Viktor and the High Council were notably absent; no doubt they considered it beneath their dignity to wait in attendance upon mere mortals. Any visitor to the castle was required to present themselves to the Elder and his illustrious court instead. They would be escorted into the great hall at Viktor's convenience and not a moment before.

Just as well, Lucian thought, grateful for Viktor's absence. He was tense enough without having to worry about the Elder's scrutiny, especially after Tanis's vague insinuations earlier. He recalled the unsettling feeling that had troubled him before, as though he and Sonja had been watched right before they had parted. Was it possible that the ubiquitous scribe knew of their secret liaisons? The very idea was enough to fill Lucian's soul with dread. Tanis had Viktor's ear. What might he have told Sonja's father already?

Perhaps he only suspects *the truth?*

A faint noise, coming from beyond the castle's walls,

immediately drove such concerns to the back of his mind. Lucian threw back his head, straining his ears to make out the disturbing sound, which nobody else in the courtyard seemed to have noticed yet. He sniffed the air.

Was that a howl he heard?

And the smell of a hungry beast?

"No," he whispered. His heart sank. He knew with certainty that his apprehensions had been fulfilled.

Sonja was in danger.

Chapter Seven

A mud-covered claw erupted from the floor of the forest. Razor-sharp talons sank into the leg of Ivan's horse, grabbing onto it with preternatural strength. The Death Dealer swore in surprise, and the horse neighed in panic, as his steed was yanked violently to the ground as though being sucked into a mire of voracious quicksand. Hundreds of pounds of screaming horseflesh hit the earth with a thunderous impact. Ivan was thrown from his saddle. His armor crashed loudly against the rocky soil.

What's happening? Sonja thought in confusion. Her helmet slipped from her fingers, ringing out as it bounced off a nearby boulder. Shocked by this sudden turn of events, she barely noticed its loss. *I don't understand!*

The stallion's collapse panicked the horses drawing the carriage. They backed away fearfully, shoving the entire coach backward. A back wheel slipped into a deep rut at the edge of the road and the carriage lurched to one side. Fragile bodies smacked against the interior of the toppled coach. The girl and her family shrieked in fright. The driver shouted uselessly at the distraught horses.

"God preserve us!" the nameless maiden cried out. "I don't want to die!"

Unlike the Death Dealer's armored destriers, the carriage horses were not trained to ignore the tumult of battle. Gnashing at their bits, the frenzied animals thrashed wildly in their frantic desire to escape the terror that seemed to have struck out of nowhere. They tugged at their restraints until, with a resounding crack, the harness rod snapped in two. The reins were yanked from the driver's grip as the terrified team bolted for safety, leaving the stranded carriage behind. The horses vanished into the fog but did not get far. Seconds later, a cacophony of savage growls and agonized wails made the team's gruesome demise horribly clear to anyone with ears. The doomed horses sounded as though they were being ripped apart by bloodthirsty fangs and claws.

Which was precisely the case.

The death cries of the butchered horses did not escape Lucian's keen ears. He realized at once that Sonja and her companions were only moments away from suffering the same fate. He ran up to the nearest Death Dealer and shouted urgently.

"Get your men out there, NOW!"

The vampire looked puzzled, and vaguely annoyed, to be addressed so by a mere lycan. Lucian realized to his dismay that no one else had heard the howling yet. The Death Dealers exchanged puzzled looks between themselves, confused by the blacksmith's intemperate outburst. No one was taking him seriously.

Fools! he thought angrily. *What's the matter with you? Can't you hear them dying?*

"Down, boy!" Kosta rode up on his horse and snatched the crossbow from Lucian's hands. He sat lazily astride the great black stallion. "I think your leash is too tight." His silver-tipped bullwhip was coiled at his side. He fingered the grip of the lash as he glowered at Lucian. The scornful look in his eyes made it clear that he had not forgotten yesterday's confrontation. He appeared eager for an excuse to teach the upstart lycan a lesson. "Step ba—"

"There are too many of them!" Lucian shouted. He tried desperately to make the sneering overseer understand. *"They'll be massacred!"*

But Kosta merely snarled and grabbed onto his whip. Lucian realized that there was no reasoning with the man, nor time enough to bandy words with the uncomprehending Death Dealers. Without a second to lose, he leapt at Kosta and knocked the startled overseer from his saddle. The vampire grunted in pain as he landed hard upon the pavement. Moving swiftly, before any of the other Death Dealers could stop him, Lucian took Kosta's place within the saddle. He thrust his boots into the stirrups and spurred the steed with his heels. Although he had seldom ridden a horse before, the stallion got the message. It took off at a gallop, nearly trampling a cluster of vampires lingering before the gate. A Death Dealer raised his sword in surprise and Lucian snatched the weapon from the vampire's hand. His other fist held onto the reins for dear life as the horse raced out of the courtyard.

"Stop him!" Kosta hollered in rage. "Don't let him get away!"

Lucian half expected to feel a crossbow bolt strike him in the back at any moment, but apparently the disorganized Death Dealers were too taken aback by the lycan's unexpected move to respond with the necessary promptness. Lucian was well beyond the drawbridge, and out of range of the castle's archers, before anyone fully grasped what had just occurred. The horse's racing hooves tore up the ground beneath them. A damp, clammy fog enveloped both horse and rider.

He didn't even look back. Nothing mattered now but getting to Sonja in time. The ferocious sounds of battle filled his ears, driving him onward. He kicked savagely at the stallion's flanks.

Hold on, Sonja! he pleaded silently. His heart pounded in his chest. *I'm coming!*

Sonja spun Hecate about as yet another of the guards' horses went down with a sickening thud. The rider—Blasko by name—tumbled to the ground as well, landing in a heap of flailing limbs and dented metal. His drawn sword flew from his fingers. Swearing profanely, he groped urgently for his weapon.

Bloody claws, rising up from the earth, tore at the downed horse's leg. Sonja stared at the carnage in shock, finally grasping what was happening all around her. *By the sacred blood of Corvinus, the werewolves are attacking us from below!*

Screams escaped the toppled carriage. Intent on defending the trapped mortals, Sonja tugged on Hecate's reins, reeling the horse around so that she was facing the coach. She drew her silver-plated sword just as, like a nightmare come to life, a berserk werewolf landed on the armored roof of the carriage. The beast grabbed the shrieking driver with two hairy forepaws and plucked him from his seat as easily as it might lift a child's doll. Before Sonja could come to the mortal's aid, the werewolf hurled the driver to the ground, where the man's skull shattered like an eggshell, spilling his brains onto the muddy earth. A crimson halo pooled around his head. He was killed instantly.

She suspected that he might be one of the lucky ones.

The beast was not alone. More werewolves dropped from the trees, attacking the carriage and its defenders. Their barbaric howls competed with the high-pitched screams coming from both the coach and the blindfolded slaves, as well as the pitiful wails of the crippled horses. Chains rattled as the terrified prisoners tugged uselessly at their bonds. They couldn't even see what was attacking them, only hear the growls of the monsters.

"Take your positions!" Sonja shouted over the din.

Her Death Dealers surged into action. They rallied around the fearless noblewoman, both on foot and on horseback. Ivan and Blasko staggered to their feet, while the remaining horsemen charged until battle. A werewolf lunged from the forest, tackling a mounted warrior named Erzsi and knocking her to the ground. Roaring, the beast slashed at her armor with daggerlike claws. Blood spurted from torn flesh and metal. Erzsi screamed her last.

The battle had only begun, Sonja realized, and they were already losing. Hot lycan blood sprayed across her face as she hacked and stabbed at the nearest creature. There was no time to recover her helmet; she had only her body armor and sword to defend her.

That would have to be enough.

The first werewolf dug his claws into the roof of the carriage. Tortured metal squealed in protest as the monster peeled back a sheet of heavy armor plating. . . .

". . . we beseech Thee, O Lord, that in the hour of our death we may be refreshed by Thy holy Sacraments and delivered from all guilt and so deserve to be received with joy into the arms of Thy tender mercy. . . ."

Inside the carriage, Natalya's parents prayed in unison as all the Powers of Darkness seemed to descend on them from without. Her mother's embroidery lay forgotten upon the floor, along with her father's parchments. Her mother's fingers clutched her rosary beads, which a returning Crusader had sworn were carved from pieces of the True Cross. Her father had paid a small fortune for the beads, much good they were doing them now. Father's head was bowed in prayer. Mother's chubby face was white as a ghost. Blood leaked from a cut on her father's brow, sustained when the carriage had tilted abruptly on its side. Natalya's own bones still ached from the jolt. A bump throbbed at the back of her head. The glass lantern was cracked across its face.

". . . though we walk through the valley of the shadow of death, we will fear no evil. Please, God, deliver our souls from the clutches of the Evil One. . . ."

Her parents' fervent orisons did nothing to alleviate the girl's terror. She was only sixteen. She was too young to die. She had never even kissed a boy yet!

"Father . . ." In the past, whenever her childish imagination had turned shadows in the nursery into lurking specters, her father had always been there to drive her fears away. His warm and comforting presence had been enough to keep the ogres at bay. But one look at his ashen features quickly informed her that she could expect no such deliverance tonight. Against real monsters, he was as helpless as any other man.

The candle sputtered out, leaving them trapped in the dark.

No! she despaired. *This can't be happening!*

A wrenching noise came from beyond. Moonlight invaded the carriage, followed by the head of an enormous wolf! A deafening roar filled the darkness. Foam sprayed from immense jaws that snapped wildly at those inside. The beast's rank breath was as hot as Perdition.

Mother dived for the floor, but Natalya froze in place, too petrified to move. Memories of Red Riding

Hood and the Big Bad Wolf flashed through her brain. She couldn't look away from the creature's cobalt eyes and gleaming white fangs. Its jaws opened wide.

The better to eat you with, my dear. . . .

The werewolf lunged at the girl, but at the last minute, Father shoved her out of the way. She tumbled onto the floor beside her mother, even as her father thrust his body between the monster and his family. The slathering jaws closed on his head and shoulders with a nauseating crunch. Blood splattered the luxurious interior of the wrecked carriage. A headless body dropped onto the embroidered seat cushions.

Father!

Cowering on the floor, while her mother feverishly prayed for their souls, Natalya suddenly remembered the expensive damask gown packed away in her luggage. She had spent hours selecting the fabric for the gown with which she had intended the dazzle the fine gentlemen of Lord Viktor's court. The finest seamstress in the village had tailored the dress especially for her.

How tragic that she would never get to wear it.

The battle was still raging when Lucian rode out of the fog into the heat of the conflict. A scene of utter chaos and carnage greeted his eyes, which swiftly took in the stranded carriage, downed horses, and embattled Death Dealers. He saw at once that the vampires were badly outnumbered. He counted at least a dozen werewolves, with who knew how many more lurking in the trees and undergrowth. His grip tightened on the hilt of his stolen sword. Searching desperately for Sonja, he did not immediately spy his love. He cursed the fog and shadows for hiding her from him.

Where are you, Sonja? Let me know you're still alive!

Directly in front of him, an injured Death Dealer was fighting a losing battle against two rabid werewolves, who had him backed up against the mutilated body of his horse. The overwhelmed vampire slashed at one wolf with his sword, while the second wolf snapped at his legs. Mud and gore smeared the knight's dented armor. One arm hung limply at his side. His sword was broken. The truncated blade was barely the length of a dagger.

Lucian hesitated for only an instant. Although there was little love lost between him and Viktor's soldiers, they needed every ally they could spare if any of them hoped to survive this bloodbath. Racing headlong down the road, he leapt from the horse and tackled the nearest monster as if it were a runaway hog. Lycan and werewolf crashed to earth together. Rolling away from the beast, he jumped to his feet and raised his sword. He gripped the hilt with both hands as he swung the blade at the other werewolf's throat. The blade sliced through tough meat and muscle, nearly severing the werewolf's head from its shoulders. A scarlet trail streamed behind the sword like the tail of a comet.

Lucian's brown eyes turned cobalt blue. A fierce growl filled his ears.

It took him a second to realize that the growl was coming from his own throat.

Unable to see a thing because of the thrice-damned hood over his head, Raze could only listen to the nightmarish clamor all around him. Once an accomplished warrior and hunter, he recognized the unmistakable sounds and smells of strife. The screams of the dying warred with the roaring of beasts. The air reeked of blood and fear.

Death is upon us.

His fellow prisoners thrashed and screamed like maniacs, tugging so hard on their chains that Raze had to struggle to keep his balance. They pulled in all directions, getting nowhere fast. At the head of the line, just behind the carriage, Raze planted his feet on the muddy ground, anchoring himself to the earth. He wasn't about to be yanked blindly into the clutches of whatever creatures were assailing the caravan.

Not while he still had an ounce of strength in his body!

Despite his nightmarish situation, he refused to panic. He was the son of a sultan and he would not disgrace his ancestors by being slaughtered as easily as a frightened antelope brought down by a lion. His wits were his only weapons now. He would die on his feet if he had to, while looking his killer bravely in the face.

But first he to get rid of this stinking hood!

Bending his thick neck toward his bound hands, he managed to snag the top of the hood with his fingertips. He held on tightly to the coarse fabric and yanked his head back. His heart leapt in excitement as his skull slipped free of the hood for the first time in hours. A smooth brown dome crowned his solid features. A short black beard carpeted his chin. He filled his lungs with the fresh night air. Shrewd brown eyes rapidly assessed the ghastly massacre being waged around him.

It was even worse than he had imagined.

Before his eyes, only a few yards away, a knight in black plate armor was dragged down from his horse by a monstrous black wolf the size of a mountain gorilla. Raze saw at once that the creatures attacking the caravan were no ordinary wolves; many of them walked erect like men and stood even taller than Raze himself. *Werewolves,* he realized, recalling eerie tales told by the other slaves while they huddled together at night. It was said that these inhuman predators had once been mortal men. . . .

Sprawled upon his back, the fallen knight flailed at the werewolf with his fists, but his blows smacked impotently against the monster's snout. Jagged fangs punched through metal as the wolf ripped the soldier's arm from its socket. Bright arterial blood sprayed from the victim's shoulder, splattering Raze and the other prisoners. Violent death throes rattled the knight's useless armor as the werewolf tore him apart limb by limb. His horse stampeded away, only to be brought down by two more werewolves. The charger's frantic whinnies were cut off abruptly.

The knight's blood felt surprisingly cold against Raze's face, more like the blood of a dead man—or an *obayifo*—than a living warrior. He reached to wipe it away, but the iron manacles weighed down his hands. Thick links of chain still bound him to the back of the carriage, making it impossible to fight back or flee. Although the werewolves seemed to be concentrating on the armed guards at the moment, Raze knew that it was only a matter of time before they feasted on the slaves as well. Chained, he didn't stand a chance against the bloodthirsty pack. Only with his hands free could he defend himself to the death.

The empty hood dropped from his fingers. Clenching his teeth, he took hold of one of the chains with both hands and pulled with all his might. . . .

Flattened against the floor of the carriage, Natalya and her mother clung to each other as they whimpered in terror. The wolf at the roof snapped and snarled, straining to squeeze its shaggy bulk through the gap in the armor. Its claws scraped against the stubborn metal. Drenched in her father's blood, Natalya squeezed her eyes shut and wondered how much it hurt to be eaten alive. Had her father suffered before he died, or had the wolf's powerful jaws killed him as swiftly as a headsman's ax? Natalya sobbed piteously. Her mother's endless prayers fell on empty ears. Tears streamed from her eyes. What mattered if she died unshriven? They were already in hell.

Where are the Death Dealers? she thought. *Why aren't they saving us?*

The entire coach rocked back and forth, like a ship tossed about upon a stormy sea, as another monster slammed into the side of the carriage again and again. A painted yellow wall bulged inward, wooden planks splintering loudly. The treasure chest slid across the floor, slamming into the maiden's side hard enough to bruise her ribs. Mother pulled Natalya under her, sheltering the girl with her own well-fed body. Her blood-soaked wimple had come loose, exposing graying blond hair. The string of rosary beads broke apart. The precious relics rolled and bounced over the quaking floor.

Another titanic blow shook the coach. Steel and timber buckled as the head and shoulders of a *second* werewolf smashed its way into the carriage. Canine jaws clamped down on Natalya's mother and tore her away from the girl. The wolf shook the older woman's body back and forth while more blood painted the interior of the carriage incarnadine.

Suddenly an orphan, Natalya was all alone in the dark.

Sonja was the last vampire still astride a horse. The rest of the Death Dealers had already been yanked to the ground. Her sword cut a bloody swath before her. A crimson stream gushed down the gutter of her double-edged blade. Hecate reared up, striking out at the swarming werewolves with her steel-shod hooves. But for every creature Sonja struck down, two more seemed to burst from the swirling mist. Her azure eyes glowed like balefire.

Was there no end to these creatures?

A heart-wrenching scream called her attention back to the besieged carriage. Squinting through the grisly haze of battle, she spied a werewolf clinging to the side of the coach. Another beast crouched upon the roof. Ruptured steel plates suggested the carriage's passengers were in mortal peril, if not already dead. Sonja remembered the innocent mortal girl she had smiled at before. She prayed that she was not too late to save her.

Hecate charged toward the carriage. The horse's thundering tread alerted the werewolf on the side of the coach. Turning away from its mortal prey, the beast growled at Sonja's approach. Gore dripped from its open jaws.

Whose blood is that? Sonja wondered. *The girl's?*

A massive paw swung at her head, its lethal claws slicing through the air. Sonja ducked beneath the claw and, in one smooth move, slashed her blade across the werewolf's abdomen. Hot blood sprayed from the gash, and the beast's steaming entrails spilled onto the ground. Howling in agony, the werewolf clutched at its guts with its clumsy mitts, even as more of its innards dangled from the grievous wound. A crimson flood gushed through its fingers. It dropped limply onto the ground beside the coach. A billowing sheet of fog covered the carcass.

Hecate trampled the body beneath her hooves. Sonja savored the monster's death.

If only she could have slain it a few moments earlier!

Off to the other side of the carriage, Raze fought for his life against the unyielding chain. Swollen veins bulged beneath his skin. Beefy muscles, hardened by years of backbreaking servitude, strained to the utmost as he dug his heels into the dirt and tugged on the chain until his aching arms and back felt as if they were being torn apart on the rack. His knuckles whitened and the rusty links dug savagely into his sweaty palms. But despite his strenuous exertions, the chain refused to give even an fraction of inch. The trapped slave feared that he wasting the last moments of his life.

Intent on his struggle, he nearly jumped out of his boots when the coach door banged open only a few feet away. The sudden noise made his heart miss a beat. A second later, a blood-soaked corpse slumped out of the carriage onto the ground. It took Raze a moment to recognize the mutilated body as the master's daughter, Natalya. The girl's throat had been torn open, her fine clothes ripped to shreds. Glazed green eyes and a tortured expression captured the unspeakable horror of her final moments. Every inch of her ravaged body was awash in blood.

May your ancestors guide your soul to Paradise, Raze thought, mourning her loss. Never mind that her father had enslaved him and treated him harshly; Raze had not known the girl at all, but no one deserved to die in so barbaric a fashion. *Let alone one so young and fair.*

A werewolf leapt from the roof of the carriage, landing a few yards away from Raze and the other prisoners. Its cobalt eyes glared at the hooded captives. Drooling black lips peeled back, baring bloody fangs. Its hackles rose.

Raze looked around for help and spotted a bearded stranger wrestling with a wolf near the back of the carriage. No knight, the man wore a tattered leather vest and trousers. His spiked collar looked even more painful than the iron ring around Raze's own throat. The stranger had one arm locked around a werewolf's throat and was struggling to keep out of the way of the beast's deadly fangs and claws while hacking at the monster with a bloody sword. Clearly, he had troubles of his own. . . .

This is it, Raze realized. It was now or never. *Freedom or death.*

Gritting his teeth, he threw himself into one last herculean effort. He yanked hard on the chain attached to his manacles and was rewarded with the sound of a loud snap at the other end of the links. He staggered backward, almost falling onto his rear, even as the ravenous werewolf pounced at him. Gaping jaws offered him a view straight down the monster's gullet.

Raze swung the severed chain like a lash. The iron links cracked against the werewolf's skull. The beast let out a hurt yelp and collapsed to the ground. Its body twitched and fell still. A bloody froth spumed from its jaws. Raze whipped the wolf again and again until he was sure it was dead, then looked up to see the bearded stranger staring at him in wonder. His strange blue eyes took Raze's measure even as he withdrew his sword from the bowels of a fallen werewolf. Steam rose from the monster's exposed entrails.

"Impressive," the man said. He lobbed his sword over to Raze before returning to the fray.

Chapter Eight

Sonja called out to the carriage's passengers, but no one answered. Concerned for their safety, and fearing the worst, she jumped down from Hecate and hurried to check on the coach. She took only a few steps, however, before the earth erupted right behind her. Sonja spun around, sword in hand, but not fast enough. A werewolf sprouted from the ground, like a mythological monster spawned from a dragon's tooth, and grabbed her from behind. A sharp pain stabbed her in the side as the creature's claws penetrated her metal cuirass. Her boots lost contact with the slippery mud as she was yanked down into a yawning pit. She hacked and stabbed at her captor even as she fell into the darkness.

Hellfire!

She landed hard upon a rough floor several feet beneath the forest. Driven back by her sword, the werewolf retreated for an instant, allowing her to hastily take stock of her surroundings. To her amazement, she found herself trapped in a network of crude tunnels stretching away into the shadows. Tangled roots hung like stalactites from the ceiling. Centipedes and other vermin wriggled through the dank clay and earth. A few faint beams of moonlight entering the underground warren via gaps in the ceiling gave her just enough light to see by. Fog tumbled through the open pits. The pungent scent of the werewolves polluted the air. She choked on the stench.

The size and extent of the tunnels astounded her. The beasts had built all this, in anticipation of this ambush?

Perhaps they're not nearly so mindless as we believed.

A quick glance informed that she was far from alone. Werewolves infested the tunnels like oversized rats, scrambling to join the battle overhead. Meanwhile, the wolf that had snared her was closing in for the kill. Blood dripping from his injured snout, the beast charged at her with murder in its eyes. . . .

Rounding the corner of the carriage, Lucian spotted Sonja at last. His heart leapt with joy and relief. *Thank the fates she's alive!* But before he could call out to her, a werewolf lunged up from out of nowhere and dragged her, kicking and shouting, beneath the earth. In an instant, she disappeared from sight.

No! Lucian raged.

He couldn't believe that he had found her, only to

have her snatched away from him at the last minute. He raced to where she had been standing only seconds before. The forest floor trembled beneath his feet and he looked down to see a moving hump of dirt shifting below the leaf litter and other detritus like a gargantuan mole. His keen ears heard a snarling werewolf racing underground—straight toward Sonja!

Empty fists clenched in frustration. What had he been thinking off, tossing his sword to that defenseless slave? Glancing around for a weapon, he spied an exhausted Death Dealer slumped against the trunk of a skeletal oak. The vampire's ebony armor was liberally splattered with blood, whether his own or his enemies' Lucian could not tell. Without pausing to ask permission, he snatched the soldier's sword from his grip and raced after the burrowing werewolf. His fist tightened around the ornate steel hilt of the weapon. Thankfully, only the blade was coated with silver.

The disarmed Death Dealer shouted in protest, but Lucian wasn't listening. Rescuing Sonja was all that mattered now.

If she wasn't already dead.

Trapped underground like a prisoner in her father's dungeons, Sonja scooted backward until she bumped into a solid wall of earth. Gnarled roots snatched at her hair. Cold vampiric blood seeped through the jagged gash in her armor. Backed against the hard-packed clay, she fought to keep the hungry werewolf at bay. The cramped tunnel made it difficult to wield her sword effectively, yet she jabbed at the beast's snapping jaws and cobalt eyes, while kicking out at the monster with her spurs. The wolf's huge head ducked and darted, searching for an opening past her defenses. Its hot breath, redolent of raw meat and marrow, sickened her. She found it impossible to believe that Lucian could possibly be related to such a vile monstrosity.

Farewell, my love, she thought. *I fear I shall not know your sweet embrace once more.* She winced at the memory of their brief quarrel earlier. It pained her to think that her final words to him had been so cold. *Please know that I always loved you. . . .*

Despite her preternatural stamina, she felt her strength flagging. The wound in her side burned like fire; blood loss sapped her energy. Her mouth felt as dry as ashes and she would have killed for a fresh flagon of hot cattle blood to restore her vitality. It had been too long since she had last refreshed herself from the castle's slaughterhouse. Alas, the foul ichor of the werewolves could not slake her thirst. The very thought turned her stomach.

Beneath her armor, her body was soaked in sweat. Her dark bangs were plastered to her smooth white brow. The heavy metal plates and chain mail felt as though they weighed at least a ton. The tip of her sword wavered uncertainly as her weary arm strained to hold it before her. Her lungs gasped for air in the claustrophobic confines of the tunnel. Sweat dripped into her eyes. She tasted salt upon her lips.

Sensing weakness, the werewolf lunged for her face. . . .

Lucian heard the monster growl. His eyes zeroed in on the telltale hump beneath the soil. Realizing that he had not a second to spare, he dived forward and *buried* the blade deep into the ground. A savage howl burst from his lips.

Die, hellspawn, die!

Sonja swung her sword, but the blade snarled in the hanging roots. Unable to wrench it free in time, she could only throw her head backward against the hard clay wall behind her as the werewolf surged forward to rip her face off. Without her helmet, nothing stood between her and beast's fangs except empty air. Spittle sprayed her cheeks.

It seemed she would not live to be an Elder after all.

Just then, when all seemed lost, a silver blade stabbed down from above, piercing the werewolf's skull. Its jaws snapped tight as it convulsed once, then died without a whimper. The sword pinned the monster's head to the floor of the tunnel. Acrid fumes rose from where the silver seared its lifeless flesh.

Sonja blinked in surprise, startled to find herself rescued from certain death.

What? How?

"Sonja!"

She recognized Lucian's voice at once, even if she could scarcely believe that her ears were not deceiving her. Squeezing past the dead werewolf, she looked up to see Lucian staring anxiously down at her through the open shaft above her. A gibbous moon haloed his worried face. Leaning over the crumbling edge of the pit, he reached for her with outstretched fingers.

The welcome sight of him renewed her spirits. She had no idea how he had come to be here, so far from the castle walls, but for now she didn't care. It was enough that he was here for her, just when she needed him most.

Leaping to her feet, she rescued her sword from the roots and gratefully took hold of his hand. His strong fingers clasped hers as he pulled her up from the tunnels. She breathed a sigh of relief as she scrambled onto the muddy surface of the crossroads, safely free of the hidden warren below. The open sky, glimpsed through the bony tree branches, was a vast improvement over the stifling confinement of the subterranean tunnels. A cold wind blew against her face. She no longer felt like she was buried alive. How on earth did the Elders endure it every hundred years?

Lucian looked her over anxiously. His eyes widened in alarm as he spied the bleeding rent in her armor.

"You are hurt."

Her hand went to her side and came away wet and sticky. Overjoyed by Lucian's miraculous arrival, she had almost forgotten how the wolf had slashed her ribs, but an excruciating pang brutally brought her back to reality. Her torn flesh throbbed painfully. She tottered unsteadily upon legs that suddenly felt as limp as cotton. The bright blue light in her eyes faded.

Damnation! What did that mangy wolf do to me?

Maintaining a stoic expression, she tried to dismiss the wound, but her legs buckled beneath her and she crumpled onto the ground. Lucian dropped to her side, visibly distressed by her collapse. Blood coursed from her side, pooling beneath them. She winced as his fingers delicately probed the wound through the gap in her armor. He didn't need to tell her how bad it was. A few more inches and the monster's claws would have disemboweled her.

A chorus of angry growls reminded them that they were literally not out of the woods yet. Looking away from Lucian's troubled face, she saw an entire pack of werewolves circling them. There had to be at least a half dozen of the relentless beasts, all intent on devouring their flesh and blood. Their cobalt eyes glowed in the dark like a swarm of lightning-bugs. Lucian took her sword and jumped to his feet to defend her. He brandished the silver blade menacingly, but the wolves did not back off. Confident that their prey could not escape them, they took their time as they cautiously closed in on the ill-starred couple. Sonja longed to fight back against the monsters, but it was all she could do to keep from passing out from blood loss. She sagged against Lucian's legs, holding onto him for support. Darkness encroached on her vision. Her eyelids drooped.

She shook her head to clear her thoughts. Her eyes searched the misty crossroads for help, but saw none forthcoming. If any of the other Death Dealers had survived, they seemed nowhere nearby. Sonja feared that she was last vampire alive in these woods.

If only for the moment . . .

She squeezed Lucian's hand as they faced the teeming pack together. She had no illusions that even his matchless strength and courage could prevail against such overwhelming odds. *At least I will not die alone,* she consoled herself. *If I must perish, let it be at my true love's side.*

But Lucian had another idea.

Dropping the sword, he reached beneath his belt and pulled something from a small woolen pouch. Sonja's eyes widened in alarm as he plucked the key from the pouch. Her heart stopped as she grasped what he intended.

"No," she murmured weakly. *It's forbidden.*

Ignoring her protests, Lucian jammed the key into the lock holding the moon shackle around his neck. A metallic click greeted the key and the collar snapped open. The silver spikes fell away from throat. He grabbed onto the open shackle and hurled it away from him.

The effect was instantaneous.

His fair skin darkened, turning a mottled shade of gray. His unruly scalp birthed a mane of coarse black fur that sprouted from his head and shoulders, then spread across his body and limbs, which themselves lengthened and grew larger in the space of a heartbeat. His blood-splattered vest and breeches came apart at the seams as he assumed the proportions of a giant. His fists curled into paws. Clawed feet shredded his leather boots.

The moon pulled on his flesh and bone, so that it flowed like the tide. His very skull underwent a grotesque metamorphosis. A canine muzzle protruded from his face. His brow sloped backward over fierce cobalt eyes. Tufted ears tapered to a point. Flattened nostrils flared above a maw full of jagged incisors. Foam dripped from his wolfen jaws.

Sonja gazed up at him in awe. Despite their past intimacies, she had never seen him like this before. Tall and strong and ferocious beyond belief, like the great beast Fenris of the Norsemen's myth. Although she had known, on an intellectual level, that Lucian was indeed a lycan, she had never imagined that the wolf inside was so wild, so . . . magnificent.

Lucian exulted in his newfound power. An overwhelming sense of exhilaration accompanied his transformation. More than two centuries had passed since he had last taken this shape, and he was no longer an insecure boy locked away in Viktor's dungeon. This time he had changed of his own accord. He flexed his shaggy limbs, feeling the inhuman strength and vitality in them. He had never felt so free.

Or so deadly.

Nevertheless, he was still sorely outnumbered. Six other werewolves stalked him warily, while more dropped from the trees or came crawling out of the tunnels. His startling metamorphosis had given the other wolves pause, but not sent them into retreat. Lucian bared his fangs and crouched defensively in front of Sonja. He realized he was in for the fight of his life. This was going to get bloody. . . .

So be it, he resolved. These beasts would get to Sonja over his dead body.

Throwing back his head, he let out a tremendous roar.

And other wolves stopped in their tracks.

Lucian couldn't believe his eyes. He held his breath as a hush fell over the werewolf horde. Their leathery snouts crinkled and they cocked their heads to the side. They lowered their eyes in submission. Lucian tried to understand what was happening. Although it seemed inconceivable, he would have sworn that the pack was *obeying* him.

One by one, the werewolves backed away, disappearing back into the forest. They leapt into the sheltering tree branches or else slunk away into fog. Within moments, to Lucian's vast astonishment, he and Sonja were alone upon the pitted roadway. Gaping cavities in the earth were all that remained of the marauding horde.

He looked down at her, fearing her reaction to his grotesque appearance. Even though the change had been their only hope, he had never wanted her to see him like this. What if she stared back at him in horror or revulsion? Now she knew that he was truly a beast and not a man. He wouldn't blame her if she never loved him again.

But, to his surprise and relief, he saw only awe in her beautiful chestnut eyes. She looked just as dumbfounded by the pack's abrupt departure as he was.

What happened there? he pondered. *Why did they listen to me?*

A large figure stumbled out of the fog, and Lucian immediately tensed for battle once more. Perhaps not all of the werewolves had abandoned the hunt after all? Then the figure stepped into a patch of moonlight and he saw that it was not a werewolf but rather the towering dark-skinned slave he had noticed before. The one who had slain a wolf with nothing more than a broken length of chain. A veritable mountain of a man, the bald warrior contemplated the werewolf and the vampire noblewoman from a safe distance. The sword Lucian had shared with him was still in his possession. Lucian wondered just how much the mortal had seen.

Does he understand that I saved us all?

The clicking of crossbow triggers intruded on the silence. A volley of silver-tipped bolts came whistling through the fog, thudding into the trunks of trees and striking sparks off the armored carriage. The clamor of pounding hooves preceded the sudden arrival of four more Death Dealers, who immediately took aim at the sole remaining werewolf before them.

Lucian.

Wait! he tried to call out, throwing up his paws, but only an inarticulate snarl escape his canine snout. Blood dripped from his claws. He realized to his dismay that it no doubt looked at though he was attacking Sonja. *You don't understand. I'm not one of* them!

The crossbows fired again. A silver quarrel zoomed toward his head with lethal precision.

Sonja leapt from the ground with blinding speed, swiping the bolt from the air only inches away from Lucian's skull. The lethal silver had no effect on her; only werewolves were poisoned by the precious metal. She flung the offending missile away from her.

Alas, a second bolt zipped below her arm and struck Lucian in the thigh. He howled in pain and grabbed for the arrow, but his clumsy paws could not take hold of the shaft. The silver arrowhead burned inside his thigh like a red-hot coal. He dropped to his knees, even as the metal stole his lycanthropic strength and stature from him. Sable fur receded from limbs and his bones contorted back into human guise. Wolfen claws retracted. Cobalt eyes dimmed to brown.

A third bolt stabbed him in the leg.

"No!" Sonja shouted. She threw herself in front of Lucian. "Stop!"

The lead horseman lowered his crossbow. A cruel chuckle revealed that he was none other than Kosta. A crooked smile showed through his Corinthian helmet. He watched with obvious satisfaction as the wounded werewolf turned back into Lucian. The naked slave writhed in agony upon the ground.

More riders emerged from the mist. Viktor rode past Kosta. Unlike the armored soldiers, the Elder wore a stately black robe and cape. A nervous-looking Tanis followed after him, riding a pale gray palfrey instead of a proper warhorse. The scribe held aloft a blazing torch. His eyes anxiously searched the woods around them. He clearly wished he were anywhere else than this treacherous crossroads. He flinched at the sight of the overturned carriage and the ravaged bodies surrounding it.

Concerned only with tending to Lucian's wounds, Sonja failed to acknowledge her father's arrival. Dropping to his side, she gently worked the barbed arrowheads from his punctured flesh and bone. Despite her delicate touch, every motion sent a fresh jolt of agony through his tortured body. Throbbing purple veins spread from each wound. Cramps and nausea gripped his innards. Sonja worked the blood-slick bolts back and forth in order to extricate them without breaking the birchwood shafts. He clenched his teeth to keep from screaming. It took all his willpower not to turn and snap at Sonja like a maddened hound.

Viktor observed the tender scene with visible distaste. His icy gaze went from Lucian's bare throat to the discarded moon shackle lying several yards away. He speared the collar with the tip of his sword and lifted it up for all to see. Anger flared in his eyes and voice.

"What is this?"

Alarmed by her father's outraged tone, Sonja rushed to explain. She looked up at him urgently. Tearful eyes beseeched his mercy. "He did it to save me!"

The vehemence of her cry only seemed to provoke him further. His eyes narrowed suspiciously, as though an ugly thought had begun to scrape at the back of his mind. Dismounting from his steed, he strode over to where Lucian lay bleeding and grabbed the lycan's hair. He jerked Lucian's head back and hissed into his face.

"Am I not the master of my house?"

His armored gauntlet slapped Lucian across the face. The force of the blow loosened the slave's teeth and sent him tumbling across the road. Lucian's head rang like a gong. He spit a mouthful of blood onto the ground. A flash of anger burnt brightly amidst the pain.

Was this his reward for saving Sonja's life?

"Father!" Sonja shouted. She stared aghast at her father, as if she didn't know who he was anymore. "Stop it!"

"*Am I not the master of my house?!*" he bellowed, as much at Sonja as at the brutalized lycan. He grabbed onto Lucian's throat and squeezed tightly. "Answer me, cur!"

Lucian struggled to lift his head from the road. A

large purple bruise discolored his face. Blood trickled from a split lip. One eye was swollen shut. His voice was hoarse and barely audible.

"I . . . yes."

"Yet you break my law." Viktor thrust the unlocked collar in Lucian's face. "After I gave you your life so many years ago." He yanked Lucian to his feet. "Your days of plush living are over, slave!"

Riding up behind Viktor, Tanis watched the humiliating spectacle with acute interest. Lucian glimpsed the scribe's sly smile and amused eyes. He seemed to be enjoying this almost as much as Kosta was.

Viktor drew back his hand to administer another crippling blow.

"Father!" Sonja grabbed his wrist. "Leave him be! I told you, he was merely—"

Viktor yanked his arm from her grip. His face was livid beneath his helmet as he spun around to confront her. "Hold your tongue!" Centuries of pent-up anger and frustration boiled over into his voice. "You have defied me for the last time."

He barked at Tanis. "Get her out of here!" Turning his back on his daughter, he nodded at Kosta and the other Death Dealers. "And take this ungrateful mongrel away!"

The knights descended on Lucian, kicking him in the ribs as they threw him back onto the ground. Rough hands rolled him onto his stomach and chained his hands and feet together. Dazed from Viktor's blow, and still smarting where the silver quarrels had pierced his flesh, Lucian lacked the strength to put up a fight. He could only hope that Viktor's temper would abate once they got back to the castle. Or had his desperate ploy with the key condemned him forever?

Kosta got down from his horse and spit on Lucian. Finally seeing his chance, he stepped vengefully on the back of the lycan's head. His heavy boot ground Lucian's face into the dirt.

Viktor did nothing to curb the overseer's cruelty. Sonja flinched, but seemed to realize that her protests on Lucian's behalf were only making things worse. Her eyes glistened moistly as she bit down on her lip and let Tanis guide her back toward Hecate, who had somehow come through the massacre with only a few more scars. Lucian watched her go.

At least I saved her life, he thought. *That's worth any punishment.*

Viktor muttered darkly beneath his breath. "I will have the skin off his back." He tossed the discarded collar over to Tanis. Venom dripped from his voice. "Dispose of this."

Leaving Lucian to Kosta's untender mercies, the Elder surveyed the ghastly carnage surrounding the carriage. Dismembered Death Dealers lay in pieces, their butchered mounts reduced to bloody heaps of bone and horseflesh. The daughter of a mortal noble was sprawled at the foot of the coach's open door, her throat torn open, her virgin blood wasted upon the mucky soil. The smell of death emanated from the interior of the carriage, which was now nothing more than an abattoir.

Viktor watched unhappily as his men rounded up a handful of mortal slaves who appeared to have come through the slaughter unscathed. Among them was a large Moor or Nubian who reluctantly surrendered a bloody sword to the knights. The Death Dealers led the prisoners away. Hoods covered the heads of all but the black giant.

Two centuries ago, Viktor would have worried about the murdered mortals coming back to life as werewolves, but, thankfully, William's curse had grown less infectious with each successive generation. Now only those who survived a werewolf's attack risked joining their loathsome ranks.

Still, there was no point in taking chances.

"Burn the bodies!" Viktor ordered. "Burn them all!"

Chapter Nine

Despite the imminent arrival of the other human nobles, practically the entire coven had turned out to witness Lucian's punishment. Burning braziers and flambeaux lit up the courtyard in front of the keep. Vampire lords and ladies, soldiers, servants, and courtesans mingled together, murmuring excitedly amongst themselves. The story of the ambush upon the caravan, and Lucian's subsequent rebellion, had spread like wildfire through the fortress. Avid spectators waited impatiently for tonight's entertainment.

Off to one side, the castle's lycan population had been herded together in the shadow of the unfinished tower and its scaffolding. Death Dealers watched over the restless slaves. Afraid to speak, the lycans shifted uneasily and exchanged furtive glances with each other.

Lucian spotted Xristo among them. The surly laborer, whom Lucian had rescued from Kosta's lash only yesterday, risked a muttered aside to his companion, a strapping lycan youth named Sabas. The men scowled unhappily at the dreadful spectacle under way before them:

Lucian hung spread-eagled between two vertical wooden posts in the center of the courtyard. Manacles of silver-iron alloy bit into his wrists and ankles. A new moon shackle pricked his neck. Naught but a grimy loincloth protected his modesty. Although the wounds from Kosta's arrows had scabbed over, his abused body remained in torment. His bare toes barely grazed the cobblestones, so that he was hanging more than standing. Gravity tugged on his depleted frame. His aching arms felt like they were being yanked from their sockets. His lips were cracked and dry. He would have sold his soul for a sip of fresh water.

Or perhaps one last kiss from Sonja.

Viktor strode up to Lucian. The Elder wore a magisterial black robe. His azure eyes dissected the chained lycan, whose life he had spared two centuries before. His gaunt face held a rueful expression. Lucian braced himself for another jarring blow, but instead Viktor cupped Lucian's chin with surprising gentleness. He lifted the lycan's face so that he could look the prisoner squarely in the eyes.

"You have stung me, Lucian, with your betrayal. You were like a son to me." He eyed the brand upon Lucian's arm, then glanced at the forbidding walls of the keep. The looming gray edifice rose like a gigantic tombstone above the hidden dungeons below. "I gave you life not ten feet from this very spot."

Under the circumstances, Lucian was feeling less than grateful. His voice croaked hoarsely. "You gave me *chains*."

"I would have thought after all these years you would have known that you cannot have one without the other." Viktor turned to Kosta, who was standing nearby, eagerly awaiting his moment. The Elder's face hardened. "Do it."

The armored overseer required no further prompting. His gray eyes gleamed with anticipation as he stalked forward brandishing a cat-o'-nine-tails. Shiny silver barbs flashed at the end of the knotted cords. His scar stood out lividly against his face. A smirk lifted the corners of his lips.

"I told you I would be there when you fell."

Lucian did not waste his breath pleading for mercy. He knew there would be none forthcoming.

Kosta stepped behind Lucian, out of the prisoner's line of sight. Lucian tried to crane his head around but the silver spikes in his collar tore at his skin. Unable to see Kosta, he could only wait tensely for the inevitable blow.

He did not have to wait long.

With a fury, Kosta brought down the lash. Nine silver-tipped cords struck Lucian's naked back, paring the flesh to the bone. Angry red welts crossed his flesh. Steam rose from scalded skin. His spine arched in agony. An audience of jaded immortals oohed and aahed in appreciation. Undead doxies giggled and licked their lips. Tanis kept a tally of the blows on a scrap of parchment.

The pain was unimaginable, yet Lucian endured the blows with stoic courage. Clenching his teeth to keep from crying out, he'd be damned if he gave the heartless vampires the satisfaction of seeing him whimper like a whipped dog. His bloodshot eyes searched the mob of spectators but found one face conspicuously absent. Desperate for something to focus on besides the brutal beating, his gaze lifted to an open window on the top floor of the keep.

But the window was empty.

The terrible reports of the whip invaded Sonja's private chambers. The opulent furnishings failed to soften the brutal cracks. She shuddered at the sound, almost as though the fearsome blows were falling upon her own immortal flesh as well. She steeled herself for her lover's screams, but heard nothing but the snap of the whip and the bloodthirsty reaction of the crowd below.

Monsters! The coven's voyeuristic enjoyment of Lucian's suffering filled her with disgust for her own kind. *It is they who are the animals, not my brave Lucian.*

The sheer injustice of it all offended her to her very core. In a better, more honest world, Lucian would have been knighted for his heroism these past two nights. But instead he was whipped and pilloried for the "crime" of doing everything in his power to defend her from the werewolves. Knowing what Lucian was going through at this very moment seared Sonja's soul more painfully than the brightest sunlight. That he should be tortured so was dreadful enough; that he was being punished for saving her broke her heart.

Tears streamed down her cheeks as she stared forlornly into the bronze-framed mirror above her vanity. Red-rimmed eyes gave away her distress. A funereal black gown fit her mood. Despair beckoned as she heard the cruel whip snap once more. In her mind's eye, she saw the caustic silver barbs scourging Lucian's precious flesh.

Be strong, my love. Know that I am with you in spirit.

Perhaps the hardest part of this ordeal was that she could not even weep openly, lest she fuel her father's suspicions. The venomous look on his face when he'd caught her tending to Lucian's wounds had chilled even her cold vampiric blood. For the first time in her two centuries of existence she had found herself fearing what her father was truly capable of . . . and how much he already knew. Did he even now have an inkling of what had transpired between her and Lucian? *Surely not,* she reasoned. The harrowing tribulation Lucian was enduring now was nothing to compared to what her father would do to him if he truly knew that a lycan had claimed his only daughter's virtue. *My father must never guess our secret, no matter how much it pains me to stand by while Lucian suffers for us both.*

Determined to put on a brave front and offer no hint of her inner turmoil, she wiped the salty tears from her cheeks. The face in the mirror froze into an icy mask, little different from the burnished steel helmet that often shielded her features from a dangerous world. Only the faint redness of her eyes bore testament to her tears. She took a deep breath to compose herself, then turned away from the mirror. She walked stiffly toward the window overlooking the courtyard. A whip cracked loudly, but she didn't even flinch.

At least not on the outside.

The whip cracked like thunder. Pain lashed Lucian's back and shoulders once more, burning like molten steel. He felt like a lump of metal on his own anvil, being tortured by the blows of a red-hot hammer. His skin sizzled every time the silver touched him. But still he refused to utter a single sound, even as his flayed body rocked beneath the impact of Kosta's lash.

Each blow elicited amused grins and titters from most of the audience. The fall of Viktor's favorite lycan was a rare diversion indeed. Only a handful of vampires frowned at the proceedings. They glanced nervously at the other lycans, as though worried that Lucian's public agonies might incite his fellow servants to revolt.

Their concern was not without basis. Among the gathered slaves, Xristo and Sabas could not bear to stand by idly while their fellow lycan was flayed before their eyes. Their faces contorted with rage, they lunged forward to intervene. But the watchful Death Dealers were ready for such an incident. Before the irate lycans could get more than a few steps, the soldiers clubbed them in the head with the butts of their crossbows. The men dropped to the ground, clutching the back of their skulls. Steel-toed boots kicked their ribs for good measure. Enjoying the sideshow, aristocratic vampires applauded.

The other lycans got the hint. They backed away from the guards, taking shelter in the shadows beneath the scaffolding. The Death Dealers hauled Sabas and Xristo up by their arms and hurled them bodily into the throng of servants. The men's limp bodies crashed to the pavement. No slave dared to come to their assistance, for fear of incurring the guards' wrath as well, so the battered lycans were left to groan and whimper upon the ground.

Rash fools! Lucian thought, observing the men's short-lived rebellion. While he appreciated their righteous anger on his behalf, he wanted no other lycan to suffer because of him. He had freely chosen to defy Viktor's edict for Sonja's sake, but the consequences of that fateful choice should be his alone. *This is my fight, not theirs.*

He looked again to the lofty window—and was rewarded with a vision of unearthly loveliness. Sonja gazed down at him from her bedchamber, which he had never dared set foot in. Although she kept her exquisite face still and impassive, so as not to betray their secret love, her moist eyes offered him a moment of solace in his ordeal. Even if there was nothing she could do to spare him, at least he could take comfort in the knowledge that he was not alone in this time of trial. Their eyes met briefly across the distance.

And then she was gone.

He watched as she disappeared behind a pair of closed velvet drapes. Could it be that she could not bear to watch anymore? Lucian scarcely blamed her. Were their positions reversed, he was not sure how long he could endure the sight of Sonja being tortured right before his eyes.

The fates forbid that such a nightmare should ever come to pass!

More blows rained down on Lucian's quivering form, each more vicious than the one before. He quickly lost count of the lashings, which blurred into an excruciating haze. He slumped in his bonds, held up only by the chains upon his wrists. Despite his earlier resolve, plaintive groans escaped his lips. Deep gashes crisscrossed his back, which was now a map recording previously uncharted realms of pain. Hot blood streamed from crimson traceries.

"Lord Viktor, hold!"

A grave-faced vampire, whom Lucian recognized as Coloman, spoke out boldly. Flanked by other members of the High Council, all with disapproving expressions, he broke away from the audience to address Viktor directly.

"What?" the Elder asked brusquely. He reluctantly tore his gaze away from the flogging.

Coloman gestured at Lucian. "Stop this. He is one of our protectors."

"They are beasts themselves," Viktor snarled. He cast a baleful glance at the other lycans, who backed away fearfully.

Coloman contemplated the huddled slaves as well. "This could stir up the others," he warned darkly. The other council members nodded in agreement. A few of them seemed to regard the restive slaves with distinct apprehension. A matronly vampiress, whose bloodline boasted several dukes and earls, clutched her jewelry as she contemplated the unwashed rabble.

"Let them stir." Viktor dismissed the Council's concerns with a wave of his hand. "Do you fear them? Believe me, it will be worse if we do *not* punish them." He turned to confront the insolent boyar. "Do you see now, Coloman? You would trust the lycans outside our walls?" He snorted derisively. "We cannot even trust them inside."

Turning his back on Coloman and the others, Viktor turned back toward Lucian and his avid tormentor. "By my count that is twenty-one!" he barked at Kosta. "Continue!"

The cruel lash tore at Lucian's flesh once more. He gritted his teeth to keep from screaming. Part of him wished he had fallen in battle against the werewolves instead.

Being torn apart by savage fangs and claws would have been bliss compared to this.

Chapter Ten

At last the ordeal was over. The crowd dispersed and uncaring Death Dealers roughly unfastened Lucian from the pillories. Barely conscious, he was only dimly aware of being dragged down into the lower reaches of the dungeons. Instead of his usual lair, he was tossed into the cavernous vault that housed the rest of the lycans. Arched recesses, stacked one atop another, were carved into the towering walls of the vault. The foul aroma of the cesspits wafted up from metal grates in the floor. Spiders, roaches, and other vermin infested the dirty straw carpeting the floor. Greenish mold streaked the rough granite walls. Brackish water trickled from the ceiling.

Reluctant to be associated with Lucian, the other lycans kept their distance. They huddled in their respective dens, watching Lucian uneasily. Only Sabas and Xristo showed any signs of concern, but, battered and bloody as they were, they were in no shape to come to Lucian's aid. He sprawled limply upon the filthy straw. Dried blood caked his back, which looked as though it had been dragged for leagues over broken rocks and glass. Red and raw, his anguished flesh could not bear even the touch of empty air. He moaned pitifully, no longer caring who might hear. Immortal though he was, Lucian wondered if he would ever be whole again. Surely no one could endure such pain and live?

Impervious iron bars divided the lycans from the human prisoners rescued from the caravan. No longer hooded, the mortals cowered in the corners of their cell, uncertain of what had befallen them. Having survived the werewolves' attack, they now found themselves in the hands of strange new masters, facing anything from servitude to execution. Vague rumors of vampirism and other deviltry had gained new life after their firsthand encounter with the werewolves in the woods. Nightmares troubled the sleep of those who had finally succumbed to fatigue. The sight of Lucian's ravaged body, streaked as it was with bloody welts, did little to assuage the prisoners' fears.

Heavy footsteps approached Lucian from the other side of the bars. He lifted his eyes to see the dark-skinned Goliath from earlier. The man crouched beside the bars dividing them. Sympathetic brown eyes surveyed the vicious scars traversing Lucian's bloody flesh. A knowing frown suggested that the stranger was all too familiar with the marks of the slavemaster's lash.

"Stay away from him!" a fearful lycan warned. "Or they will punish you, too!"

The giant ignored the other slave's outburst. He dipped a soiled rag in a rusty copper bowl filled with water for the prisoners, then held it out to Lucian. Grateful for the stranger's kindness, and dying of thirst, Lucian tried to reach out for the damp rag but lacked the strength to even lift his arm. Every movement, no matter how slight, left him gasping in pain. His naked back felt like it was being flayed anew. Unable to speak, he collapsed against the cold stone floor.

The stranger nodded. Understanding Lucian's plight, he reached between the bars and held the rag over the other prisoner's mouth. He squeezed the soaked fabric, releasing a thin stream of tepid water that fell like manna from heaven upon Lucian's cracked and swollen lips. The tortured lycan gulped down the water hungrily. No wine or ale had ever tasted sweeter.

Thank you, my friend, Lucian thought. He didn't even know the giant's name yet, but the mortal's courage and compassion had already elevated him in Lucian's eyes. *Bless you for your kindness.*

Would that the vampires could be so humane.

Viktor entered Sonja's chambers without knocking. She quickly wiped the tears from her eyes before turning to greet him. Alas, the motion was not swift enough to escape her father's notice. He eyed her suspiciously.

"Your concern for Lucian was most touching," he noted. "A mere slave . . ."

"Was it?" She hastily consulted her reflection in the

mirror and was relieved to find her emotions well hidden. She kept her voice cool and imperious, as befitted her station. "I suppose. Well, he had just saved my life. And was it not you who told me that I should show a little gratitude in such instances?" A hint of anger showed upon her features. "And what of yourself? Have *you* no gratitude to one who rescued your daughter?"

"I am awash in it," he declared archly. "That he still lives shows the breadth of my magnanimity. Were it any other circumstance, I would have fed him in pieces to his own kind."

The ghastly image seized her imagination; it took all her self-control not to shudder in response. Her stomach turned and she feared she might gag. The sheer venom in her father's voice appalled her. *Surely he cannot be serious.*

"But now his punishment is over?" She strove to sound as though the question was merely of academic interest to her, and not a matter of life or death. "He will be freed?"

"Freed?" He glared at her in disbelief, sounding shocked that any daughter of his could be so naive. "Your judgment is clouded, Sonja. One does not keep order with foolish sentiment. Lucian was forbidden to remove his collar, yet he did so"—he raised a hand to forestall any objections—"for however fine a reason. He will remain in prison."

Just like William, she realized. *Condemned for all eternity.*

He examined her face carefully. Feeling like a prisoner in the dock, Sonja said nothing lest she accidentally give voice to her despair. She kept her guilt and anguish bottled up behind the impassive mask of a noble born. *Lucian, my dearest. What has my love brought you to?*

Her father's eyes narrowed. He appeared not wholly convinced by her semblance of calm. When he spoke again, his words seemed laced with hidden meaning:

"A cautionary tale."

Was he speaking solely of Lucian's transgression, or of something more?

Sonja nodded. For Lucian's sake, she feigned assent, although it rent her very soul to do so. Uncertain how much longer she could contain her grief, she prayed that her father would not tarry much longer. Shaken by the fearful news she had just received, she wanted desperately to be alone with her sorrow.

There must be some way to save him! There has to be!

To her relief, Viktor appeared pleased that she had not challenged his decision. His severe expression lightened somewhat. Turning away from her, he headed for the door, pausing only for one last admonition.

"Janosh and the rest of the nobles will arrive soon. Your presence is *expected.*"

His emphatic tone made it clear that this was not a request.

Moonlight entered the dungeon through a rusty metal grate high up on the wall. Rats scurried in the corners of his cell as Lucian painfully hauled himself up into a sitting position. A damp stone wall felt cool against his throbbing back. Several hours had passed since the flogging and his strength was slowly returning. The scars left by Kosta's whip were already healing over. His skin itched as it slowly knit itself back together. Although he still felt as weak as a half-dead mortal, it seemed as though he had survived the ordeal. What else Viktor had in store for him, however, was an entirely different question. Lucian feared his punishment had only begun.

Just so long as Sonja escapes any reprisals, he thought. *That's all I ask.*

He wrung a few more drops from the damp rag, then handed it back to his new friend. The kindly mortal, who called himself Raze, sat opposite from Lucian on the other side of the prison bars. He returned the rag to the now empty bowl. His wary eyes examined the fading welts upon Lucian's shoulders. The lycan's miraculous recovery clearly had not escaped his notice.

"I saw what you did out there," Lucian said, finally able to speak once more. He recalled how Raze had singlehandedly slain an attacking werewolf with naught but a length of chain. "Very brave for a human."

Raze shrugged, as though he had merely done what was necessary. Lucian was impressed by the human's stoicism. Unlike the other mortals locked up with him, the black man had not succumbed to panic or despair. Even now, trapped in these oppressive dungeons, he seemed to be merely biding his time. Not even a ravening pack of werewolves had broken his spirit.

"Have you ever come across them before?" Lucian asked.

"Only in stories." The man's voice was impossibly deep, especially for a mortal. He made even the gruffest lycan sound like a castrato by comparison. "Stories I never believed."

Lucian was aware that, outside the castle walls, many mortals regarded both vampires and werewolves as nothing but myths, akin to basilisks or dragons. Having spent his immortality defined by his bloodline, he had always found this notion difficult to grasp, but apparently it was so. *What must it be like,* he pondered, *not to live under the sway of the vampires every day of your life?*

"Were you not afraid of them?"

"Yes," Raze admitted. "But I wanted to live."

So it seems, Lucian thought. He wondered again how much Raze had seen of Lucian's own inhuman transformation during the battle. "Are you afraid of me?"

Raze took a moment before answering. His gaze went again to the vanishing scars on Lucian's shoulders.

"Yes."

Lucian appreciated the mortal's honesty. "Well, do not be." He smiled slyly. "I will not bite . . . much."

Raze blinked in alarm, then realized Lucian was joking. Still, he regarded the caged lycan with a certain wariness. "And you are . . . like them?"

"No!" Lucian insisted. The very thought still offended him. "A lycan, yes. But not like them. Nothing like them." He sought to explain the vital difference between himself and the wild werewolves. "Those you fought tonight were animals. The spawn of William, the first true werewolf. Pure-bloods, if you will. No trace of humanity left in them. Savage, mindless beasts."

He suddenly realized that he sounded much like Viktor.

Perhaps too much so.

"Or so it has been told," he murmured, as much to himself as to Raze. For the first time, he questioned the fundamentals of the twilight world in which he had been raised. The lingering ache in his back and shoulders certainly belied the vampires' claims to being more civilized and cultured than their feral brethren. Could it be that the renegade werewolves were not entirely unreasoning beasts as he had always believed?

Raze's own curiosity interrupted his musings. "But I saw you." He gestured at other human prisoners sharing his cell. The pathetic mortals eavesdropped on their conversation with varying degrees of horror and fascination. "We saw how you were with them." The memory caused him shake his head in disbelief, as though he still had difficulty accepting the evidence of his eyes. "They *obeyed* you."

Lucian remembered the pack turning tail after he roared at them. That unlikely turn of events still amazed and puzzled him, although he'd had precious little chance to ponder the matter since. Getting shot with a crossbow and flogged within an inch of his life had understandably driven that mystery from his mind . . . until now.

"Yes," he said. "They did."

A pair of bored Death Dealers guarded the entrance to the dungeons. Their sour faces suggested that they resented being stuck with such a thankless duty on the very night that the castle was welcoming the surviving nobles. They sat at a rickety wooden table, rolling dice and exchanging dirty jokes. A ring of large metal keys hung on a hook behind them, below a glowing lantern. Silver-tipped pikes leaned against a nearby wall, within easy reach of their hands. A flagon of lukewarm blood and two leather tankards rested on the table between them. Growls and heated voices came from the cells beyond the guard station as a loud argument broke out somewhere in the dungeon. The annoyed sentries shouted and pounded on the walls to quiet the prisoners.

"Rutting savages," one of the soldiers groused. "You'd think they'd mind their manners after what happened to that blacksmith."

"What do you expect?" the other guard said. "They're nothing but animals."

The night's tedium was broken unexpectedly by two female vampires who came creeping down the stairs to join them. One of the women, a flaxen-haired beauty named Luka, was Sonja's lady-in-waiting. A red velvet gown flattered her shapely figure. Her companion was of less noble birth, being merely a petite, redheaded chambermaid by the name of Malvina. A plain linen kirtle denoted her lowly status but showed off her feminine charms nonetheless. The delicate fragrance of the women's perfume sweetened the fetid atmosphere.

They boldly approached the guards, who were too delighted by their comely visitors to question their good fortune. Armor rattled as they eagerly jumped to their feet and hastily offered the ladies the flagon of blood. Declining the proffered refreshment, Luka insinuated herself between the two soldiers and whispered huskily in their ears, while Malvina flirted shamelessly with both men, batting her eyes and licking her pearly fangs. Lustful grins broke out across the guards' faces. Greedy hands grabbed the women's waists. They clearly liked whatever Luka had proposed.

"Follow me," she enticed them. "You shall not regret it."

All thought of duty forgotten, the men let their new companions lead them away into the murky privacy of an adjacent corridor. Hushed laughter echoed off the somber gray walls. A saucy hand slapped Malvina's rump. Just before the revelers disappeared into the shadows, however, Luka glanced back the way she'd came. Her sultry violet eyes briefly made contact with . . .

Sonja, who lurked in the stairwell until the gullible sentries were safely distant. She held her breath and counted to fifty before stepping out of hiding. She peered about anxiously, but was relieved to discover that the way was clear. No hidden eyes waited to expose her.

Bless you, Luka, she thought sincerely. The faithful attendant had proven her loyalty a thousandfold tonight, while a generous bribe had ensured Malvina's cooperation. Sonja had not trusted either woman with the true nature of her bond with Lucian; she had merely claimed to be concerned with the well-being of an innocent lycan who had twice saved her life. Thankfully, Luka had accepted this explanation without question, although Sonja feared she had caught a flicker of suspicion in the other woman's eyes. If all went according to plan, the two women would keep the guards occupied long enough for Sonja to carry out her mission.

That they were willing to endure the grubby attentions of the soldiers for her sake filled her with gratitude. *I am deeply in their debt.*

Sonja knew she was taking a terrible risk, especially with her father expecting her at tonight's reception, but she simply *had* to see for herself that Lucian had survived Kosta's sadistic excesses. The thought of her valiant lover suffering alone in the dark had been more than she could bear. She had to see him, comfort him, if only for a few precious minutes.

Moving quickly yet stealthily, she made her way through the dimly lit dungeons. Downtrodden lycans averted their eyes as she passed, although she thought she heard a few muted snarls and curses as well. Her status as Viktor's daughter, and a Death Dealer to boot, clearly earned her few friends in these wretched quarters. And small wonder; decades had passed since she had last ventured into the dungeons, which the elite of the castle seldom had occasion to visit, but she found herself troubled by the squalid sights and sounds and smells all around her. The rank odor of piss, feces, and unwashed bodies offended her nostrils. Fungus infested the damp stone walls. She gagged at the stench. Regurgitated blood climbed up her throat. The conditions in which the lycans were kept were enough to appall anyone whose eyes had been opened to the injustice of their sorry lot. Here was the ugly underside of life at Castle Corvinus, far removed from the decadent luxury of her father's court.

How have I never noticed this before?

As though drawn by an invisible cord linking their souls, she swiftly discovered Lucian slumped against the wall of a malodorous cell. Although dismayed to find him locked away in so dismal a setting, she was relieved to see, at least at first glance, that his horrific ordeal had not left him dead or crippled. Although pale and drawn, his noble face shone like a beacon in the harsh confines of the dungeon. Love brought a lump to her throat.

His bloodshot eyes bulged at the sight of her. He staggered to his feet, wincing only slightly as he did so, and grabbed onto the slime-encrusted bars between them. The other lycans retreated into the gloomy corners of the cell, evidently wanting nothing to do with this unlikely meeting. Her father's "cautionary tale" had clearly been absorbed by the cowed slaves, just as he had intended. None of them wanted the same brutal treatment Lucian had received.

And who can blame them?

Worry showed on Lucian's face. "You should not be here."

"I had to." Her throat tightened. Guilt stabbed her heart. "I am sorry, Lucian." She tried to peer around him to get a glimpse of his injuries. He looked unscathed, but the tenebrous gloom made it difficult to see for certain. "Your back . . . Are you . . . ? "

He turned around to show her a bare back marred by only a few faint red marks. "I am all right."

Praise the House of Corvinus, she thought, grateful for the immortal bloodline that granted both lycans and vampires the ability to heal from almost any injury. Never before had she realized just how great an ability this was. Perhaps because she had never come this close to losing someone she loved.

"But your key . . . This is all my fault." She lowered her eyes, unable to meet his gaze. "If I had not gone out . . ."

"Then you would not be who you are." His loving voice held no hint of anger or recrimination. "Look at me."

Relief flooded her heart. Could it truly be that he did not blame her for all that had befallen him? Lifting her gaze from the floor, she found only warmth and understanding in his intense brown eyes.

"It was knowing that I would see your lovely face again, when it was over, that gave me the strength to endure my punishment. This is not your fault," he insisted. His expression darkened, however, and his voice grew more somber. "But . . . I cannot remain here." He glanced around at the moldy walls hemming him in. Dangling chains and manacles spoke of centuries of torture and subjugation. He tugged at the moon shackle around his neck. "I have to leave this place."

Sonja swallowed hard, feeling more conflicted than ever. She understood now why Lucian desired so passionately to escape from captivity. Indeed, if her father had his way, Lucian would never again set foot outside this dungeon. He would be entombed forever, just like William himself. And yet the prospect of such a drastic ploy still filled her with dread.

"My father," she warned him. "He will be watching you now more than ever."

Lucian nodded solemnly. He stroked his beard thoughtfully. "What about your Death Dealers? Are there none you trust?"

She shook her head. The best and most faithful of

her soldiers had died in the werewolves' ambush, and for the rest . . . "Their fear of Viktor is greater than their loyalty to me, unfortunately."

Lucian took her at her word, accepting that she knew the ins and outs of the soldiery better than he. He massaged his furrowed brow as he racked his brains for another solution. Sonja could also think of no other recourse. There was always Luka, of course, but Sonja was uncertain how far she could push the other woman's loyalty. Abetting a clandestine visit to the dungeons was one thing; defying an Elder's decree to liberate a condemned lycan was something else altogether. She could hardly ask Luka to commit treason on her behalf.

Could she?

A sudden inspiration struck Lucian. "Tanis!"

What? Sonja thought, startled by the suggestion. *That scheming toady?* For a moment, she feared that Lucian had taken leave of his senses. Tanis was the very last person she would have thought of as a potential ally. "He cannot be trusted."

"No," he agreed readily. "But Tanis knows about us."

By the dark gods, no! The shocking revelation hit her with the force of a battering ram. She gasped out loud as a profound chill raced down her spine. Her ivory face grew whiter still. Her jaw dropped and she struggled to catch her breath. Her hand went to her chest, where her undead heart skipped a beat. This was a disaster beyond reckoning. Lucian might as well have foretold the end of the world. She whispered hoarsely.

"How?"

"I have no idea," he admitted. "But if he still has not

told your father, then it means he wants something. Find out what it is."

Sonja nodded gravely. There was something to what Lucian said. *Tanis cannot possibly have informed on us yet, or Lucian would not still be alive.* Nor would she have escaped her father's wrath either; Sonja was unsure just how severely she would be punished for her transgression, but surely her father would not be able to overlook so grievous a violation of the Covenant. That she was still free to move about the castle of her own volition, and not awaiting the judgment of the Council, suggested that Tanis was indeed keeping his secrets to himself. But what sort of game was the ambitious scribe playing?

And for what stakes?

Chapter Eleven

*T*he Great Hall awaited the arrival of the human nobles. Vampires, resplendent in fine black silks and sat-
ins, lined the walls of the vast chamber and loitered
alongside the towering stone archways and pillars. Viktor sat proudly atop his throne, while the High Council
was seated to either side of the throne in two rows of
six chairs each. As ever, Tanis stood at the Elder's left
hand, his quill poised to record the events for posterity.
Flames crackled atop the chandeliers and within
wrought-iron braziers. Death Dealers were stationed at
every entrance. No lycans were in attendance; these
festivities were not for their eyes. A pair of large double
doors barred the far end of the hall.

Viktor's nails drummed impatiently upon the arm of
his throne. Although the rest of the Council was al-

ready in attendance, Sonja was missing as usual. *Damn that girl!* he fumed. *Did I not expressly inform her that her presence was expected here?*

He was about to send Tanis in search of her once more, when a rustle of fabric heralded her tardy arrival. Sonja hastily took her place among the other council members, to the right of the throne, as Viktor suppressed a sigh of relief. Though she had tested his patience somewhat, he chose to take her last-minute appearance as progress of a sort; that she had shown up at all was a definite improvement over her recent acts of disobedience. Perhaps she had finally taken his fatherly advice to heart?

A pity that I had to make an example of Lucian to remind her of her duty.

Furthermore, he was pleased to see that she had dressed appropriately. A rich burgundy surcoat, draped over a gown of shimmering metallic mail, befitted her regal status. A golden chain girded her slender waist. The crescent-shaped pendant upon her bosom looked freshly polished. Viktor enjoyed a private joke as he recalled the true significance of the pendant, which only a handful of living souls suspected. Little did his daughter know that she wore the key to William's hidden prison around her neck. *Nor shall she ever know. Not even when she becomes an Elder.*

That secret belonged to Viktor alone.

Watching his daughter, he saw her glance across the room at Tanis. Preoccupied with his clerical duties, the scribe failed to notice Sonja's interest and she quickly looked away. *Curious,* Viktor thought. *What business could Sonja have with Tanis? I thought she despised him.*

A bell tolled midnight, distracting Viktor from this latest mystery. He decided that he had kept the mortals waiting long enough.

"Bring them in," he commanded.

The ponderous doors creaked open and a fanfare of trumpets announced the arrival of the delegation. A procession of middle-aged mortals entered the hall. Unlike the vampires, who preferred garments of darker hue, the nobles were bedecked in costly robes dyed in a variety of richly extravagant colors. Voluminous quantities of fabric with fur trimmings attested to their prosperity. Burnished metal badges proclaimed their rank and honors. They marched forward two by two, carrying several heavy wooden chests between them. Acutely conscious of their dignity, they struggled not to let their exertions show upon their faces, even though many of them were visibly straining to support the caskets, any one of which a vampire or lycan could have lifted with ease. Their heavy tread echoed off the imposing stone walls. A few of the men glanced nervously at the throng of vampires observing their entrance.

Good, Viktor thought, pleased by the apparent weight of the chests. *That bodes well for the size of the tribute.*

The nobles laid the cases before his throne. Once unlocked, their lids opened to reveal an impressive accumulation of gleaming silver coins that shone like moonlight. Each noble stood behind his own gift to his liege, save for one of their number who appeared to have come empty-handed. Casmir Janosh, perhaps the wealthiest of Viktor's vassals, posed beside his fellow mortals, yet no treasure chest rested before him. A portly man with a balding pate, he wore an olive-green robe over a white linen tunic. His rotund proportions hardly bespoke poverty; he did not seem to have missed any meals.

Viktor leaned forward in his throne. He gestured at the empty space at the mortal's feet. "Dear Janosh, do you not own the largest silver mine in these lands?"

"It has been overrun, milord." The negligent mortal stepped forward to explain. Beads of perspiration dotted his brow and he tugged nervously on the fur-lined collar of his robe. "Our workers . . . infected, turned to beasts!"

Viktor scowled at the news. William's accursed spawn were growing bolder if they dared to raid a *silver* mine. Or were they simply too crazed by bloodlust to consider the threat posed by such a location? None of which excused Janosh's temerity in trying to shirk his feudal duties. How dare the man think he could cheat the coven of its rightful due?

"Most unfortunate," the Elder observed, "and costly." He stroked his chin thoughtfully before rendering a decision. "I think that half the rights to your mine should cover the expense of our assistance."

Janosh flushed with anger. Greed overcame his good sense. "Your assistance? We all saw the funeral pyres on our way here. And where is our good friend, Baron Covasha, and his family? Did you truly think that you could hide his ghastly fate from us? The wolves are at your door as well!" Caught up in the heat of the moment, he brazenly challenged Viktor in front of the other nobles. "Why should I pay tribute when you cannot so much as protect your own house? You have bled me dry already!"

Assorted vampires snickered at the mortal's unfortunate turn of phrase.

"Hardly," Viktor replied.

Janosh blanched but declined to beg for the Elder's mercy. No doubt he realized that he had already gone too far to turn back now. He turned to his fellow nobles for support.

"We have all heard the stories." He pointed an accusing finger at Viktor. His voice took on a more strident tone. "Look into his eyes. Cannot you see the evil in them? The tales are true, this place is cursed!" His frantic gaze swept over the entire coven. "They are no more human than the devils that invade our lands!"

Many of the council members smirked in amusement, although Coloman and Sonja, among others, did not seem to approve of the way this unfortunate drama was playing out. The other humans looked increasingly uncomfortable. They averted their eyes from the ranting nobleman and backed away from him as though he carried the plague. The more devout of them fingered jeweled crosses and crucifixes, clearly laboring under the mistaken belief that such superstitious talismans could defend them against the undead. None spoke up in Janosh's defense.

He blanched as he saw that he was alone in his rebellion.

Viktor savored the man's desperation. It seemed that Lucian was not the only upstart who needed to be made an example of tonight. He rose from his throne and descended a short flight of steps to the floor of the hall. A sinister smile slid across his face as he strode up to Janosh. The nobleman's eyes darted back and forth, as though searching for a way out, but there would be no escape for him. No strategist, he had chosen his battleground poorly, and would now pay the price for that fatal error in judgment.

"If devils you call us, rest assured . . ." Viktor seized the man's neck with one hand and physically lifted him from the floor. Janosh's plump legs dangled in the air. He choked as Viktor's fist tightly squeezed his throat. Blood seeped from beneath the Elder's sharpened nails. Viktor mocked the thrashing nobleman in his grip. "Better the devil you know."

Janosh's bloodshot eyes bulged from their sockets. His ruddy face turned an ugly shade of purple. He grabbed Viktor's wrist with both hands but was unable to pry the Elder's powerful fingers from his throat. Fear showed in his eyes, yet he strove to hide it still. Viktor almost admired his stubborn belligerence.

"U-unhand me!" he blustered.

"Certainly," Viktor said.

With a sweep of his arm, he flung Janosh across the chamber. The noble's overfed body smacked into a granite column as though hurled by a catapult. His bald pate cracked open like an egg. Chips of stone flew from the pillar. The noble's lifeless body crumpled to the floor with a satisfying thud. A crimson trail streaked the damaged stone column, where a newly formed crater testified to the force of the collision. Viktor's mouth watered at the scent of freshly spilled human blood. Excited vampires, their eyes aglow, licked their lips.

Some night soon, Viktor thought, *when these present crises no longer require my immediate attention, perhaps I will reward myself with a visit to one of the neighboring villages.* Although the Covenant expressly forbade preying on unwilling mortals, for fear of inciting a witch-hunt that might consume them all, Viktor had been known to quietly break this rule on occasion. Rank had its privileges, after all, and Janosh's demise had whetted his appetite for human prey. *One cannot live on steer's blood alone. . . .*

But first there was an important lesson to be taught, to any foolish mortal who might also be contemplating a change in the social order. Viktor raised his arms to address the remaining human nobles.

"Now . . . does anyone else wish to be heard?"

The trembling men could not bow their heads fast enough.

Janosh's broken body left a crimson trail in its wake as a pair of Death Dealers dragged it out of the great hall. Viktor had left the corpse lying on the floor for the remainder of the nobles' visit, as an object lesson to his fellow mortals, but now it was nothing more than carrion. The humans had hastily departed Castle Corvinus following their audience with Viktor, choosing to brave the perilous roads and wilderness rather than spend another hour enjoying the "hospitality" of the coven. Disappointed vampires and council members had trickled out of the chamber as well, seeking their own private diversions, so that the hall was now all but empty. Janosh's blood still stained the floor and column, however, and the reek of mortality lingered in the air.

First Lucian, now that unfortunate mortal, Sonja thought. *Will this ghastly night never end?*

Standing by the throne, she contemplated the gory streaks left behind by Janosh's remains. The abrupt slaying of the recalcitrant noble troubled her. Janosh had been foolish to defy her father, but surely there could have been a less drastic way to discipline him? Tonight's ugly events had shown her a ruthless side of her father that she had always overlooked before. *When did he become so cruel, so callous?*

Or had he always been thus, and she had simply been too blind to notice?

She and her father had the great hall to themselves. At his request, she had stayed behind when the other council members had retired for the evening. Now he came up behind her and laid a gentle hand on her shoulder. For the first time in her life, she flinched at his touch.

"Morning is upon us, my child," Viktor said in a conciliatory tone. "It is time we left this wretched night behind."

On that at least they were in agreement. "Gladly."

He turned her around to face him. His azure eyes examined her fondly.

"You are the most fearless warrior I have ever seen. And you make me proud. But you were born into your elevated position. You have no idea what it means to earn it." He fingered the golden pendant about her neck. "There are difficult decisions ahead of us. I would like your help with one of them."

She supposed that, in his own way, he was reaching out to her. Despite the atrocities she had witnessed tonight, she could not help feeling slightly touched by his obvious desire to mend the rift between them. "Of course, Father."

"With Lucian gone," Viktor declared, "we need to promote another lycan in his place."

The warmth of the moment vanished abruptly, supplanted by a sudden foreboding that she did her best to conceal. "Father, what do you mean 'gone'?"

Was not lifetime imprisonment punishment enough?

"Coloman fears that he will stir up the other lycans," he said with deliberate casualness. His eyes searched her face for any untoward reaction. "We must remove him expeditiously."

Sonja realized she was being tested. It took all her discipline to keep her dismay from showing upon her face. "This is difficult," she said coolly. "He has been with us for so long." She pretended to give the matter some thought, as though replacing Lucian was simply a minor household arrangement. "Perhaps Thrasos? Or Gyorg? They would be most trustworthy."

Her blasé tone hid an almost overwhelming sense of panic. Was her father truly intending to have Lucian put to death? Or perhaps buried alive in some forgotten oubliette like William? Either prospect filled her with despair.

Let it not be so!

Her answer seemed to satisfy her father, however. "Excellent suggestions. I will consider them strongly." Smiling, he leaned forward and kissed her on the forehead before leaving her alone in the bloodstained hall with only her hidden fears and guilt to keep her company. A bell tolled the hour, heralding the dawn.

Time was running out for her and Lucian.

Returning to her chambers, Sonja pondered her options. Her mind was awhirl; it seemed that over the last few hours her entire world had turned upside-down. It struck her as tragically ironic that, after two centuries of immortality, it had taken only one night to reduce her life to tatters.

To think that only yesterday Lucian and I made love in the old tower . . .

Heavy drapes and wooden shutters shielded the room from the lethal sunlight outside. A blazing hearth kept out the winter's chill. A lighted candelabra cast dancing shadows upon the intricate runes adorning the walls. A plush carpet absorbed her footsteps as she returned her burgundy surcoat to an imported mahogany armoire across from the vanity. As she did so, her swinging pendant tapped against the wooden door of the wardrobe. Lifting the amulet off her chest, she stared at it in melancholy. Memories of happier times flooded over her:

No more than a child, she beams up at her father as he gently places the pendant around her neck. The gift is perhaps the most beautiful thing she has ever seen; that her father trusts her with so precious an object makes her feel very special indeed. She vows to cherish it always. Bending low, he softly kisses her on the cheek and she throws her tiny arms around him, treating him to the biggest hug she can manage. A warm chuckle greets her embrace and he lifts her easily from the floor.

Snug in her father's comfortable arms, she feels secure in his undying love. . . .

The idyllic memory faded, leaving her back in the present. Sonja's throat tightened and she wiped a tear from her eye. Everything had seemed so simple once; why must she now choose between her heritage and her love? Her father and Lucian?

She glanced around the opulent bedchamber, perhaps for the very last time. The familiar furnishings tugged at her heart, which felt torn in two directions. Treasured heirlooms, many of them inherited from her mother, ornamented the shelves and dressers. Her armor was mounted proudly upon its rack. Her favorite incense perfumed the air. Castle Corvinus had been the only home she had ever known, but there was no future for her or Lucian here. And no hope for Lucian at all unless she took decisive action before night fell once more.

Tanis, she thought. *I must find Tanis.*

Casting her doubts aside, she made up her mind at last. The pendant slipped from her fingers, falling back onto her bosom, as she closed the door of the armoire. She would not be needing her fine attire any longer. A gown of chain mail was all she required now.

And a sharpened dagger.

The castle archives were Tanis's exclusive domain. Centuries' worth of ancient scrolls and manuscripts, many dating back to the very birth of the coven, were squirreled away in the numerous wrought-iron pigeonholes lining the walls. Literacy being both rare and underappreciated in these benighted times, few besides Tanis ever consulted the dusty chronicles. Which was just as it should be, as far as he was concerned. There were secrets buried in the archives that were best left undisturbed.

At least for the present.

The scribe sat at his desk, diligently chronicling tonight's memorable events on an unrolled sheet of parchment. Inkwells and goose quills cluttered the desktop, alongside loose scraps of paper, leather-bound tomes, and other scholarly paraphernalia. A flickering beeswax candle had burned down almost to its base, the melted wax spreading out like a greasy fungus across the bottom of the candle holder. A penknife waited to sharpen the points of the quills as required. An empty goblet needed refilling.

Pausing to dip his quill in an inkwell, Tanis yawned and rubbed his eyes. It had been a long night and he was eager to retire to his own quarters, but he felt compelled to record the day's happenings while his memory was still fresh. The devil was in the details, as the saying went, and he was loath to let any crucial nuance be lost to history.

Now then, he mused, *how best to describe Janosh's untimely demise?*

Inspiration struck and he put pen to paper once more:

"The insolent mortal, whose overweening pride and avarice led him to forget the sacred obligations he owed his liege, met his just reward when Lord Viktor, in all his awful glory, smote him before the transfixed gaze of his entire court. The varlet's brains were dashed against the unforgiving walls of the great hall as the mighty Elder delivered swift and terrible justice to the unworthy noble. . . ."

Intent upon his literary efforts, the scribe failed to hear the stealthy approach of footsteps behind him—until a powerful hand suddenly grabbed him by the collar and flung him against a nearby rack of scrolls. The impact rattled the dusty shelves. Something cold and sharp pressed beneath his chin and he looked down in alarm to see a long steel dagger at his throat. Sonja glared at him, her unsmiling face only inches from his own. Cold brown eyes threatened him with instant extinction. An armored elbow dug into his chest.

"What have you told my father?" she demanded.

Tanis suddenly regretted taunting Lucian earlier. His brain raced feverishly to fashion a suitable response. Should he confess to his knowledge, or feign ignorance? It was hard to think clearly with a knife at his throat.

He did not answer quickly enough for Sonja, who nicked his skin with the edge of her blade. A trickle of blood ran down his neck, mingling with the cold sweat breaking out across his pallid flesh.

"What have you told him?"

"Nothing," he insisted. The murderous look in her eyes convinced him that lying to her would be a very bad idea.

She withdrew the blade by just a hair. "Why?"

"Wh-why what?"

"Why have you told him nothing?" She spoke cautiously, reluctant to divulge any more than necessary. "I have heard you have secrets."

Tanis wondered why she had not killed him already. Could it be that she required something from him, perhaps information as to just how secret her scandalous love affair remained? A trace of his usual sardonic attitude crept back into his voice as he surmised that it might still be possible to talk his way out of this prickly situation.

"Everyone has secrets, milady," he observed, mustering a shaky smile. "I have more than most."

"About me?"

"A few, yes," he confessed.

Sonja nodded, as though he had merely confirmed something she had already suspected. "And why keep them secret?"

He faltered, uncertain how best to answer that query. Dare he confess that he had not yet figured out the best way to exploit that knowledge? What if she chose to silence him once and for all?

These are dangerous waters indeed. . . .

She seemed to find his hesitation amusing. A heartless smirk lifted the corners of her ruby lips. "Or is that a secret, too?"

The dagger dug into his flesh once more. Tanis gulped and felt the edge of the blade scrape against his Adam's apple. He remembered staring down the length of Sonja's sword several hours ago, when he had attempted to block her at the gate. As before, he sensed that she was not bluffing.

"This game we are playing is boring," she stated flatly. "And I am not a good loser, as I am sure you know."

Fearing for his life, Tanis broke his silence. "Would your father welcome the man who brought him news that his beloved daughter was consorting with a lycan?"

He snorted at the idea. "He is not well known for his gratitude. So"—he decided to lay all his cards on the table—"I am not yet in a position to use your secrets to my benefit."

Sonja's eyes narrowed. "What sort of benefit?"

He sensed that they were getting to nub of this tense negotiation. Perhaps these were precisely the sort of answers Sonja had come looking for?

"There are twelve council seats," he said carefully.

Sonja grasped his meaning. "And we do not die often."

"Sadly, no." Alas, a hierarchy of immortals offered few opportunities for advancement. No new member had been admitted to the Council since Sonja herself had achieved her majority.

"So what if I simply gave up my seat at Council?" she suggested. "Left it to you."

Was she serious? Tanis was hesitant to look a gift horse in the mouth, yet this sounded too good to be true. "And why would you do that?"

Sonja withdrew the dagger. She stepped backward to permit him a little more breathing room. A wisp of a smile suggested that she had more of a talent for politics and intrigue than she had ever demonstrated before.

"Can you keep a secret?" she asked.

Touché, he thought. After a distressing start, this meeting was rapidly becoming more to his liking. He nodded and smiled back at her.

"I might need something in exchange," she volunteered.

He was all ears.

Chapter Twelve

*E*ven locked away in the dungeon, Lucian sensed the sun go down. Moonlight infiltrated the flea-infested cell he shared with the other slaves. Nightfall meant feeding time as well; scowling guards banged on the walls to rouse the lycans from slumber, then hurled buckets of raw meat and vegetables through the bars. The rancid fare splattered onto the grubby straw bedding. Lucian was dismayed by his fellow lycans' table manners as they descended on the food like wild animals, elbowing each other aside in their eagerness to claim the choicest bits of the miserable slop. Bloody juices ran down their chins as they crammed the meat into their mouths with bare hands. Gnawing on the bones, they noisily slurped down the marrow.

Lucian's stomach growled. He had eaten nothing

since his beating yesterday, and his depleted body required sustenance, yet he was reluctant to take part in the degrading feeding frenzy. He kept his distance, hoping to salvage a few scraps after the rest of the pack was done gorging themselves. Perhaps there would still be a few rancid vegetables or half-chewed bones left.

To his surprise, however, Xristo snagged a meaty rib and, instead of tearing into it himself, lobbed it over to Lucian. The tempting morsel flew over the heads of the other lycans, who snatched at it unsuccessfully, before landing in Lucian's outstretched hands. He was both moved and startled by the young lycan's generosity; apparently Xristo had not forgotten how Lucian had stood up for him before.

Who would have guessed, Lucian thought, *that an illiterate lycan slave could show more character than Lord Viktor himself?*

He nodded gratefully at Xristo, then sniffed the bloody rib, which seemed rather fresher than the lycans' usual victuals. His eyes widened in surprise. *This is not horsemeat,* he realized. His finger traced the curve of his own rib cage as he examined the bone more carefully. *By the moon, this is human flesh!*

Such was hardly their customary fare. Lucian could only wonder what some mortal had done to end up on their menu. Whom had Viktor literally fed to the dogs?

He sniffed the meat again. Its mortal origins gave him pause, but ultimately he decided that he was in no position to be finicky. He needed to regain his strength if he want to escape this hellish prison. Putting his scruples aside, he tore at the bloody rib with his teeth.

After all, he rationalized, this was hardly the first time he had tasted human flesh.

It was even more delicious than he remembered. . . .

Still, he thought it best not to illuminate Raze on the true nature of his repast. After feeding the lycans, the guards moved on to provide the human prisoners with moldy vegetables and loaves of stale black bread. As before, Raze sat across from Lucian as he chewed on a wilted head of cabbage. The iron bars between them had proved little impediment to their growing friendship.

The giant remained impressed by the speed with which Lucian had recovered from the merciless flogging. By now, the welts left by Kosta's cat-o'-nine-tails had vanished entirely.

"Will you live forever?" Raze asked.

"I have been asking myself that question for nearly two centuries," Lucian admitted. "I feared that today I might find the answer."

Raze was obviously intrigued by his strange new ally. "You were born like this?"

"The first of my kind. I grew to a man and have aged little since. And all in captivity," he added bitterly. Indeed, for all he knew, he had been born in this very cell, or one very much like it. "Viktor's little experiment. Our bite, it seems, is infectious. He used me to create others. They created more. And soon he had his 'daylight guardians,' as the vampires call us." He snorted at the lofty-sounding appellation. "Daylight guardian? Sounds rather more tasteful than slave, does it not?"

175

Before Raze could answer, a fierce fight broke out in one of the adjoining cages. Two surly lycans vied for a hefty chunk of meat that bore a suspicious resemblance to a human heart. A bear-sized older lycan by the name of Vasily clutched the dripping heart under one arm, while fending off a younger challenger, Ferenz, who was determined to wrest the tempting prize from him. Vasily's hair had been shaved by the lycans to rid him of lice, while Ferenz boasted a mane of greasy red tresses. Bestial growls and snarls came from the men as they circled each other like crazed mastiffs fighting over a bone. Ferenz grabbed at the heart, despite the slashing nails and bared fangs of the larger man. Tufts of hair and skin went flying as they traded vicious scratches and bites, to the tumultuous delight of the other lycans, who hooted and hollered at the frenzied combatants. The gleeful prisoners clustered around the ferocious brawl, rudely jostling each other in their eagerness to get a better view. Blood splattered the faces of the spectators, which only excited them further. Such barbaric spectacles were what passed for entertainment in these quarters.

"Get 'im!" a jubilant lycan roared, although it was unclear which combatant he was rooting for. "Rip his guts out!"

"That's it!" another called out. He stamped his feet upon the floor and waved a bloody leg bone in encouragement. A plump black rat, which had come sneaking in for scraps, scurried for safety. "Don't let him get away with that! Go for his throat!"

A handful of guards lingered to watch the show as well. They laughed and applauded, while placing bets on which lycan would come out on top, and whether one or both would end up dead or maimed. "Fifteen coppers says the bald one loses an eye," a soldier wagered, provoking another round of furious betting. Crude jeers mocked the lycans' respective prowess and ancestry, until an impatient shout from the vampires' commander forced them to reluctantly abandon their sport. Rattling coins were thrust back into purses.

Disgraceful, Lucian thought. He watched the grumbling soldiers exit the dungeons. Tossing aside the human rib, which his bloody teeth had already stripped to the bone, he waited until the brawlers in the next cage came within reach, then grabbed Vasily through the bars and locked his elbow beneath the man's neck. Seeing his opportunity, Ferenz started to lunge for the heart, but Lucian warned him off with a threatening growl. His fierce gaze drove the red-maned lycan back and quieted the raucous crowd, although not a few of the overexcited lycans glowered at Lucian for interrupting their fun. Disappointed faces bared their fangs.

"We are not animals," he whispered intensely, then raised his voice so that all could hear. *"We are not animals!"*

A hush fell over the dungeons as his words struck home.

"Is this what you want?" he challenged his brothers. "To be their entertainment? Their playthings? Their pets?" Scorn dripped from his voice as he forced them to confront the harsh reality of their wretched lives. "Cowering beneath the whip and then fighting amongst ourselves? Is that what you truly desire?"

Vasily struggled to free himself from the headlock Lucian had him in. His hairless skull bounced against the hard steel bars. He snarled spitefully. "Easy for you to say, blacksmith!"

Lucian ignored the brawler's rebuke. He released Vasily and shoved him away. The man staggered into the crowd, while massaging his bruised throat. He crammed the pulped remains of the coveted heart into his mouth. Blood trickled down his chin.

"I have lived by their rules for my entire life," Lucian confessed. "I have envied them, protected them, even crafted the weapons they use to slay our brothers in the forest. And for what? To be treated like an animal?" He shook his head. "No."

Not anymore, he vowed. *Not even if I live for centuries to come.*

The other lycans listened to him in rapt fascination, as did Raze and his fellow humans. Any lingering resentment faded from the faces of the audience as they fell under the spell of Lucian's words. Xristo and Sabas came forward, nodding in agreement. Lucian was glad to see that their wounds also had healed.

"We *do* have a choice." He gestured at their sordid abode. "We can choose to be more than this. We can choose to be free—in here." He thumped his chest, directly above his heart, then tapped the side of his skull as well. "And in here." He paused to let that provocative notion sink in before spelling it out for them. His voice rang out passionately as he raised his arms in exhortation. "We can be slaves—or we can be lycans!"

His oppressed brethren stared at him in astonishment. No lycan had ever spoken like this before. Even

Vasily was now gaping at the former blacksmith in stupefied awe.

"Which is it?" he demanded of them.

Their dumbfounded silence encouraged him. Had he succeeded in stirring something within them? Perhaps a newfound desire to aspire to better things? To stop acting like the uncivilized beasts the vampires had reduced them to?

Lucian could only hope.

The moment was broken, however, when the vampires returned to the dungeon. Four stone-faced Death Dealers stomped toward Lucian's cell. Both humans and lycans scurried back to the corners of their cells, save for Sabas and Xristo, who lingered near Lucian. Raze stood by Lucian as well, albeit on the opposite side of the iron bars.

Now what? Lucian wondered. He cursed the knights' miserable timing. *I was getting through to the others. I know I was!*

Three of the soldiers stood guard with crossbows and raised whips as the fourth unlocked Lucian's cage. Rusty hinges squeaked loudly. The barred door swung open.

The leader of the guards nodded at Lucian.

"Out!"

Xristos and Sabas tensed, as though inclined to come to Lucian's defense once more, but Lucian quietly caught their gaze and shook his head. Now was not the time; he had no desire to see the two men brutalized on his behalf again. Keeping a wary eye on the guards' crossbows, Lucian let himself be escorted out of his cell—perhaps to his execution? Raze clutched the iron bars of his own cage as he watched the guards take Lucian away.

Lucian silently bid his new friend farewell.

He had no idea what the Death Dealers wanted of him and knew better than to ask. Any unsolicited query would doubtless earn him nothing more than a smack across the face or perhaps a fresh blow from their silver-tipped lashes. Still, he could not help worrying about the vampires' intention. *What does Viktor have in store for me now?* he fretted. *More torture, or perhaps a summary beheading?*

Not even an immortal could survive having his head parted from his shoulders. Or being drawn and quartered like a common thief.

The guards led him to a lonely cell on another level of the dungeon. They locked him inside, then departed wordlessly. Lucian found himself alone in a cage of his own. A quick inspection of the premises revealed that the cell had once been used as a torture chamber. An iron maiden, its interior lined with rusty spikes, reclined against one wall. A dilapidated rack had once been used to stretch human or lycan bodies apart. Metal pincers lay beside an overturned brazier. Suspicious brown stains covered the floor, walls, and ceiling. A fractured human skull rested in a niche upon the wall. A spider had made its home in an empty eye socket. Uncertain what was happening, Lucian morosely surveyed his solitary new domain. Was he was destined to live out the rest of his immortality in this isolated chamber?

He would not be the first to meet this fate. Legend had it that William himself, the savage progenitor of their breed, was even now buried alive in some hidden dungeon whose true location was known only to Viktor himself. Lucian wondered if he was also destined to become nothing more than a cautionary myth for others of his kind.

How ironic, he reflected, *that the first of the werewolves and the first of the lycans should come to the same end. And both at the hands of the same draconian Elder.*

Lucian had just about convinced himself that he was condemned never to look upon another living soul again when a key rattled in the lock. He spun around to find Tanis standing outside the cell along with another figure. A hooded cloak concealed the other vampire's face and figure. The scribe opened the door to admit his companion to the cell. He glanced about nervously, as though fearful of being discovered at any moment. He tucked an iron key back into the folds of his robe.

"Two minutes," he said in a low voice. "Any more is too risky."

The hooded figure nodded and entered the cell. Tanis closed the door and wasted no time vacating the premises. His stealthy footsteps receded into the distance.

Lucian faced his visitor. He sniffed the air, catching a whiff of lavender. The familiar scent proclaimed Sonja's identity even before she threw back the hood to reveal her beautiful face. His heart leapt at the sight of her. He rushed forward to embrace her. They clung to each other as though their immortal lives depended on it.

"I'm sorry," she murmured. Her voice was hoarse, as

though she had been crying for hours. "I would have come sooner, but it took time for Tanis to arrange this meeting. There was no other way. . . ."

He silenced her apologies with a passionate kiss. For a precious moment, they lost themselves in the kiss, their mouths hungrily seeking each other out. The fire of their desire welded them together like metals in a forge. Lucian wished they could make the moment last forever, but he knew they had vital matters to discuss in the brief time remaining to them. He reluctantly tore himself away from her cool red lips.

"Tanis?" he asked.

"You were right," she confirmed. "He'll help us for a seat on the Council."

Lucian was impressed by the scribe's ambition. "And your father knows nothing?"

"I'm sure of it."

That was the best news he had heard in days. As long as Viktor remained ignorant of their love, he and Sonja had time to plan their escape. For the first time since feeling Kosta's silver arrowhead pierce his thigh, Lucian allowed himself a flicker of hope. "This can work."

"Lucian." She hugged him with all her vampiric strength. "It has to."

The sheer determination in her eyes and voice inspired him anew. All her doubts seemed to have melted away since last they spoke. He felt his spirits soar. *Our love cannot be conquered. Together, we can make this happen!*

And not just for the two of them alone.

"I think that some of the others will come with me," he informed her. "Sabas, Xristo, the human Raze . . ."

She pulled away slightly. A worried look crossed her face. "My love . . ."

He recalled how his impassioned oratory had affected the other lycans. "In time, I'm certain that I can convince more—"

"Lucian, there is no time," she interrupted. The urgency in her voice cut through his deliberations. "My father will have you killed tomorrow—after the humans have been turned."

Her stark declaration could not be ignored. He did not bother to ask how she knew this. The certainty—and fear—in her voice was enough to convince him.

Apparently Viktor wanted him dead after all.

"You must leave at sunrise," she insisted.

"Sunrise?" That was only hours away. Lucian didn't understand. How could they contrive their escape in so short a time? Especially since Sonja could not venture out into the daylight without risking incineration. "But . . . how will you . . . ?"

She shook her head. "The important thing is that you stay alive. You know the best chance you have is when Viktor and the Death Dealers sleep. I will be at my father's side when you go."

But to leave this place—without you? He weighed her words in silence, unable to refute their wisdom. As much as he hated the idea of being parted from her again, he knew she was right. There was no manner in which they could safely depart the castle together, not without betraying their secret and raising all of her father's Death Dealers in swift pursuit. Their new life together would be over even before it had begun. Yet recognizing the truth did not make it any less bitter. He gazed mournfully into her eyes, wishing with all his heart that there was another way. *What good is life and freedom without you in my arms?*

Her own eyes moistened. Her voice caught in her throat. "If this succeeds," she promised, drawing him closer, "I will join you after the sun sets in three days' time. There is a clearing by the river. I will meet you there."

Lucian vaguely remembered spotting the river, which flowed down from the craggy mountain peaks, during his frantic ride through the forest the night before. Her stated intention did little reassure to him, though, and he could tell by the anguished look in her own eyes that she also knew just how easily their plans could go awry. They both realized that they might never see each other again.

"And if it doesn't succeed?" he asked.

She buried her hands in his disheveled hair and claimed his lips once more. She gave him a fierce kiss intended to last for all eternity if need be. His senses were reeling by the time she finally pulled away. Her azure eyes blazed in the darkness.

"I *will* meet you in the clearing," she vowed.

Chapter Thirteen

After Sonja left, the Death Dealers returned Lucian to his original cell. His fellow lycans still populated the dungeon; apparently they would not be put to work tonight. Lucian guessed that Viktor preferred to keep the other slaves confined until he was certain there would be no further insurrections. No doubt the calculating Elder hoped that Lucian's death would put an end to any unrest among the lycans.

It seems I am to be a cautionary lesson, Lucian mused. *To keep my brothers in their place.*

He was not there long before Tanis visited the dungeon again, now accompanied by Kosta and a half dozen Death Dealers. The duplicitous scribe scrupulously avoided looking at Lucian, concentrating on

Raze and the other human prisoners instead. He gestured at the mortals.

"Remove them."

Anxious gasps and whimpers escaped the humans' cell. Kosta's men unlocked the gate and herded them out into the corridor, cracking their whips as necessary. Manacles chained the slaves' wrists together. A couple of the more panicky mortals tried to retreat to the corners of their cell, but a few swift blows swiftly broke down their resistance. Raze, on the other hand, knew better than to put up a fight against the armed knights. His mighty frame towered over the vampires, but he was no match for their swords and crossbows. He shot Lucian an inquiring look as he exited the cell.

Lucian could only shake his head sadly. He feared he knew what horrific trial awaited Raze and the other humans now, but there was nothing he could do to avert their fate. He could but hope that the stalwart African would survive the harrowing with his proud spirit intact.

"Be brave, human," Lucian said. *Would that I could spare you this!*

Kosta and his soldiers led the mortals away, but Tanis lingered behind. He sidled up to Lucian's cell and whispered to him through the bars. A contemptuous sneer twisted his vulpine features. "Do you know what your problem is?"

"How much time do you have?" Lucian said wryly.

Tanis answered his own question. "You have no respect for the natural order of things."

"Things change," Lucian replied. He realized now that the strict hierarchy of their society was nothing more than an insidious fiction designed to keep the lycans subject to the vampires' tyrannical whims. If that was "the natural order of things," then to blazes with it!

Tanis was not inclined to debate the issue. "Yes. Be ready when they do."

The scribe glanced about to make certain that no one was watching, then retrieved a wadded scrap of leather from beneath his black velvet doublet. He quietly tossed the small parcel through the bars. It skittered across the floor before coming to rest at Lucian's feet.

"Consider it a parting gift," Tanis whispered.

Without another word, he turned and scurried from the dungeon. Lucian waited until he was out of sight before rescuing the bundle from the floor. Turning his back on the corridor, he furtively unwrapped the parcel.

Inside the rumpled leather was the key to his spiked collar. Perhaps the same one he had forged in his own smithy.

His fist closed tightly around the key.

Raze felt like he was back in the caravan, marching to an uncertain fate, as the guards escorted the chained humans down into an even lower level of the sprawling dungeons. Frequent kicks and prods kept the procession moving, despite the apprehensions of the frightened mortals. Visions of blood-sucking fangs sinking into his jugular passed through Raze's mind as he wondered where they were being taken—and for what malignant purpose. *At least we're not hooded this time,* he thought. His muscular arms tested the chains binding his wrists.

They came to a large vaulted chamber facing a stone archway. The flickering light of mounted torches failed to penetrate the shadowy cell beyond the archway. Lord Viktor, whom Raze recognized from the battle at the crossroads, waited to one side. The Elder's gaunt, pale face and cold-blooded hauteur were the epitome of what Raze imagined a vampire lord to be like. His scribe, a slight man with shifty eyes who reminded Raze of a jackal fawning on a lion, soon joined the Elder by means of a side corridor. He nodded apologetically at Viktor before taking his place at the tyrant's side. Viktor seemed only mildly annoyed by his servant's tardiness.

The ruler of the vampires looked over the assembled prisoners, his gaze briefly lingering on Raze. The chained captive remembered how Viktor had coldly ordered the bodies of the werewolves' victims buried. According to Lucian, Viktor was a vampire to be feared and, looking into the Elder's pitiless blue eyes, Raze saw no reason to doubt that assessment. Was it not Viktor who had ordered Lucian whipped nearly unto death?

"Proceed," the Elder commanded.

The Death Dealers prodded the slaves toward the waiting doorway. Chains rattled in the darkness and a low growl sent a fresh jolt of fear through the helpless prisoners. They turned and tried to flee from the beckoning cell, but the guards blocked their retreat. A swarthy Turk named Nasir, who had been captured during the Crusades, was dragged to the front of the line. His frightened eyes peered into the cell.

Lurid cobalt eyes glared back at him.

"No!" Nasir shrieked. *"Don't! No!"*

A shaggy black werewolf, indistinguishable from the ones who had attacked the caravan, lunged from the cell, only to be held back by a sturdy chain around his neck. The beast reared up onto its hind legs and slashed at the air with gigantic forepaws. Slobber dripped from its gaping jaws.

"Please, for the love of God!" Nasir begged, but to no avail. The Death Dealers shoved him forward—and the wolf's gleaming fangs sank into his shoulder. Blood spurted onto the walls and ceiling as Nasir screamed like a damned soul trapped in the bowels of hell.

Which was not far from the case.

Aside from Raze, the other prisoners erupted into hysterics. The vampires cracked their whips to keep the panicked slaves in line. An armored knight wrenched Nasir from the werewolf's jaws before the beast could rip him to shreds entirely, and a second human was hurled to the monster with equally gruesome results. Raze watched in horror as, one by one, the prisoners were bitten by the wolf, then tossed into an adjacent cell. The infected slaves writhed upon the floor, convulsing and foaming at the mouth. Blood streamed from their bite marks, flooding the dungeon. The spreading crimson pool excited the assembled vampires, who eyed the blood with undisguised rapacity. They licked their lips, offering glimpses of sharp white fangs.

No vampire tended the victims' wounds. Instead the Death Dealers clamped slave collars onto the thrashing prisoners. *They're turning us into lycans,* Raze grasped, *just like Lucian and the others!*

Despite his customary reserve, he felt a growing sense of panic as his own turn drew near. The man in front of him, a convicted poacher named Zoltan, was shoved into the werewolf's clutches. Unsated by its previous victims, the monster took a chunk out of Zoltan's shoulder before the soldiers tore the bleeding slave from its grasp. A metal truncheon poked Raze between the shoulder blades. The werewolf eyed the huge slave hungrily.

No! Raze thought. *You shall not taste my flesh!*

Exploding into action, he spun around and swung the chains between his wrists into the skull of the Death Dealer behind him. The improvised weapon struck like a mace, shattering the vampire's neck with a loud crack. The soldier dropped to the floor like the dead man he was. Azure eyes widened with horror as the vampire realized he was paralyzed from the neck down. *Can a vampire heal from that?* Raze wondered.

He hoped not.

Swearing profanely, a second guard charged at Raze, but, moving with surprising agility for a man his size, Raze dodged the attack and looped the chain over the vampire's neck. He twisted it like a garrote until he heard the man's vertebrae shatter. A strangled gasp escaped his lips. Blood gushed from his mouth.

That's two, Raze thought. He tossed the throttled vampire aside.

By now, however, the other soldiers had united to

subdue the unruly prisoner. A whip cracked against Raze's broad shoulders, sending a staggering jolt of agony through his body. A steel-shod fist slammed into his jaw, while a leather boot kicked his legs out from under him. Refusing to surrender, he swung his chain again, but the vampires were ready for him now. An alert soldier grabbed hold of the chain with preternatural speed and yanked it hard. Raze's hands were almost torn from his wrists and he fell forward onto his face. His forehead smacked against the hard stone floor. A heel dug into his back, pinning him down. Another vampire kicked him in the side. A rib cracked, the pain nearly blinding. He tried to get back up again but was overwhelmed by the vampires' superior strength and numbers. Grunting defiantly, he spit a mouthful of blood and broken teeth onto the ground.

Devils! he cursed them. *Fiends from hell!*

The vampires were done with him, though. His broken rib shifted painfully as they hauled him to his feet and carried him toward the waiting werewolf, who drooled in anticipation. Raze squirmed in the soldiers' grasp and dug his own heels into the floor, but he was carried forward nonetheless. He felt the werewolf's hot breath upon his face. Raze's heart pounded in fear. Fresh blood smeared the monster's muzzle.

Its gore-stained fangs were only a footstep away.

Lucian was conferring softly with Xristo and Sabas through the bars of their respective cages when the mortal slaves were thrown back into their cells. Festering bite marks on their shoulders, which were already healing over, revealed that they had now joined the ranks of the lycans, whether they liked it or not. Lucian could smell the taint of the wolf spreading through their veins. They were clammy and pale and shaking as though with ague. Prodigious quantities of sweat soaked through their ragged garments. They panted like dogs in the heat.

Not all of them would survive the infection, Lucian knew. Once the bite of a werewolf had been universally contagious, but now, centuries after the initial plague, it sometimes killed instead of transforming a mortal into a lycan. Was it that the wolfen strain was growing weaker over the course of generations, he wondered, or was it simply that humans were developing a fatal resistance to the plague? Perhaps someday their bite would bring death more often than it brought immortality.

I'll never know, he mused, *unless I escape this prison soon.*

One of the transformed slaves—a Saracen by the look of him—scratched at the ugly red scab upon his shoulder. His sweaty face bore an expression of utter confusion. That fact that he was still alive baffled him. "What . . . what did they do to us?"

"You will find out soon enough," Sabas said bitterly. Lucian recalled that the sinewy young lycan had once been a mortal himself, before his entire family had been sold into slavery to pay off a debt owed by a human noble to Lady Amelia. That had been over one hundred and fifty years ago. An ornate letter *A* was branded on his upper arm.

Raze seemed to have a better understanding of what

had been done to his fellows. "They turned us into . . . like you?"

"Yes," Lucian confirmed. He lowered his voice to avoid being overheard by any vampire guard. "The time has come. At sunrise I leave this place. And anyone willing to take the risk may follow me."

One cell over, Xristo and Sabas were busy recruiting other lycans to join their cause. Conspiratorial whispers were greeted with murmured assents. They nodded at Lucian before going back to spreading the word. Lucian hoped he could trust them only to approach those lycans who were receptive to their message. One traitor hoping to curry favor with the vampires, could get them all beheaded in no time. *Then again,* he reflected, *those two probably know their fellow laborers better than I do. . . .*

"There is a new life waiting outside these walls, my friend," he promised Raze. "You can be part of it. One of us. If you wish it."

Raze pondered Lucian's offer. "I will fight with you, Lucian . . . as I am."

Excellent, Lucian thought. He could ask no more of the redoubtable giant. His gaze swept over the forlorn dungeon, where Sabas and Xristo continued to make the case for freedom to those who might be willing to listen to it. Lycan eyes, some filled with hope, others with anxiety, stared back at him. *This is about more than just Sonja and me,* Lucian realized. He felt the weight of his entire breed resting on his shoulders. *Can I count on my fellow lycans? Dare they place their faith in me?*

Everything depended on what happened at sunrise.

Chapter Fourteen

A bell warned of dawn's approach, but Kosta judged he had time enough to make one last final inspection of the dungeon before retiring to the barracks. He swaggered past the lycans' dingy cells, cracking his whip to remind them who was in charge. As far as he was concerned, Viktor and the council had been too soft on the lycans in recent years. It was past time to put them back in their place.

He peered through the bars at the latest batch of slaves, whom he looked forward to literally whipping into shape. "New dogs today," he taunted the former mortals. By nightfall, those who had survived the infection would be ready to be put to work. "Let's see how you look."

Too cowed to reply, the newborn lycans merely

huddled in their cells. Most of them seemed to be recovering from the werewolf's bite, although a few were curled up on the floor in obvious distress. They moaned and quivered amidst pools of stinking vomit. A rank odor revealed that many of the infected slaves had soiled themselves. Kosta reminded himself to have the cells flushed out after the initial fever ran its course. The transition from human to lycan was seldom an easy one. . . .

Moving on to Lucian's cell, Kosta relished the memory of flaying the upstart blacksmith to the bone the night before. Tonight would be even better; preparations were already under way to have Lucian burned at the stake in the middle of the courtyard. A cruel smile came over Kosta's face as he visualized Lucian screaming in torment as the flames consumed him. The overseer prayed that Lord Viktor would grant him the privilege of personally lighting the bonfire.

I always knew that arrogant mongrel would get what he deserved one day, Kosta thought. *Lord Viktor should have known better than to indulge Lucian the way he did. Fear is the only way to keep these mangy curs in line.*

But as he looked more closely at the blacksmith's cell, he was dismayed to see that the door was slightly ajar. *What the devil?* His gloved fist tightened on the grip of his whip. A suspicious scowl replaced his smile. He warily approached the door.

"You're too late," Sabas taunted him from the adjoining cell. Kosta recognized the youth as one of the lycans who had tried to defend Lucian during the flogging. His equally insolent companion stood by him, openly laughing at the vampire. "He has already gone."

No! Kosta thought in alarm. Lord Viktor would have his hide if Lucian had indeed escaped. *How can this be? It's not possible!*

Throwing caution to the wind, he kicked the door open and rushed into the cell—only to find an angry werewolf waiting for him!

The beast, who could only be Lucian, lunged from the shadows. Kosta's gray eyes widened in fear. Caught by surprise, he had no time to defend himself. His whip flew from his hand as the werewolf's slavering jaws ripped the flesh from his skull.

He died screaming.

Cold vampire blood dripped down Lucian's chin as he gazed down at the headless body of the unwary overseer. No longer wolfen in shape, he stood naked over the corpse. Kosta's mutilated skull lay on the floor several feet away. His face had been completely stripped from the bone. Bits of skin and cartilage were still stuck between Lucian's teeth. He spit an ear out onto the floor.

Who has fallen the lowest now? Lucian thought.

Recalling how Kosta's vicious cat-o'-nine-tails had flayed his hide only yesterday night, Lucian derived no little satisfaction from the vampire's death. A crimson flood pooled beneath the decapitated remains. Kosta's many cruelties, against both Lucian and his fellow lycans, had at last been avenged.

If I have my way, he thought, *Kosta will not be the last vampire to feel my fangs.*

The other lycans gazed at Lucian in awe. Kosta had terrorized some of them for centuries, but he had lasted only moments against Lucian's unleashed wrath. Flickers of excitement—and apprehension—played across their stunned faces. No doubt many of them feared what the other vampires would to do to them in retribution. Xristo and Sabas, on the other hand, could barely contain their glee, hugging and punching each other in jubilation. Raze nodded grimly in approval.

Lucian held up the key for all to see. His own collar lay discarded upon the floor of his cell. He disdainfully kicked it in the corner. The sight of the key captivated his rapt audience. It was more than just a forged piece of metal; it was freedom itself. Lucian felt his destiny unfolding as he roared triumphantly.

"Are you with me?"

Cheers greeted his fervent exhortation, along with some fretful muttering. Hastily dressing himself, Lucian retrieved Kosta's keys from his belt and set about freeing the other lycans. Prison doors swung open. He handed off the keys to the dungeon to Xristo, who finished unlocking the cells. Lucian was tempted to remove the other slaves' collars as well, but feared they lacked the time. He did not want to linger here any longer than necessary. Given the hour, and the dungeon's thick stone walls, it was unlikely that any vampire had heard Kosta's dying screams, but Lucian and his allies would not be truly safe until they were well clear of Castle Corvinus.

Haste and surprise are our best weapons, Lucian mused. *We must not waste them.*

In the end, nearly two dozen lycans agreed to join in the escape, while the rest chose to remain in their cells rather than risk being caught by the vampires. Lucian was disappointed by those who proved faint of heart, but was gratified that none seemed inclined to betray them. Lycan loyalty stretched that far at least. Unlike Tanis, who had gladly double-crossed his own kind for the sake of political advantage.

To think I ever admired the vampires, Lucian thought ruefully. Aside from Sonja, not one of them was worth the immortal blood that flowed through their veins. *They are truly the demons the mortals believe them to be.*

Sniffing freedom, he led his motley band of rebels through the castle's subterranean corridors. Their lack of weapons concerned him. They would have to rely on the rising sun to clear all obstacles from their path, just as Sonja intended.

Sonja.

He could not help wondering just where his love was at this very moment. Alone in her bedchamber, unable to sleep for worry? Knowing her warrior spirit, he could only imagine how it pained her to stand by helplessly while he risked his life thus. He wished there was some way he could communicate to her that their plan was working . . . at least so far.

Three days, he reminded himself. *We will be together in three days. . . .*

All was going well, until they rounded a corner and found themselves confronted by two startled Death Dealers. The vampires' jaws dropped in alarm, flashing yellow fangs. They reached for their swords, but Lucian's reflexes were faster. He sprang forward and slammed their heads together with all his strength. Steel helmets collided, producing a ringing sound not unlike the sound of a hammer hitting an anvil. The dented metal helms smacked against the floor as the men dropped like marionettes whose strings had been cut. Sabas whistled in appreciation. Snatching a knife from one of the unconscious vampires' belts, he cheerfully slashed their throats. A crimson fountain sprayed the walls and ceiling before the ill-fated guards breathed their last. He kicked the corpses in the head for good measure.

Well done, Lucian thought, applauding his comrade's ruthlessness. *It's past time these bloodsuckers learn that even tamed wolves can bite.*

Lucian claimed one of the soldier's swords and handed the other one over to Raze. Xristo tucked a bronze dagger into his belt. Lucian was tempted to strip the knights of their armor but chose not to take the time. He had silenced the soldiers before they had cried out, but had anyone heard the commotion? What if there were other Death Dealers about?

Let us not tempt fate by tarrying too long.

Trampling over the butchered vampires, the lycans abandoned the dungeons. They crept stealthily up a spiral staircase. Lucian's plan was to reach the hidden tunnel behind his smithy, but first they had to traverse a long covered gallery on the ground floor of the castle. The dense stone walls of the keep were on their left while thick wooden shutters faced the courtyard side of the gallery. An oaken door beckoned at the end of the corridor.

Almost there, Lucian thought. He raised a finger to his lips to remind the other men to keep silent. The eager lycans were trying to move silently but not entirely succeeding. Lucian winced at the sound of their footsteps echoing off the cold stone walls. One of the newer lycans, a Turk named Nasir, coughed hoarsely. His clammy complexion and febrile eyes suggested that he had not yet recovered from the infection. He stumbled against a wooden shutter, which rattled alarmingly. Lucian shot him a withering glance.

By the gods, he prayed, *let no one have heard that!*

The sky was lightening on the horizon as the Death Dealers patrolled the ramparts. Sandor, the captain of the night guard, glanced impatiently at the nearest stairwell. Where were the lycan sentries meant to relieve them? He had dispatched two men to fetch the daylight guardians several minutes ago, and yet the lycans had not arrived to take their posts upon the walls.

Was something amiss?

His men paced restlessly by the loaded ballistas. They looked to him in confusion, and understandably so. They could see as well as he could that the sun would be rising soon. Unless the lycans assumed their posts quickly, the vampires would be forced to leave the castle walls undefended, a grievous dereliction of duty that had not occurred for more than two hundred years. Surely the lycans realized the terrible risk they were taking.

Something's wrong, he realized. *Very wrong indeed.*

A jarring noise came from the courtyard below. Sandor's eyes zeroed in on the wooden shutters guarding the ground floor of the keep. Were those footsteps he heard in the gallerys?

"Rotate the ballistas!" he ordered. "Now!"

* * *

The lycans were halfway down the gallery when a silver-tipped harpoon burst through the wooden shutters, impaling three of the fugitives. The massive bolt stretched across the narrow corridor like a barricade. Wooden splinters struck several other lycans, who suddenly found themselves trapped behind the harpoon and their skewered comrades. Dying lycans wailed in agony.

The uproar startled Lucian, who spun around to witness the appalling sight. He instantly recognized the bolt as coming from one of the gargantuan siege bows atop the ramparts. *The guards are onto us,* he realized. *They're turning the ballistas around toward the courtyard!*

A second harpoon exploded through the shutters, killing two more lycans and embedding itself in the stone wall on the opposite side of the passageway. A half dozen more bolts instantly followed, as yet more ballistas targeted the gallery. Within seconds, six or seven lycans were impaled upon the lethal harpoons. The sturdy hafts of the bolts, as well as the transfixed bodies of their victims, formed a row of fences, cutting off half of the escapees from Lucian and the others. Panicked lycans tried to squeeze past the obstacles, only to find their way hopelessly blocked. The floor of the corridor was soon slick with blood. A harpoon pierced Nasir's chest, pinning him to the wall like a butterfly on display. A scarlet river streamed down his front.

His clumsiness had cost him his life.

Then, just when Lucian thought things could not get any worse, a door at the rear of the corridor banged open. A squad of Death Dealers, armed with hand-held crossbows, fired at the trapped lycans from behind. Silver-tipped bolts thudded into the backs of the fugitives, who were cut down like wheat. Frantic lycans clawed hopelessly at the harpoons in front of them, before being struck by the soldiers' arrows. They slipped and fell amidst the flowing blood. Their collapsed bodies added to the obstacles filling the corridor. More bolts flew past the harpoons at the lycans on the other side of the barrier. Sparks flared as the silver missiles ricocheted off the walls. A stray quarrel whistled past Lucian's ear. He ducked to avoid a second shaft.

Amidst the pandemonium, Raze rushed back to rescue their trapped comrades. "Stay strong!" he exhorted them. "I am coming!" Lucian was impressed by the man's courage and loyalty but refused to let him throw away his life in a hopeless cause. He tugged on Raze's shoulder. A silver bolt barely missed the slave's bald dome. A desperate lycan, whom Lucian recognized as one of the other slaves from the caravan, reached through the harpoon shafts.

"Help me!" the man pleaded. "Don't leave me here!"

Raze wavered, uncertain where his duty lay.

"There is nothing you can do!" Lucian shouted over the screams of the dying. He physically dragged Raze away from the barricades, while shouting back at the comrades they were forced to abandon. "My brothers, I will be back for you!"

Reaching the exit at the far end of the gallery, Xristo yanked open the doors and beckoned frantically for Lucian and the others to join them. Sabas snatched a flying arrow from the air and hurled it angrily to the floor. Glancing around quickly, Lucian saw that maybe ten additional lycans had survived the massacre. "Up the stairs!" he commanded. Clearly, there was no way they could cross the courtyard without being cut down by the archers upon the ramparts. A stairway ahead offered the only way out. "Move!"

He glanced back over his shoulder at the grisly array of impaled lycans filling the gallery. In death, the skewered casualties served as a grisly shield between the surviving lycans and the Death Dealers, but this temporary benefit came at a terrible cost. Lucian felt a stab of guilt for leading these poor slaves to their doom; he promised their souls that their awful sacrifice would not be in vain.

The vampires will pay for this, he vowed. *I swear it on my life!*

He turned and fled the gallery.

Viktor was meditating in the crypt when a Death Dealer barged in unannounced. Snarling at the interruption, the Elder rose angrily from his throne. How dare this lowly foot soldier disturb his privacy?

"Milord!" the guard blurted, before Viktor could discipline him for his effrontery. "Lucian is escaping!"

A rooster crowed in the courtyard. The warning bell sounded again. Lucian sensed the sun rising as he and the other fugitives raced down a corridor on the second floor of the keep, which was mostly given over to storerooms and larders. A shuttered window called out to him from the end of the hall. Daylight leaked through the wooden slats. A tight smile crossed his face. Freedom was so close he could taste it.

We're going to make it. . . .

Then a pair of Death Dealers rushed from a stairwell, barring their way. "Halt, dogs!" they ordered. "Surrender your weapons!"

Lucian didn't even slow down. Without breaking his stride, he hit the soldiers like a battering ram, driving them backward through the shuttered window. Timber splintered with the impact of the three men's bodies as they tumbled into the open air outside. The dawn's rosy glow hurt Lucian's eyes, but that was nothing compared to the devastating effect the unfiltered sunlight had upon the falling vampires. Their pale flesh burst into flames. Smoke gushed from the creases of their armor. The soldiers wailed like fallen angels as they were cremated inside their metal suits. They fell like comets toward the rocky slopes below.

Unharmed by the daylight, Lucian touched down nimbly on a rugged ledge just beyond the castle walls. A cloud of chalky white ash, which was all that remained of the incinerated Death Dealers, descended upon his head and shoulders. Scorched pieces of armor bounced off the rocks. Lucian spit out a mouthful of gritty ash. He wiped the powdered remains from his face.

Two more vampires dead!

Glancing up at the castle, he saw the other lycans leap from the shattered window. Raze brushed himself off and nodded at Lucian. He gripped the hilt of his sword as the rest of the lycans dropped beside them.

Lucian was glad to see that more than a dozen of his comrades had survived so far, although a few had been wounded by silver arrows during the slaughter in the gallery. A hairy-chested lycan named Rainar grimaced in pain as he yanked a bloody bolt from his shoulder. Smoke rose from his seared flesh. Lucian sympathized with the man's pain, having endured the excruciating sting of Kosta's arrows that night at the crossroads. Still, the injury didn't seem life-threatening. . . .

There will be time enough to tend to our wounded later, he decided. *First we need to reach the safety of the forest.*

Turning his back on the castle walls, he eyed the mountain slope before them. At the foot of the mountain, a barren plain stretched between them and the sheltering wilderness. He knew they would not be truly free until they reached the forest.

But at least they had the dawn on their side. Even now, the sun was cresting the horizon, heralding the first day of the rest of their immortality. The warm glow of the sun felt like a benediction as the lycans scrambled down the mountainside toward freedom.

The guardhouse atop the front gate offered a commanding view of the mountainous terrain below the castle. Flanked by an elite regiment of Death Dealers, Viktor strode through the gatehouse toward the battlements beyond. The fortified garrison, which was wedged in between two flanking towers, held room enough for an entire company of defenders. Crude cots and tables provided a few creature comforts for the guards stationed above the gate. An iron winch stood by to raise or lower the portcullis as needed. The ominous red glow on the horizon gave Victor pause, however, and he hesitated before the doorway leading out onto the ramparts. Daylight had been his enemy for centuries now and he had not survived so long by tempting fate unnecessarily. He lingered prudently in the shadow of the doorway.

Until he spied Lucian leading an entire pack of lycans away from the castle.

Fury erupted inside him. "Get them!" he roared at the nearest Death Dealer, who looked uncertainly at the sunlit palisade. The soldier's cowardice enraged Viktor. Lucian and his traitorous followers were getting away. They had to be stopped . . . now!

He shoved the recalcitrant guard out the doorway, hoping there was still time to halt Lucian's escape with a well-aimed crossbow bolt. But the sun's relentless advance reduced such hopes to ashes, along with the unlucky guard. The soldier ignited like a human torch. Shrieking and flailing about in his death throes, he tumbled between two weathered stone merlons and plummeted over the side of the wall. Smoke and flames trailed behind him as he crashed to earth many feet below.

Damnation! Viktor cursed. The knight's death upset him less than the fact that the man had failed to kill Lucian first. *The fates themselves are conspiring against me!*

The Death Dealer's fiery descent caught Lucian's attention. Viktor watched in frustration as the fleeing lycan looked back over his shoulder at the smoldering remains of the soldier. A worried expression on his face, Lucian peered up at the guardhouse atop the gates.

"Go!" he shouted to his men. "Now!"

Viktor's eyes met Lucian's. They glared at each other across the distance. No more than a hundred yards separated them, yet, thanks to the rising sun, it might as well have been leagues for all Viktor could do to stop the fugitives. The accursed daylight crept inexorably across the ramparts toward the entrance of the guardhouse, shielding the rebels from Viktor's dreadful wrath. The Elder's guards retreated from the doorway, but Viktor remained frozen in place, not yet willing to concede this battle to Lucian and his seditious rabble. "Milord!" a soldier entreated him, urging him to seek safety from the sun's deadly rays. She tugged nervously on Viktor's arm.

He shook off the Death Dealer's hand. His rage rooted him to the spot. His gnashed his fangs. His fists were clenched at his sides, his sharpened nails digging into his palms. He stood frozen in the doorway, glowering at the escaping rebels, even as a golden beam swept over his hand. Smoke rose from his ancient flesh, which sizzled and blackened at the sun's pernicious touch. He hissed through his teeth.

Ignoring the pain, he refused to unlock his gaze from Lucian's. The arrogant blacksmith glared back at him, equally determined not to give ground. An infuriating smirk came over Lucian's face as the sun fought his battle for him. He stepped forward boldly, taunting Viktor, and shook his fist in defiance.

Turncoat! Betrayer! Viktor fumed silently. *I should have killed you along with the bitch that bore you!*

The lycan's blatant ingratitude stung more fiercely than the sunlight, which was even now creeping toward his face, but at last Viktor could ignore the agonizing glare no longer. Nursing his burnt hand, he withdrew into the comforting gloom of the guardhouse, where he seethed in impotent frustration. As long as the sun remained in the sky, there was nothing he could to prevent Lucian and his filthy allies from making good their escape. They had thwarted him . . . for now.

This is not over, he vowed. *Lucian will pay for his audacity even if I have to hunt down every werewolf on the continent. He'll plead for death before I'm through with him!*

But first he had to find out just how this inexcusable travesty had come to pass.

Lucian savored the sight of Viktor retreating into the shadows. It was a small victory but a victory nonetheless. And probably the first time an Elder had been humbled by a lycan since the days of William.

With luck, it would not be the last.

He basked in the sunlight, feeling the warmth of the morning upon his face. Their escape had been fraught with danger and cost the lives of many innocent lycans, but they had succeeded in the end. Now all that remained was for Sonja to join them, three nights hence.

For the first time in two centuries, Lucian faced a future of unlimited possibilities. No doubt Viktor would attempt to hunt them down, but first the vengeful Elder had to find them. Lucian felt confident in his abilities to elude the Death Dealers; if the werewolves of the wild had managed to thrive for centuries despite the vampires' best efforts, surely he and his fellow lycans could fight back against Viktor's troops as well. A new era dawned, for both himself and all lycans. He couldn't wait to see what tomorrow held in store.

Turning his back on the castle, perhaps forever, he led them all toward the distant forest.

A new day dawned.

Chapter Fifteen

*V*iktor's hand had already healed by the time he reached the dungeons, but the memory of Lucian's escape still rankled him. He gazed down at Kosta's headless body, while his men disposed of the two dead guards they'd found in the corridor leading to Lucian's cell. Cracked skulls and slashed throats testified to the manner of their demise, while the nature of Kosta's murderer was equally apparent; Viktor had seen enough mauled corpses over the centuries to recognize the victim of a werewolf when he saw one. The fang marks on the overseers's skull, as well as a few shed tufts of thick black fur, allowed the scowling Elder to easily reconstruct the attack in his mind. A discarded moon shackle, lying in the corner of the cell, left little doubt as to the identity of the beast that had savaged Kosta.

Lucian, Viktor fumed. *Free of his collar once again.*

He cursed himself for not having the seditious blacksmith put to death instead of flogged the night of the mortal nobles' visit. He had delayed in doing what was necessary, and Kosta had paid the price. Viktor resolved not to make that mistake again. But how had Lucian managed to remove his collar in the first place?

"Tanis!" he snarled. *"Tanis!"*

A trio of unsmiling Death Dealers escorted the nervous-looking scribe into the cell. Disheveled hair and garments suggested that he had been abruptly roused from slumber. Viktor had immediately dispatched the soldiers to fetch Tanis upon Lucian's escape. Now he angrily plucked the open collar from the floor and waved it in the scribe's face.

"Where is the key I gave you for this?"

Tanis swallowed hard. He wrung his hands together anxiously. "I . . . I locked that up in the armory myself."

"Then how was this opened?" Viktor demanded. The scribe's obvious anxiety seemed to him a sure sign of guilt.

Tanis stammered in response. "I . . . I have no idea."

"I do," Viktor stated. There was only one obvious conclusion. "You gave him the key." He turned to the captain of the guard, his mind made up. Someone had to pay for this morning's catastrophe. "Kill him."

"No!" Tanis yelped, even as the knight drew his sword. The scribe dropped to his knees amidst the bloody straw. He clasped his hands as he shrilly pleaded his innocence. "No, milord! Check the armory! There has to be some explanation!"

Viktor pondered the other vampire's words. Could it be that he was being too hasty in his judgment? The guard raised his sword above his head, taking aim at Tanis's throat, but Viktor held up his hand to forestall the fatal blow. The knight lowered the sword and stepped away.

"Show me," Viktor said.

The forest clearing felt like paradise compared to the stinking dungeons of Castle Corvinus. Interlaced tree branches offered shade from the sun. Soft green moss carpeted the boulders and fallen logs upon which the weary fugitives rested. A spongy layer of fallen leaves and other detritus muffled their tread. A babbling stream quenched their thirst. Birdsong filled the air. A cool breeze rustled through the trees and bushes. Nature had blessed the lycans' first day of freedom with a clear blue sky. It felt good to be alive.

A lock clicked open as Sabas removed his moon shackle with Lucian's key. He hurled the spike-lined collar away from him before lobbing the key over to Xristo, who eagerly liberated himself from his own shackle. The husky young lycan gaped in wonder at the verdant wilderness surrounding them. He spoke in a hush:

"I have never been outside the walls before."

Neither had most of the castle's original crop of lycans, Lucian reflected. "Enjoy it while you can, Xristo. Because soon enough we are going to have to fight our way back in."

Raze and the others looked up in surprise. Many leapt to their feet in alarm. They glanced fearfully in the direction of the castle. Lucian held up a hand to silence their objections.

"We did not all make it out," he reminded them, "and I will not leave our brothers to rot back there. We humiliated Viktor. It is they who will pay the cost."

Indeed, even those lycans who did not join in the escape would likely have a harder time of it now. The Death Dealers and the other vampires were not likely to forgive the deaths of several of their own. All lycans would be treated much more harshly, if only to discourage the possibility of further revolts. Kosta was dead, but some other sadistic vampire was bound to take his place. Sandor, perhaps, or Soren.

All the more reason to overthrow the vampires once and for all.

"But we were lucky to get out of there alive," Sabas protested. He sounded none too eager to face the Death Dealers again. He gestured around him. "There are but a handful of us. We have few weapons. . . ."

"True," Lucian admitted. "For now." He had already conceived of a plan to expand their ranks, however. "I know of many who would join us." He turned to Raze, who was resting his considerable bulk upon a fallen log. Cracked nutshells littered the ground at the giant's feet. "The noble who brought you here?" Lucian asked. "Can you lead us back to his estate?"

Raze gave the matter some thought before answering. Lucian recalled that the slaves had been blinded by hoods on their grueling trek to the castle.

"Yes," Raze said finally.

That was just what Lucian wanted to hear. Large estates meant plenty of desperate serfs and slaves, who might be looking for a way to better their lot in life. And possibly tempted by the prospect of immortality and unlimited power. *That sounds like the makings of an army to me,* he thought. *An army of lycans.*

"Good."

Tanis's hands shook as the fumbled with the padlock on the door to the armory on the second floor of the keep. Twice he dropped the key before he managed to unclasp the lock. His close brush with execution had left him deeply shaken, and sorely regretting his illicit bargain with Sonja. It was as if he could still feel the Death Dealer's blade poised above the back of his neck. His heart raced like a scared rabbit. His mouth felt as dry as dust.

No council seat is worth this, he thought miserably. *Is it?*

A sturdy oak door swung open, offering a glimpse of the armory beyond. Viktor stepped aside and, with exaggerated politeness, gestured for Tanis to proceed him. The tremulous scribe felt the Elder's suspicious eyes upon him as he stepped into the armory and lit a lantern mounted by the door. The glow from the lantern illuminated a cramped, windowless chamber that housed the better part of the castle's excess arms. Racks of double-edged swords were lined up against the walls. Stacked quivers held supplies of arrows. Crossbows hung upon the walls. Parchment scrolls, laid out atop an angled writing desk, kept inventory of the weapons—and the precious silver used in their construction. Because of the value of the silver blades and arrowheads, Viktor preferred to keep the extra arms locked away from greedy servants. Truth be told, Tanis had occasionally melted down a quarrel or two to dispose of a gambling debt.

Today, however, he ignored the impressive array of weapons as he rummaged hastily through various shelves and cubbyholes. Loose parchments and quills tumbled onto the floor. A stuck drawer rattled beneath the desktop as he fought with it. "It has to be here," he insisted breathlessly, while Viktor loomed ominously in the doorway. Sweat dripped from Tanis's brow. His face was pale as death. "I'm positive I put it here . . . it has to be . . ." He tugged frantically at the stubborn drawer, which finally slid out into the open. He dived on its contents like a man searching for the only antidote to a lethal poison. *"Here!"*

Salvation in hand, he held up Lucian's key—which Viktor had confiscated from the lycan blacksmith after the unfortunate incident at the crossroads. Tanis eagerly handed the key over to the Elder.

Viktor scowled as he examined the key. He appeared almost disappointed to find evidence exonerating the accused scribe. No doubt he disliked being proven wrong. Tanis held his breath as he tensely awaited Viktor's judgment. He tried not to look *too* guilty.

Only Sonja knows what part I played in Lucian's escape, Tanis tried to assure himself. *And she will never tell. . . .*

"He must have made another key," Viktor concluded at last. Sighing, he tucked the key into his belt. He smiled unconvincingly at Tanis. "I never doubted you."

A transparent lie, but not one Tanis cared to dispute. He bowed respectfully as Viktor stalked out of the armory, accompanied by a clatter of Death Dealers. Tanis waited until the echoes of the knights' heavy tread faded away before he collapsed onto a nearby bench. Gasping in relief, he wiped the perspiration from his brow. His inner garments were soaked with sweat. A moment passed before he permitted himself a small, sly smile.

He had gotten away with it!

Thank the gods that he had thought to forge an extra copy of the key.

Chapter Sixteen

Lucian stood atop a mossy boulder, looking down on a mob of rugged-looking mortal men who stared up at him in awe and excitement. Sunlight filtered through a mesh of overhanging pine branches as he posed at the edge of the forest, overlooking barren fields and orchards. A column of thick black smoke rose on the horizon. As hoped, they had found the estate of Raze's former master in disarray following the noble's brutal death two nights past.

"Now I have no wish to remove one shackle from around your necks, only to replace it with one of my own," Lucian told the wide-eyed peasants. With their unwashed faces and rough woolen garments, they bore a distinct resemblance to lycan slaves. He doubted that the average mortal could tell them apart. "You have a choice. You can run and hide, or you can stay and fight. Any man who fights with me will have his freedom. And if he wishes it, immortality!"

Not all of the discontented serfs accepted his offer, but enough were tempted to make this afternoon's expedition worth the trip. Most were restless young striplings who were all too eager to abandon their hopeless lives in search of liberty and adventure, although a few older men joined them as well. The mortals brandished scythes and pitchforks and other weapons liberated from the late Baron Covash's extensive farms and estate. Some balked at being converted into lycans—at least for the time being—but Lucian welcomed their loyalty nonetheless.

We need all the allies we can muster.

Wasting no time, he led them back to the clearing, where he was pleased to discover that the lycan camp was coming together. Canvas tarps, salvaged from neighboring villages, had been strung between the trees to form crude shelters. Skinned rabbits, squirrels, and other game were roasting over open campfires. Most of the lycans still preferred their meat raw, but Lucian had allowed Raze and the newer lycans to cook their food, provided the fires were put out well before nightfall. He did not want the smoke from the flames to attract their enemies once the Death Dealers were abroad once more. It would be necessary to post sentries as well, once the sun went down.

Viktor and his men shall not catch us sleeping, he vowed.

Feeling rather like Robin Hood, whose fabled exploits had reached even the Carpathian Mountains,

Lucian inspected his growing band of rebels. Between the escaped prisoners and the new recruits, their ranks had swelled to more than thirty men. Wounded lycans had already recovered from their injuries. Many had fashioned crude staffs and cudgels from the raw timber.

But would that be enough to overcome the vampires?

Probably not, Lucian thought. He turned toward Raze, who was seated on a nearby boulder. "We need more men."

The giant nodded in agreement. He polished his stolen sword with a crude whetstone. "There are more estates to the west of here."

More humans? Lucian guessed that Raze had been conferring with the mortals. No doubt they knew of other oppressed communities of peasants, bound in bitter subjugation to their masters' lands. It seemed that human serfs and lycans had much in common. . . .

"Go to them and see how many will join us," he agreed. Viktor and his Death Dealers would not be defeated easily; only a sizable army could overthrow them. "I will meet you back here in two days' time."

Raze eyed him quizzically. This was the first he had heard of Lucian departing. "Where are you going?"

Better you should not know that, Lucian thought. What he had in mind might well alarm Raze and the others. Indeed, Lucian had his own doubts regarding the wisdom of his plan. He shot his friend a look that discouraged any further queries. He handed Raze his sword.

"I will return in two days," he repeated.

In time for my rendezvous with Sonja. . . .

Without further explanation, he left the camp in Raze's charge and trekked off into the wilderness. Hours passed as he traversed the forest, occasionally pausing to refresh himself from a gurgling stream or spring. After centuries spent toiling over a hot forge, he enjoyed stretching his legs and wandering freely of his own volition. His bare neck did not miss the constant pricking of his slave collar. He wondered why he had waited so long to free himself.

But today's expedition was not just about exercising his newfound autonomy. He had a more serious purpose in mind as well. A plan had come to his mind that, should it come to fruition, might well give them a crucial edge over their undead foes. The scheme was not without risks, to be sure, but he had felt compelled to pursue it. Too much was at stake to hesitate now.

Human allies are all very well and good, he mused, *but we need something more.*

Twilight began to chase the light from the sky. Kneeling, he searched the forest floor for tracks and spoor. He closed his eyes and sniffed the air.

Yes, he thought. *Somewhere nearby . . .*

Viktor rose promptly at sunset. Troubled by the morning's events, he had slept little during the day. He knew he would not rest easily until he had gotten to the bottom of Lucian's baffling escape—and seen the traitor put to death.

Lucian's smithy struck him as the logical place to continue his investigation. Viktor prowled the deserted shop, sniffing disdainfully at the sooty apparatus. He glared at the cold and lifeless forge, which the missing blacksmith had doubtless employed to fashion his forbidden key. Lucian had always been clever for a lycan.

Too clever, in retrospect.

The devil take me as a fool, Viktor thought, *if I ever trust another lycan again. . . .*

Alas, the cluttered smithy offered no clues as to how Lucian managed to smuggle a second key into the dungeons. Deep in his heart, Viktor suspected that some nefarious accomplice must have assisted in the prisoners' escape, but who? Tanis had been the obvious, and most conveniently expendable, suspect, yet no damning evidence had attached itself to the scribe's name. Which left open one other ghastly possibility, which Viktor could scarcely bring himself to entertain.

No, he thought. *Not her.*

That was unthinkable.

Searching for some other explanation, he stepped around to the rear of the smithy. His trod upon a rusty metal grate, which clanked loudly beneath his foot. He glanced down at the grille, which seemed to lead down into a drainage chute below.

Hark! he thought. *What's this?*

He tried the grate again and it wobbled loosely above the drain. Perhaps too loosely?

His eyes narrowed in suspicion.

Nightfall found Lucian in a narrow valley nestled at the base of a high limestone cliff that stretched many feet above his head. Ferns and brambles sprouted from the rubble at the base of the precipice. Darkness shrouded the wilderness as the temperature dropped severely. The wind, which had seemed pleasant by day, now had a chilly bite to it. His breath frosted before his lips. An owl hooted in the treetops.

The nocturnal forest raised unnerving memories of the bloody massacre at the crossroads only two nights ago. Not for the first time, Lucian wondered if he was making a serious mistake. Death and danger lurked in these woods at night. Perhaps he would have been wiser to have stayed back at the camp with Raze and the others.

But, no, he had come too far already to turn back now. Following his nose, he traced a faint musky aroma to a deep cleft in the face of the cliff. He paused and sniffed the air again. The smell was definitely coming from somewhere inside the cave. His keen ears detected sounds of movement from within, as well as a raspy noise that sounded like the breathing of a dragon.

Or a werewolf.

This is it, he realized. Taking a deep breath to steady his nerves, he slipped through the open fissure. Stygian darkness, only slightly relieved by a narrow shaft of moonlight, enveloped him and he had to feel his way along a winding passageway. Water dripped down damp curtains of calcified stone. Stalactites hung overhead like the fangs of a sleeping dragon. Gaping sinkholes threatened to swallow him forever. Twisted rock formations, carved out by the ceaseless passage of time, looked like lurking demons in the fading light.

Lucian was unpleasantly reminded of the forgotten catacombs beneath Castle Corvinus.

Even after his eyes adjusted to the gloom, he could still barely make out anything at all. Something cracked beneath his boot, and he glanced down to see a suspiciously human-looking jawbone. More bones were scattered across the floor of the cavern. Fang marks gouged the skeletal remains, which had been cracked open and stripped clean of their marrow. Lucian wondered if his own bones would soon join the ghastly refuse. The bestial odor grew overpowering, while the raspy sound of heavy breathing drowned out the rapid beating of Lucian's heart. Squinting in the dark, he rounded a corner, then froze in his tracks.

Glowing cobalt eyes stared back at him.

Scores of werewolves—the feral spawn of William—crowded an immense grotto that rivaled the great hall of Castle Corvinus in size. The savage beasts were everywhere, crouched on numerous ledges and formations, or lurking within countless murky antechambers. Their hackles rose as they regarded the intruder in their midst. Their lips peeled back, revealing yellow fangs. Hostile growls echoed off the petrified walls of the cavern.

The sheer size of the pack took Lucian by surprise. His human instincts urged him to turn and flee, but the wolf in him sensed instinctively that to do so would be suicide. Above all else, he must not show fear. His mind flashed back to his confrontation with the pack only two nights ago. Against all odds, he had faced the ravening horde down. But could he do so again?

I must, he realized. *My life depends on it.*

A low snarl came from his right, only a few inches away from his ear. Lucian gulped and fought down panic. Turning slowly, he found himself face-to-face with an enormous werewolf. The terrifying monster towered above him. Its jaws looked big enough to bite off his head with a single snap.

Don't move, Lucian thought. He didn't even dare try to transform for fear of provoking the beast. The werewolf was close enough to slay him in an instant, before he could finish shifting into wolfen form himself. Lucian had left his sword behind, in order to avoid provoking the werewolves, but now he regretted that decision. Armed only with his own resolve, he summoned a memory of Sonja to give him strength. He imagined her pale face shining down on him like the moon. *Forgive me, my love, if this desperate ploy costs us our future together.*

A hush fell over the grotto as the rest of the pack watched the scene expectantly. The looming werewolf lowered its shaggy head toward Lucian. Its rank breath accosted his nostrils. Saliva dripped onto his shoulder. The monster sniffed the intruder. Its protruding muzzle crinkled in confusion. Lucian took that as a good sign.

That and the fact that the werewolf hadn't killed him yet . . .

Raze sat by the campfire sharpening his ax. New recruits toted whatever scythes, pitchforks, and swords they had managed to salvage from their former homes, clinging to their weapons as they came to grips with their new lives in the forbidding wilderness. Raze's dark eyes scanned the threatening shadows around them. He had not forgotten Viktor or his Death Dealers. Lucian had rescued them from the vampires before, but their leader was not here to protect them tonight. They would have to rely on their own strength and courage.

Raze offered a silent prayer to the watchful spirits of his ancestors. *Protect us from pale-skinned demons in the shape of men.*

The prayer bolstered his spirits—until a chorus of fierce howls rang out, from somewhere in the hidden depths of the forest. Raze shuddered at the sound, and the men around him gasped and murmured fearfully. The baying seemed to fill the air around them. The primal music of the wolves sent a chill down his spine.

Raze silenced the men with a wave of his hand. He listened carefully to the canine ululations echoing through the woods. His memory flashed back to the fearsome howls that had preceded the attack at the crossroads. Was it just his imagination or was there a slightly different quality to the howling tonight? The high-pitched baying sounded less like the hunting song of a bloodthirsty pack and more like . . .

A celebration?

Viktor's expensive robes stank like the drainage tunnels through which he had just waded, but the Elder paid no heed to the unsavory odor. He had more important things on his mind as he surveyed the turret of the abandoned watchtower. Lucian's trail had led to the deserted ruins, which showed evidence of recent habitation. Bat droppings had been swept discreetly into a corner. Centuries of dust had lately been disturbed. Day-old bloodstains speckled the floor. Evidence of a heated struggle?

It seemed that Lucian had been coming and going from the castle for some time, all beneath the unsuspecting noses of his betters. Viktor chided himself for his naïveté. Clearly, Lucian had many secrets. To what dire purpose had this secret lair been put?

An abominable suspicion haunted the back of his mind, but the troubled Elder was not yet ready to give voice to his deepest fear. *It cannot be,* he thought plaintively. *Not my own daughter!*

Wolves howled in the distance, mocking him.

Chapter Seventeen

Only two nights more, Sonja thought.

Alone in her bedchamber, she could not wait to be reunited with Lucian again. The next few days stretched before her like a prison sentence. Clad in a sheath of fine mesh chain mail, she paced restlessly about her quarters. She supposed that, for appearance's sake, she should best go about her life as though nothing were troubling her, but the thought of indulging in idle gossip with Luka and the other vampire ladies repulsed her; how could she feign nonchalance while her lover was a hunted fugitive? Despite her father's prohibitions, she was sorely tempted to go riding out in search of Lucian tonight, days earlier than they had planned. Even if she failed to find him, it would be a blessed relief to escape the noxious atmosphere of the castle, where Lucian's escape was the talk of the court, and every vampire save for her counted the days until his "inevitable" capture and execution. If she had to hear another bloodthirsty aristocrat go on in gory detail about what ought to be done to Lucian and the other rebel lycans, she was going to start cracking skulls!

The shadowy gloom of the chamber depressed her, so she crossed to the vanity to light some more candles. The warmth of the flames reminded her of Lucian's passionate embrace, and she took a moment to bask in the memory of their nights together. Her blood quickened in anticipation of their upcoming reunion. The prospect of seeing him again lifted her spirits somewhat—until she turned away from the candles to find her father standing only a few feet away.

She gasped and clutched her heart. Lost in thought, she had not even heard him enter. *What is he doing here?* she fretted anxiously. It was not like him to invade her bedchamber without knocking. *Is he spying on me?*

"Did I startle you, my dear?" he said blandly. "I am sorry."

"No, no," she assured him, attempting to regain her composure. "Not at all, Father. I just did not . . . no . . ."

Pensive blue eyes examined her. His gaunt face bore an inscrutable expression. She shrunk before his penetrating gaze, feeling exposed and vulnerable. Almost naked.

"It occurs to me," he mused aloud, "that I have been thoughtless. So wrapped up in my own anguish over Lucian's betrayal that I gave no thought to your own feelings."

"My feelings?" Sonja said warily. *Is this a trap? Has Tanis betrayed me?*

"These lycans," he reflected. "They worm their way into our lives, somehow making us forget the travesty of their birth. I myself was fond of Lucian. If he had been as we are, why, he could have been anything. A Death Dealer perhaps."

His praise for Lucian rang hollow to Sonja, given how cruelly he had treated the innocent lycan over the past few nights. Still, she strove to keep her ire to herself. "Yes, perhaps."

"But he was *not* as we are, was he?" His voice took on a darker, more suspicious tone. "Did you help him escape?"

The abruptness of the accusation took her aback. "Help him?" She pretended to be offended by the suggestion. "Of course not."

She felt a sudden urge to flee her father's presence. Glancing toward the door, she was stunned to see two armored Death Dealers standing in the doorway. Cold, implacable eyes gazed back at her from behind their helmets. Sonja realized she was a prisoner in her own chambers.

Her voice faltered. "Father, please."

"Are you lying to me?" he asked.

"No! I am not . . . I would not!" She tried urgently to placate him. "I know I have done many things against your will, Father. But he is a *lycan.*"

She filled her voice with a contempt she no longer felt. As though the very idea that she might ally herself with such a creature was ridiculous.

Her father weighed her words as he came up behind her. No doubt he wanted to believe her; perhaps that would be enough to quell his suspicions. Peering back over her shoulder, Sonja experienced a rush of relief as his stern expression slowly melted. A rueful smile lifted his thin lips. He leaned forward as though to kiss her warmly on the cheek.

"I am so sorry, my dear . . ."

Sonja's tense muscles relaxed. She prepared to graciously accept his apology.

". . . but you leave me with no choice."

What? She started in alarm and tried to pull away from him, but his powerful hands held her fast. Before she could even try to defend herself, he sank his fangs into her neck. She gasped out loud as her own father sucked the blood from her jugular!

No! she thought in stunned disbelief. *This can't be happening!*

The shocking assault was over in a heartbeat but left Sonja feeling dazed and violated. He released his grip and she threw herself away from him in horror. Her hand went to her neck, which was wet and sticky to the touch. Blood trickled down the side of her throat. Nausea gripped her and she staggered away from him toward the door. Her gorge rose. She thought she might vomit.

How could he do this to me? His own flesh and blood!

The intimidating Death Dealers barred her escape. They stepped inside the chamber and slammed the door shut behind them. Their swords slid from their scabbards. If either guard was appalled by the obscene spectacle they had just witnessed, they gave no sign of it. Sonja realized she could count on no mercy from the grim-faced soldiers. These were her father's men, not hers.

She was on her own.

Trembling, she turned to face her father. A crimson smear stained his lips. He casually wiped her blood from his teeth. A shadow gave his face a satanic cast.

Sonja didn't even recognize him anymore.

"This will only take a moment," he said.

Viktor closed his eyes and let Sonja's blood memories wash over him. The images came in a torrent, flooding his consciousness with scattered fragments of his daughter's past. He saw the world through her eyes, felt what she felt, heard what she heard. The more powerful the memory, the more vivid the experience:

No more than a child, she beams up at him as he gently places the pendant around her neck. She throws her tiny arms around him. . . .

Standing beside her father on the balcony, she watches wide-eyed as a handsome lycan youth snatches a silver arrow out of the air. "Lucian," she murmurs, tasting his name upon her lips. "Lucian. . . ."

Snarling werewolves chase her though a moonlit forest. A frenzied horse pants beneath her. Silver stars fly from the tip of her blade to strike an oncoming werewolf in the face. The beast howls in agony as he crashes to the ground in front of the speeding charger. . . .

She gasps in ecstasy as Lucian grinds her against the wall of the watchtower. His muscular chest caresses her breasts. Their naked bodies collide as she takes him deeply inside her. Her passion rises to an almost unbearable peak. Her flesh quickens. Her blood sings with every thrust. No other lover has ever thrilled her so!

Viktor's eyes snapped open. His face contorted in disgust. He spit the telltale blood onto the floor as though it were the foulest of poisons. His entire body quivered with hurt and rage. Pulsing red veins streaked his eyes as he glared at Sonja, who quailed before his unleashed wrath. She had never seen him so irate, not even when he had killed that foolish nobleman before the entire Council.

He knows, she realizes. *He knows it all.*

"Father?" She was at a loss for words, unable to explain what to him must be inconceivable. How could she explain the depths of her passion for a creature he regarded as even less than human? "I am sorry."

An animal cry ripped from his throat as he flew at her like a hurricane. His fist clamped around her throat as he threw her onto the nearby bed. Even the hardened Death Dealers backed away fearfully, frightened by the Elder's volcanic fury. He held her down upon the bed. Her bleeding neck stained the sheets. She screamed loudly enough to be heard all over the castle.

"I wanted to believe your lies!" her railed at her. Bloody spittle sprayed her face. His sharp nails dug into her neck. "I suspected, but I knew it could not be. Not my own daughter!" Angry tears leaked from his eyes. His voice was hoarse with emotion. *"How could you?"*

There was only one true answer. "Father, I love him."

"Do not speak those words!" His livid face twisted into a demonic mask. His voice cracked as though his heart was breaking. "You betrayed me! To be with an *animal!*"

He let go of her neck and she huddled atop the bed, weeping. Claw marks scarred her throat. Blood stained the bodice of her gown. Violent sobs racked her body as she realized that all hope was lost.

We are undone, my love.

Her father swayed upon his legs, seemingly overcome by the damning memories he had stolen from her mind. For a moment she thought that he might collapse altogether, then he stiffened and gazed down on her in judgment. A note of sadness dispelled the anger in his voice. He shook his head mournfully.

"I loved you more than anything," he said before sweeping out of the room. The door slammed shut behind him. He barked at the guards in the hall. "She does not leave this room!"

Sonja found herself under house arrest. How now was she to make her rendezvous with Lucian? He would be expecting her in two nights' time.

Her distraught gaze went to the shuttered window. Nearby, a hooded riding cloak hung upon a hook. . . .

Lucian smelled the smoke from the campfires even before he reached the clearing by the river. The smell of roast venison made his mouth water. After an exuberant night hunting wild game with the pack, he wasn't exactly famished, but he had worked up an appetite hiking back to the camp and a bite of breakfast sounded appealing. Chirping birds greeted the morning. He savored the feel of the sun on his face; there had been times last night when he had feared that he would not live to see another dawn.

But instead I laid the groundwork for a new alliance. . . .

He heard Raze, Sabas, and Xristo conferring around the campfire. A twig snapped beneath his boot and the men leapt to their feet in alarm. They snatched up swords and axes, then relaxed as they spotted Lucian emerging from the brush. The young lycans called out to him enthusiastically, while the stoic African merely raised a hand in greeting. Lucian appreciated their welcome, but was mildly dismayed at how easily he had taken them by surprise. Apparently, he needed to tighten security around the camp.

They were safe enough from the vampires by day, true, but that didn't mean that Viktor couldn't hire human mercenaries to exterminate them. *I wouldn't put it past him,* Lucian thought. *If we can enlist mortal allies, so can our foes.*

Joining his comrades by the fire, he looked over his growing army. He was pleased to see that their unlikely band of humans and lycans now numbered nearly fifty men. Their arms had improved as well; instead of sticks and stones, many of the rebels now sported swords, maces, bows, axes, scythes, pitchforks, and other weapons, all presumably appropriated from the estates of their former masters. He nodded approvingly at Raze. The mortal had clearly been busy in Lucian's absence.

"At this rate, we'll have enough men within a week," Sabas said proudly.

Perhaps, Lucian thought. *And not just men . . .* He wondered when best to let Raze and others in on the results of last night's expedition. They had good reason to fear the wild werewolves. And might not welcome the idea of casting their lot with them.

Another thought crossed his mind. "Has there been any sign of Sonja?"

Raze shook his head. "Nothing."

"With respect, Lucian," Xristo said, "I do not see the wisdom in waiting for her." He frowned at the thought of bringing Viktor's daughter into their midst. "She is not one of us."

Lucian had anticipated this reaction. "She is the one who set us free."

"But she is a vampire!" Xristo protested. Unable to contain himself, he jumped to his feet. He glowered at the nearby river, where Lucian hoped to soon rendezvous with Sonja. "If she has betrayed you, she could lead them to us!"

Betray us? Lucian would not hear his beloved slandered thus. Rising in anger, he grabbed Xristo by the throat and swung him into the trunk of a sturdy oak. The jarring impact shook the tree, causing nuts and branches to rain down on them. Xristo squirmed helplessly in Lucian's grasp. All around the camp, humans and lycans were riveted by their leader's outburst. He raised his voice so that all would hear—and understand that his love for Sonja was not to be questioned.

"Death Dealers will undoubtedly be on the hunt,"

he stated bluntly. "And they will eventually find us. But not by *her* doing." He tightened his grip on Xristo's throat to ensure that he had the husky lycan's full attention. "I trust Sonja with my life. And as long as I am in command, so shall you."

Xristo nodded meekly.

The High Council convened in the crypt immediately after sundown. The tension in the air was fairly palpable. It seemed to Viktor that Coloman and his fellow malcontents could not wait to assail him with their usual litany of grievances.

"Lucian has sacked two estates in Brashov, milord," Orsova reported. Carrier pigeons had brought word of the rebels' audacious raids. "And made off with the contents of their armories. The human slaves have joined his ranks."

Shocked gasps and exclamations greeted this dismaying news. Coloman was quick to take the floor. "Freedom is as much a disease as William's abhorrent pestilence," he declaimed. "You need to bring your unruly pet back."

His acerbic tone clearly placed the blame for Lucian's misdeeds squarely on Viktor's shoulder. That he had earlier argued for increased lenience regarding the lycans had been conveniently forgotten, making him a hypocrite as well as a conniver.

"Thank you, Coloman," Viktor said sarcastically. "The obvious had escaped me." He sat brooding upon his throne, too absorbed in grief to want to waste time parrying words with Coloman and his ilk. He had more serious matters on his mind than the mewlings of these pampered weaklings. "But I need not lift a finger to quash this insurrection. Lucian will return to this castle of his own free will." His throat tightened and his eyes grew dark with mixed anger and sorrow. "I have something he wants."

Chapter Eighteen

*H*oofbeats echoed through the forest.

Lucian and the other rebels seized their weapons. Fear swept over the campsite, with many of the men looking poised to run. Others snarled as they girded themselves for battle. Fangs and claws extended as several of the lycans shifted into wolfen form. Lucian traded a worried look with Raze. Was this the raid they had been expecting for days now? Had the Death Dealers found them at last?

I think not, Lucian thought. The resounding *clop-clop* coming toward them sounded like the advance of a single rider, not the thunderous charge of an invading force. He signaled the men to stand ready as he rushed forward to meet the horseman—or woman. A thrilling possibility caused his heart to beat wildly in anticipation. Could this be Sonja, one night earlier than planned? *Who else would know where to find us?*

He peered hopefully into the shadows, and was rewarded by the sight of a solitary horsewoman riding into the clearing. A hooded burgundy riding cloak hid the newcomer's identity. Slender white hands gripped the reins of an ebony-black palfrey.

Lucian's face lit up. He raced to meet her.

Sonja, my love!

The woman pulled back on the reins, bringing her horse to a halt.

"Milady," he greeted her.

She threw back her hood, revealing flaxen hair and cold violet eyes. Lucian's heart sank in disappointment. "Luka?" He recognized Sonja's lady-in-waiting from the castle. According to Sonja, the elegant blond vampiress had played a small part in Sonja's efforts to visit him in the dungeons. He feared to think what Luka's presence here meant for their hopes for the future. "What is it? Where is she?"

Luka eyed with obvious discomfort the scruffy outlaws loitering behind Lucian. No doubt she was acutely aware of just how vulnerable she was at this moment. Tearing her fretful gaze away from the lycan band, she addressed Lucian coolly. Both fear and anger peppered her voice. As a vampire, she had no love for his kind.

"Sonja has been arrested," she declared. "Her father knows . . . about the two of you."

The news staggered Lucian. He reached out to steady himself against a moss-covered tree trunk. This

242

was the moment he had been dreading ever since their first stolen kiss. He could readily imagine Viktor's virulent reaction.

"He will kill her."

Luka nodded. Her acid tone made it clear that she held Lucian personally responsible for her lady's misfortune. "I thought you should know."

Without another word, she wheeled her horse around and kicked it into motion. Lucian stared bleakly after her as she rode off with all deliberate speed. The horse's pounding hooves left a cloud of dust and fallen leaves in its wake.

Oh, Sonja, he lamented. *What have I done to you?*

Raze watched unhappily as Lucian prepared for war. Black leather armor encased his body. Twin swords were strapped across his back. The lycan's eyes burned with fierce determination, while all about the camp his followers debated their leader's sanity. Raze could feel the anxious eyes of the camp upon them. A buzz of angry mutters and complaints simmered in the background. Intent on rescuing his woman, Lucian seemed oblivious to his army's discontent.

"It is a trap," Raze warned him. "You know that."

Lucian did not dispute this, but showed no sign of abandoning his suicidal quest. "I will not let her die alone."

Raze remembered glimpsing the vampire during the battle at the crossroads. Lucian had challenged an entire pack of werewolves to defend Sonja then; now it seemed he was willing to take on Viktor and his entire army in the same cause. The giant admired his friend's devotion to the lady, even as he feared that it would lead Lucian to his death. And perhaps bring about the end of everything they had achieved so far.

He gestured at the lycans gathered behind them. "They followed you here, Lucian. If you go, we will lose them."

"No, we will not." Lucian reassured him. "Let me tell you a secret, my friend. They only *thought* they followed me. What they truly followed was the idea of being free. That is why they are here. Not me."

Thunder rumbled in the distance, warning of an impending storm. The unsettled atmosphere matched the turbulence building within Viktor's soul as he brooded upon his throne in the great hall. Sensing the Elder's mood, the other vampires kept their distance. Only a handful of courtiers and courtesans populated the hall, most preferring to mingle elsewhere. Even Tanis was nowhere to be seen; the scribe had sequestered himself in the archives following his close call in the armory. A goblet of fresh steer's blood, still warm from the slaughterhouse, did nothing to lift Viktor's mood. There was nothing left now but to wait.

And to wonder mournfully how he might have averted these dire events.

The captain of the guard entered the hall. Viktor had sent for him in hopes of news. He cocked his head expectantly.

Yes?

The soldier knew what the Elder was waiting for. "Nothing yet, milord."

Viktor nodded grimly. He took another sip of blood.

Soon, he thought. *Lucian will be here soon enough.*

Castle Corvinus loomed upon the mountaintop like the gateway to hell. Lurking at the fringe of the forest, hidden behind the trunk of naked elm tree, Lucian peered up at his former home and prison. He had hoped never to return to this place except at the head of a conquering army, yet circumstances had dictated otherwise. His men were not yet ready to lay siege to the fortress and he dared not risk their own lives and liberty for the sake of his own love. Indeed, despite the allegiance of Raze and the others, Lucian suspected that he might well have driven his troops to mutiny had he asked them to fight to the death for the sake of an endangered vampire.

No, he mused. *This task is mine, and mine alone.*

Lightning flashed to the south, briefly turning the night to day. A strong wind whipped up the twigs and leaves around his boots. Skeletal branches creaked and rustled before the oncoming gale. The air was tense and electric. A second boom of thunder sounded louder and more near. The storm was obviously close behind him.

Good, Lucian thought. With luck, the tempest would mask his approach.

Peeking out from behind the tree, he spied an alert Death Dealer patrolling the battlements above the front gate. Loaded ballistas waited to rain down death upon the winding path leading up to the castle. The vampire looked out over the desolate terrain, but apparently saw nothing amiss. Lucian waited until the sentry moved on before darting from the shelter of the forest toward the base of the mountain. He sprinted with preternatural speed, fearing all the while the cry of a watchful guard or the fatal pang of an arrow through his chest, until he reached the steep gray cliff beneath the castle's walls. Breathing hard, he flattened himself against the solid granite. Only four nights ago, he recalled, he had scaled these very walls to enjoy his passionate tryst with Sonja. If only he had known then what ghastly trials lay before them next!

We should have fled that very night, he thought, *and never returned.*

He took a moment to ready himself, then began to climb.

Thankfully, the rain had not yet begun to fall.

Vayer was relatively new to the Death Dealers, having served as a squire for some seventy years before being elevated to the corps by Marcus himself. He wondered why he had been assigned to stand guard over the lycan blacksmith's old forge, but he was not about to question his superior's orders. If Captain Sandor wanted him to spend the night watching over an abandoned smithy, then that was what he was going to do. *Could be worse,* he thought. *I could be risking life and limb fighting werewolves in the woods.*

Tonight his only enemy was boredom.

He spat upon the ground, barely missing the metal

grate a few inches away from his feet. The grate had felt loose when he had accidentally trod on it before. He wondered if he should mention that to anybody.

Another crack of thunder split the night. Vayer looked up, grateful for the rough-hewn stone roof above his head. *Sounds like a hell of a storm,* he thought. Thank the Elders he was indoors and not up on the ramparts tonight!

The deafening boom almost drowned out the sound of clanking against the wall behind him. He looked down in surprise to see the rusty metal grate lying askew. "What the devil?" He fumbled for his sword.

A powerful hand grabbed his ankle. He yelped in surprise as he was yanked down the drain. . . .

His glorious career as a Death Dealer ended permanently.

Two more Death Dealers were posted in the hall outside the Lady Sonja's quarters. The noblewoman had been confined to her chambers upon the orders of Lord Viktor himself. Rumors were rampant throughout the castle as to what the Elder's daughter might have done to warrant her imprisonment, but if half of what the gossips said was true, the guards figured she was lucky not to be spending the night in the dungeons instead.

Could it be true that she had actually coupled with a lycan? The senior guard, a grizzled veteran named Lazar, shook his head at the very notion. *Filthy slut,* he groused silently. Were she anyone else's daughter she'd already have been branded as a whore for such a wanton perversion of nature. But that was always the way of things, wasn't it? The goddamn aristocrats got away with crimes an honest soldier would be flayed alive for even thinking of.

Not that he would ever dare to say so aloud, of course. Especially if he thought an Elder might hear.

He pictured Lady Sonja and the slave together. Once you got over the sheer sacrilege of it all, it was hard not to find the provocative rumors vaguely arousing. Salacious fantasies frolicked across his imagination, producing a bulge in his breeches. He licked his lips as he wondered how exactly a lycan rutted with a vampire. *Probably took her from behind,* he supposed, *like a dog in heat. . . .*

A faint noise, coming from just around the corner, interrupted his lubricious reverie. Lazar exchanged glances with his partner, a Wallachian vampire named Dmitri. Drawing his sword, Dmitri hurried to investigate, leaving Lazar behind to stand guard over the bedchamber. Long moments passed as he waited tensely for the other soldier to return. He strained his ears to hear over the thunder rumbling outside.

Was that a muffled cry he heard? Or the sound of an armored body hitting the ground?

"Dmitri?"

No answer came from around the corner.

Locked within her chambers, Sonja sat forlornly at the edge of her bed. Her hand went to her throat. Although the bite marks and scratches had long since healed, leaving the skin smooth and unblemished once more, the emotional scars left by her father's attack had not yet faded. She wondered if they ever would. A fresh gown had not cleansed her from the violation she had endured at her own father's hands. Even now, she could still feel his sharp fangs penetrating her flesh. . . .

She knew she would never be able to see him the same way again.

Dark shadows haunted her eyes; she had slept little since the attack, and what meager slumber she had managed to attain had been troubled by disturbing dreams in which a demonic bat, wearing her father's face, sucked the last drops of blood from her body. Her anguished gaze went to the door. Every part of her wanted to flee Castle Corvinus and never return, yet she knew that the Death Dealers outside would not permit it. She could only await her father's judgment and tremble at the thought of what terrible punishment lay ahead for her. A vicious flogging such as Lucian had endured—or perhaps something worse?

Surely not! she strove to convince herself. Even after all that had come between them, surely her father would not order her death. *I am still his only child!*

But after what had happened last night, in this very bedchamber, she could no longer be sure of anything. Her entire world had been shaken to its core . . . and in more ways than one. Her hand drifted across her belly. Her stomach, which had been unsettled for many nights now, troubled her once more. She felt an unfamiliar stirring within her.

At least Lucian is safe, she thought. That knowledge was all that comforted her in these trying hours. She prayed to the heavens that he would not be reckless enough to try to rescue her. *Leave me, my love. Do not sacrifice your freedom for my sake.*

Footsteps sounded outside the suite.

"Dmitri?" Lazar called out again, louder this time. Once again, his hail was met with silence. *Damnation*, he cursed. He wavered, torn between staying at his post and finding out what had happened to this partner. *He better not have snuck off to relieve himself!*

Finally, he could abide the suspense no longer. Checking to make sure that Sonja's door was securely locked from the outside, he drew his own sword and cautiously crept down the drafty corridor. His former arousal wilted completely as he wondered what had become of the other Death Dealer. Rounding the corner, he discovered that a torch had gone out, leaving the hall shrouded in inky shadows. He peered warily into the dark. Was that breathing he heard up ahead?

"Dmitri? Are you there?"

A flurry of motion, moving almost faster than the eye could see, was the only warning he received before something cold and sharp sliced across his throat, just above his protective steel gorget. A cold red waterfall cascaded down his front. He crumpled to the floor in a heap.

Stealthy feet stepped over his corpse.

Sonja stared intently at the door. Minutes had passed since she had heard the guards stomp away to investigate the crash. At first, dark imaginings had sent a chill through her heart. Had her father dispatched an assassin to quietly rid his bloodline of a humiliating embarrassment, or was her sire himself returning to "question" her further? In truth, she had not known which dire circumstance would have been preferable.

But her courage had returned as another possibility leapt to mind. She held her breath, hoping against hope.

Please let it be so, she prayed. *It must be so. . . .*

A metal latch was drawn back on the other side of the door. The creaking wooden barrier swung open and Lucian rushed inside. Fresh blood stained the double-edged sword in his hand. His muddy leather gear and boots dripped onto the carpet. Concerned brown eyes sought her out. "Are you all right?" he asked anxiously.

Already clad for battle, she now wore a leather surcoat and boots over a suit of fine chain mail that clung to her body like a second skin. As plate armor did not lend itself to stealth, she had not donned her heavier gear. Her pendant was tucked between her breasts. She drew her own sword from its scabbard.

"I knew it was you," she declared.

Joy and relief washed over her. She ran to him and clung to him in a fervid embrace. She could feel the comforting warmth of his body even through his tough leather garb. Their lips found each other and they fed hungrily upon their love until her fears at last reasserted themselves.

"You . . ." She pulled her face away from his. "But you should not have come." Guilt coursed through her veins as she grasped the tremendous risk he was taking on her behalf. "You were *free.*"

He shook his head. "Not without you."

That was all she needed to hear to restore her spirits. They lost themselves in another kiss before they finally broke apart once more. It dawned on her that this was the first time Lucian had ever dared set foot in her bedchamber, but, alas, there was no time to share it with him. Commotion sounded in the hall outside. Footsteps pounded up the stairs toward her chambers.

"We have to go," he insisted. "Now."

If it was not already too late . . .

Chapter Nineteen

*S*andor rushed up the stairs, followed by a trio of loyal Death Dealers. A chambermaid had reported a disturbance on the top floor of the castle, not far from where Lady Sonja had been confined to her quarters. The captain hoped that the noise was simply the result of some clumsy accident, but he feared the worst.

How could that lycan have gotten past my guards?

His heart sank as he spotted the prone body of a soldier lying in a darkened corridor leading to Lady Sonja's quarters. A crimson pool surrounded the murdered Death Dealer's body. Bloody boot prints led away down the hall. One of Sandor's men knelt to check on their fallen comrade, but the captain knew better than to waste time on a corpse. Not while an intruder stalked the castle.

"Lucian," he muttered under his breath. It could be no one else.

Just as the Elder predicted.

He wondered momentarily what had become of the second guard, only to have his fears confirmed by the sight of the vampire's severed head, lying several feet away from the man's truncated body. Glazed blue eyes gazed blankly up at the captain as he rushed past the carnage toward Sonja's quarters. The horrified gasps and curses of his men followed him down the adjoining hall. *First Kosta, now this,* Sandor thought. He was starting to lose count of just how many vampires Lucian and his rebels had killed. . . .

"Treacherous dog!"

He skidded to a halt outside the open door to Lady Sonja's chambers. Scarlet boot prints crossed the threshold, but Sandor trampled over them in his haste to check out the interior of the suite. It took him only moments to confirm the ghastly truth.

Lady Sonja—and her murderous lover—were gone.

A pair of Death Dealers crouched beside the open drain behind the smithy. They muttered in confusion as they called out for their missing comrade. Peering down into the inky blackness of the drainage tunnels below, they were taken unawares by Lucian and Sonja, who rushed silently out of the shadows like demons freshly conjured from the abyss. Twin swords cut the knights down before they could raise an alarm. Slashed throats spilled crimson cataracts onto the sooty floor of the workshop.

Lucian plucked a burning torch from a sconce as he

stepped over the soldiers' bodies. Lightning flashed outside the smithy, followed almost immediately by a deafening crack of thunder. The storm, it seemed, was almost upon them.

Sonja wiped the blood from the blade Lucian had provided for her. He stood by chivalrously as she swiftly lowered herself into the waiting chute. He had already warned her not to be startled by the dead soldier waiting at the bottom of the drain. They exchanged a silent look before she disappeared down the drain. He gave her a few minutes, then followed after her.

The first faint lashings of rain pelted the roof of the smithy.

Sandor came rushing into the great hall, tracking blood onto the floor. Judging from the captain's apparent lack of wounds, Viktor judged that the enticing red splatter was not his own. The soldier's agitated manner suggested that Viktor's plans had at last come to fruition.

"Milord!" Sandor cried out in dismay. He prostrated himself before the Elder's throne. "Your daughter has escaped!"

The consternation on the captain's face was almost amusing. He looked as though he expected to be fed to the wolves for his failure. Instead Viktor calmly sipped on his crimson quaff.

"Ah," he said, completely unperturbed. "Of course she has."

The waiting was over. . . .

The rain was coming down in force now, flooding the ancient catacombs and drainage tunnels. Hand-in-hand, Lucian and Sonja waded through the icy torrent. The rising yellow sewage washed crumbling skeletons from their funerary niches. Skulls and bones floated past them. A drowned rat bumped against Lucian's leg.

Freedom, and a new life together, perhaps as man and wife, awaited at the end of the tunnels. Lucian found it hard to believe that they had already come so far without being stopped. It was almost too easy. . . .

Suddenly, a metal grate in the ceiling, no more than ten feet ahead of them, was wrenched open from above. The fugitive lovers jumped backward in alarm. Torchlight invaded the tunnel, followed by a large wooden barrel, which crashed down into the catacombs from high above their heads. The barrel smashed against the floor of the sewer, splintering into dozens of wooden staves. Thick black oil spilled into the frothing water.

No! Lucian thought, realizing at once what was in store. He tugged frantically at Sonja's arm, dragging her away from the spreading oil. Just as he feared, a blazing torch was tossed after the barrel. The torch ignited the oil and broken timbers, which burst into flame like a vampire in the sun.

A scorching blast of heat and smoke drove Lucian and Sonja back the way they'd come. They choked on the noxious fumes. Lucian's mustache and beard felt singed. "This way!" he shouted over the roar of the fire as he pulled Sonja from the crackling orange conflagration, which chased after them like a thing alive. Cobwebs flared up briefly before crumbling to ash. Burning rats shrieked in agony.

This is the trap Raze warned me of, Lucian realized. *Viktor has us right where he wants us!*

Many feet above them, in the rain-swept courtyard, Sandor and his Death Dealers readied another barrel. The soaked vampires struggled to keep their torches lit despite the driving rain and wind. Lightning slashed across the night sky. Thunderclaps rattled the stained-glass windows of the keep. Water gushed from the mouths of the sculpted grotesques perched upon the eaves.

Seemingly impervious to the boisterous tempest raging all around him, Viktor looked on grimly as the soldiers carried out his plan. Lucian had proven just as predictable as anticipated, relying on his hidden escape route one time too many. *Apparently,* he thought wryly, *you can't teach an old wolf new tricks. . . .*

He pointed imperiously at another metal grate. "That one."

Lucian and Sonja raced through a cramped side tunnel. The squeeze was tight enough that they had to go through one at a time. Lucian shoved Sonja ahead of him, while feeling the heat of the flames against his back. He felt as though he was trapped in a dragon's lair, with the serpent's fiery breath bearing down on them.

They had wriggled through a narrow gap when a second barrel came plummeting down in front of them. Oil splattered the walls as the barrel broke apart only a few yards ahead of Sonja. A flung torch set the spilled liquid ablaze. The dragon breathed again, even closer than before. Swirling orange and yellow flames lit up the catacombs. Lucian threw up his hand to protect his face from the searing heat. Sonja cried out in fear.

Blood-sucking bastard! Lucian thought angrily, shocked by Viktor's ruthless tactics. *Does he mean to burn his own daughter alive?*

He looked around desperately, wondering which way to turn. They were trapped like rats between the raging fires, which were converging on them rapidly. Metal scraped against stone directly above their heads. Glancing up at the ceiling, Lucian eyed a newly opened shaft overhead. He tensed in anticipation of another fiery assault from above, but, to his surprise, a third barrel did not crash down into the sewers. Rain alone poured down the open drain. It was as if Viktor was giving them a way out.

But what was waiting for them above?

Lucian clenched his fists in frustration. He realized they were playing right into Viktor's hands, but what else were they to do? The blazes were inching closer to them with every second, turning the tunnels into an underground forge. He could see the dancing red flames reflected in Sonja's watery eyes. They sagged against each other, all but overcome by the heat and smoke. The suffocating fumes irritated his eyes and lungs. The chain mail clinging to Sonja's body grew hot to the touch. She whimpered in pain. Her pale skin began to redden. . . .

He glanced again at the grate above. The encroaching infernos left them no other choice. He shared an urgent look with Sonja, who nodded in agreement.

Come what may, they had to abandon the tunnels—or be reduced to ashes!

* * *

Viktor had deliberately left the shaft undisturbed. Ten armed Death Dealers were stationed around the open drain, ready to apprehend any fugitive who tried to climb out of it. His dark robes were drenched from the deluge, but he paid no heed to the violent weather. The fearsome storm was nothing compared to the tempest in his own heart. Not until Lucian paid for defiling his daughter would the vengeful Elder think of anything else.

Come, Lucian, he urged the lycan silently. *Bring Sonja back to me—and face your just deserts!*

As though in response, a rampaging figure burst from the drain.

Lucian leapt from the tunnels as though fired from a catapult. As expected, he found an entire contingent of Death Dealers waiting for him. Outnumbered, he relied on speed and savagery to try to even the odds. Whirling like a dervish, he slashed out at the soldiers with his sword. The blade struck like lightning, targeting the cracks and crevices in the knights' armor. Blood streamed down the gutter of the blade as he speared one vampire in the eye, then yanked the sword back in time to ram the pommel into the face of a vampire behind him. Fangs shattered beneath the blow, and the soldier staggered backward, clutching his mouth. A third soldier swung a sword at Lucian's head, but the lycan ducked beneath the blow and drove his own sword up beneath the vampire's chin, spearing his brain. The guard convulsed once before toppling backward onto the rain-slick paving stones. The heavy armor clattered against the floor of the courtyard. Lucian tugged his sword free of the carcass.

Never corner a wolf, he thought, *unless you want to get bit.*

Taken aback by the sheer ferocity of Lucian's attack, the remaining Death Dealers stumbled about in confusion. They lunged clumsily at the elusive lycan, getting in each other's way. An irate commander shouted for reinforcements, drawing more Death Dealers from the keep and ramparts. A small army charged across the bailey toward Lucian, who caught a glimpse of Viktor himself standing to one side, observing the chaos from a safe distance. Lucian was tempted to hurl his sword across the courtyard at the tyrannical Elder, but that would have left him unarmed against the horde of Death Dealers. Instead he glanced behind him to see Sonja bursting up from the drain after him. A gout of fire licked her heels as she sailed over the heads of the distracted guards. A shining silver sword gleamed in her hand.

"GO!" he shouted at her.

Having drawn all the soldiers down upon him, the way seemed clear for Sonja to make a break for it. Lucian had no illusions that he could hold off the Death Dealers much longer—he was too badly outnumbered—but perhaps he could buy enough time to allow Sonja to escape? He would gladly trade his life for hers.

Howling like a wolf, he jabbed his sword straight through a soldier's metal breastplate. He had forged the vampires' armor after all, and knew exactly where the weak spots were. The driving rain washed the vampire's blood down the open drains. Lucian's lips peeled back to bare his fangs. His eyes flashed cobalt.

All right, he challenged the oncoming soldiers. *Who's next?*

The cold rain and wind came as a shock after the inferno in the tunnels. Sonja sprung like a gazelle across the courtyard as she joined Lucian in battle against the soldiers. Never for a minute did she consider leaving him to fight alone. She knew full well that her father would surely have Lucian tortured to death for his "crimes," assuming he survived his uneven battle against the merciless Death Dealers. *Not while I still live,* she vowed. They would perish together, if need be. Like the hero and heroine of some tragic Nordic myth.

A knight came at her, swinging a heavy mace. He stayed his hand too long, no doubt hesitant to strike down an Elder's daughter, and she ran him through without hesitation. The look of betrayal on his face, as he collapsed onto the cobblestones, cut her to the quick. Although a warrior born, she had never killed another vampire before.

I had no choice, she thought. Her free hand went to her belly. Although not even Lucian knew the truth, more lives than theirs hung in the balance tonight. *Our forbidden love has yielded more than just tragedy. It has also brought new life into the world.*

Side-by-side, she and Lucian fought the Death Dealers. Her heart swelled with pride as, out of the corner of her eye, she saw her lover hold his own against her father's hand-picked guards. The odds were against them, but you would never know it from the courageous way he threw himself into the fray. Vampire blood flooded the gutters. This, she promised herself, was how she wanted them both to be remembered: fearless and indomitable.

Fight on my love, she thought. *Fight for our future together.*

Her sword danced like a living flame, cutting and thrusting through the guards. Death Dealers dropped at her feet and, for an instant, she found herself triumphant. Her gaze went to the ramparts. The massive siege bows were unmanned. It appeared that every soldier on duty was busily engaged in the strife surrounding her. If she and Lucian could just make it to the top of the palisade, one leap would put Castle Corvinus and all its dangers behind them. The way seemed clear.

Then her father's fist slammed into her face.

One minute Viktor was lurking on the periphery of the conflict, letting his soldiers do his fighting for him. The next, he disappeared from sight as swiftly as a bat on the wing. Fearing the worst, Lucian risked a glance at Sonja and was dismayed to see the Elder striking his daughter. Lightning heralded Viktor's sudden attack. Lucian saw their desperate plan coming apart before his eyes.

"Sonja!" he cried out in despair. "No!"

His lapse in attention cost him dearly. He took his eyes off his foes too long, and they swiftly took advantage of his mistake. An armored fist punched his jaw, knocking his head to one side, while another soldier clubbed the back of his skull with a studded mace. A steel-toed boot delivered a vicious kick to his privates. The butt of a crossbow rammed the base of his spine. His head ringing, he dropped to his knees and retched on the pavement. Everything went black for a heartbeat. A fist seized his hair by the handful and yanked his head back up again. When his vision cleared, he found a ring of loaded crossbows surrounding his skull like a crown of thorns. A flash of lightning illuminated the inchlong silver arrowheads pointed at his skull. The surly expressions of the Death Dealers dared him to provoke them further. Their fingers were poised upon the triggers of their crossbows.

His sword slipped from his fingers.

Lucian's fight was over, but Sonja's had only just begun. Across the courtyard, she faced off against her father, who stood between her and the gates. A pair of ponderous stone towers framed his imposing figure. His somber robes and severe expression gave him the look of some nocturnal bird of prey. Rain ran down the blade of the silver-plated broadsword in his hand. Her face stung from his blow.

She slowly lifted her own sword. "I do not want this, Father."

"How dare you raise your hand to me!" Anger flashed in his eyes. "I am still your father!"

Sonja did not deny it. Despite all that had transpired over the past few nights, the bonds of kinship still had a hold upon her heart. Two hundred years of loving memories could not be easily shoved aside. Yet it was clear from his unforgiving mien that he was not going to let her depart without a fight, and she could no longer abide the cruel injustice of his rule. Not when it demanded the death of her one true love.

Very well, she resolved. *Let my sword speak for me.*

The blade sliced through the rain. He parried with his own sword, blocking her blow. Sparks flew as metal rang against metal. She flipped her sword, just as she had while being chased by the werewolves four nights ago, and rammed its ornate hilt into his chest. Wincing, he stumbled backward into a stone wall. His sword arm sagged and for an instant his heart lay bare before her. She drew back her sword to deliver the fatal thrust, but a flicker of doubt stayed her hand. Could she truly end her father's life?

She hesitated only for a heartbeat, but that was one moment too long. Snarling, Viktor rebounded from the wall and lunged at her like a demon. She went for the kill, but he batted the thrust away with his own sword and swung back savagely. Rain flew from their blades with every counterattack and riposte. Sheets of rain rendered the cobblestones treacherously slick. Thunder punctuated the clash of steel against steel. The wind whipped Sonja's hair about.

Her lover wanted her free. Her father would not let her go.

But only she knew all that was truly at stake. . . .

Their heated duel drew the attention of the nearby Death Dealers. The vampire soldiers gaped in amazement at the unlikely spectacle of the Elder trading blows with his own daughter. None rushed to join the battle; all sensed that there was nothing to be gained by getting in the middle of this deadly family dispute.

When the high and mighty warred against each other, the smart immortal kept out of the way. . . .

Only Lucian yearned to throw himself into the melee, but the guards' crossbows kept him at bay. He stepped forward instinctively, only to be brought up short by the silver points pressing against his throat—like a lethal variant on the moon shackles he had once worn.

He could only look on helplessly as Sonja fought for her life.

"Do you think you can defeat me?" Viktor said incredulously. He sneered at her through their crossed swords, their contorted faces only inches apart. Their matching azure eyes glowed with equal intensity. Ivory fangs betrayed their vampiric natures. He forced her backward across the bailey, toward the weathered stone steps leading up to the ramparts. His blade bounced off the guard of her hilt, sparing her fingers. A forceful cross almost knocked her sword from her grasp. "I am older and stronger."

"I don't want to defeat you!" she insisted. Why was he forcing her to fight him like this? *Let me go and I'll never trouble you again!*

A skillful feint failed to penetrate his defenses. He charged at her head-on, driving her halfway up the stairs. His blade thrust at her shoulder, but she spun about, dodging the blow, and swung her sword at his side. The vigor of the attack forced him to vault back onto a landing to avoid being cut in twain. His soggy black robes fluttered in the wind like the wings of an enormous bat.

A bat with my father's face, sucking the blood from my veins . . .

A disturbing fragment of her earlier nightmare flashed through her brain. Pressing her advantage, she lunged after her father. She slashed repeatedly at his guard, like Lucian pounding on his anvil. Again and again, her sword rained down against his, in arc after blinding arc, as he parried each blow at the last minute, only seconds before they slashed his face to ribbons. Sonja began to think that she truly had a chance of defeating her father.

If only she could bring herself to kill him!

Lucian watched the frenetic duel in an agony of helplessness. Silver arrowheads dug into this neck, scalding his skin, as the armed Death Dealers hemmed him in on all sides. His bloodied face was racked with worry. He clenched his fists in frustration.

Sonja was fighting for her life and there was nothing he could do!

With an explosive burst of strength, Viktor propelled Sonja backward, regaining the offensive. His sword came whistling through the rain at her neck. Sonja parried in time, but the jarring impact sent a jolt through her arm. Gasping, she gave ground and stumbled backward a few steps. Her blade momentarily drooped toward the floor.

Seeing an opening, Viktor charged again, but she ducked beneath the blow and spun around behind him. *Hah!* she thought. *Too much confidence makes you careless, Father.* Before he even realized that he had fallen for another feint, she brought down the flat of her sword hard against the back of his hand. He hissed in pain as he lost his grip on his sword. The blade slid across the slippery landing before tumbling off the stairs. Sonja heard it clatter to the ground many feet below.

Viktor wheeled about to find Sonja's sword leveled at his throat. His eyes widened in shock. He swallowed hard, stunned to find himself at his daughter's mercy.

How does it feel, Father, to look death in the eye?

Death Dealers belatedly rushed to his defense, racing up the steps with their swords raised high. Sonja shot them a warning look. Her fierce blue eyes dared them to test her resolve. She kept her face as cold and implacable as the rain beating down on her. Her dark hair fell wetly across her pale white countenance as she struck a defiant pose, resembling a warrior goddess whom only a fool would cross. The soldiers got the message and kept their distance. None wanted to be responsible for the death of an Elder.

Neither do I, she thought. *But I will if I have to.*

Despite the sword at his throat, her father swiftly regained his composure. His face hardened into a stony mask. His voice was cold as ice. "Killing me will not save your precious lycan."

"I do not wish to kill you, Father." She made one last attempt to reason with him, and possibly avert more bloodshed. "There is another way. Please, call off your men"—she placed a hand upon her belly—"for the sake of your grandchild."

Viktor's jaw dropped. Startled exclamations blurted from the Death Dealers. The soldiers stared at each other in disbelief, too shocked by her unforeseen revelation even to try to conceal their feelings from their master. Sonja realized that she just undermined the very foundations of the Covenant, perhaps for all time.

But would the truth, in fact, set them free?

Lucian could not believe his ears. Sonja was with child? How was that even possible? Lycan and vampire were two completely different breeds, or so he had always believed. The blood of wolf and bat could never mingle; they were eternal opposites.

But Sonja and I have already put the lie to that myth, have we not?

He recalled their frenzied lovemaking in the watchtower only a few nights ago. Was that when his seed had taken root in her womb, or had it been during one of their earlier trysts? How long had she known of this unexpected blessing?

No matter, he thought. All that concerned him now was that Sonja lived to raise their child far from here. But would Viktor ever allow that to come to pass?

Lucian doubted it.

Now, more than ever, he longed to rush to her side. But, alas, the ring of crossbows trapped him where he was. He could only watch impotently as Sonja pleaded for their child's freedom. Their eyes met briefly and they shared a single poignant moment as he tried to convey to her just how much their shared miracle meant to him as well. He was a father now, who wanted his bride and offspring to have everything it was in his power to offer them.

Sadly, at this dreadful instant, that was nothing at all.

"A miracle, Father," Sonja proclaimed, her sword still at her sire's throat. Her voice caught in her throat. "A union of the bloodlines."

She prayed that, despite everything, news of his heir would soften her father's heart. Vampire births were rare and treasured events, and even more so where the nobility was concerned. With her free hand, she tried to place her father's hand against her armored belly, but he yanked it away in disgust. Her hopes were crushed by her father's vitriolic reaction. His initial look of shock swiftly gave way to an expression of utter disgust and condemnation, exceeding even his violent response to his discovery of her illicit liaisons with Lucian. He glared venomously at her even as he shook his head in dismay.

"I curse the day your mother gave her life to bring you into this world," he said bitterly. Icy contempt, leavened only slightly by a trace of unspoken sorrow, dripped from his voice. "This . . . *thing* inside you is a monstrosity."

His harsh words stung more painfully than the brightest sunlight. Sonja realized at last that there could be no hope for a reconciliation between them. She had to choose between her father's life or her child's.

Which was no choice at all.

"So be it," she said coldly, steeling herself to do what must be done. The memory of his fangs rending her throat gave her the strength she needed to put aside her past devotion. *He brought this on himself,* she decided. *His tyranny and prejudice force my hand.*

She drew back her sword.

Lucian was not surprised by Viktor's virulent words. He knew too well how deeply Viktor loathed all lycans. The fiendish Elder was never going to acknowledge a half-breed bastard as his heir, no matter what Sonja might have hoped. Her love for her father had blinded her to the true depths of his evil.

Kill him, he silently entreated her. *Kill him now!*

His eyes widened in alarm as he spied Viktor slyly reaching behind him to draw a long silver dagger from a concealed sleeve at the back of his robe. Distracted by her father's scathing rebuke, Sonja failed to notice Viktor hiding the knife behind his back. Ironically, Lucian recognized the doubled-edged blade as his own work. Its keen edge would slice through vampire flesh as readily as any lycan's.

Damn you, Viktor! She's your daughter! He lunged forward, heedless of the crossbows around his neck. Their silver points gouged his throat as he shouted in panic. "SONJA!"

The butt of a crossbow struck his skull, producing a blinding explosion of pain. He tumbled forward onto all fours, scraping his palms on the rough stones. A heavy boot dug into his back, grinding him into the wet pavement. Crossbows targeted his head once more. The tip of a quarrel jabbed the nape of his neck.

A smirking Death Dealer kicked him in the ribs.

"SONJA!"

Lucian's urgent cry commanded her attention. Looking away from her father, just for instant, she pivoted in time to see Lucian beaten to the ground by his unfeeling captors. The force of their blows rang out even over the pealing thunder. A pentacle of crossbows were aimed at his prone body. The guards looked as if they were about to execute him on the spot.

No! she thought. *Lucian!*

Her fears for his life proved her undoing. Seizing his opportunity, her father swept her blade away with his arm, then whirled behind her ere she knew what was happening. His arm encircled her waist. A knife somehow appeared against her throat. She felt the edge of the dagger press against her jugular, not quite drawing blood. One move, she realized, and he could slit her throat open.

"This is over!" he barked. He relieved her of her sword, then nodded at the guards below. "Remove him!"

Her head and shoulders sagged in defeat. An awful chill sank into her bones. She sobbed openly as Lucian was dragged off to the dungeons by the brutal Death Dealers. His spilt blood was washed away by the storm, which finally began to abate. Unable even to lift his head, he looked more dead than alive. She feared that death by combat would have been a kinder fate than what lay in store for him.

Why did you come back for me? You were free . . . and safe.

Now both of them would pay the price for their transgressions, as would their unborn child.

The guards on the steps came forward and clamped a pair of heavy manacles around her wrists; the dense metal was strong enough to bind even a lycan—or a vampire. Only once she was securely chained did her father remove the dagger from her throat. He bent low to whisper in her ear, his damning words meant for her alone.

"Do you understand what you have done?" Anguish warred with anger in his voice. "This night was never about you. It was about *him*. I could have given him to the Council and swept everything else away. In time, the rumors about you would have been forgotten. But not now." He yanked his hand away from her belly as though the very touch of her repelled him. "Not after *that*."

He stepped back and gestured for the soldiers to take her away.

Chapter Twenty

They were together again, after a fashion.

Lucian and Sonja shared adjoining cells in the lowest level of the dungeons. Two rows of iron bars denied them the comfort of each other's arms, as he sat across from her, much as he had once done with Raze. Her wrists were chained to the bars of her cage, so that she could not even reach the bowl of cold, congealed ox blood lying before her. A wide gap separated their cells. No matter how far he stretched, his fingers could not reach hers. Only their eyes met.

That will have to be enough, he thought. *Little as it is.*

The sight of her locked away in this fetid hellhole tore at his heart. Stripped of her fine armor and boots, she had only a tattered linen shift to protect her from the chill and grime of the dungeon. The striped blue-

and-green garment was hardly fit for a beggarwoman, let alone a noblewoman. Her golden pendant shone incongruously against the threadbare fabric. That she had been allowed to keep the jeweled ornament could only be a sentimental whim on Viktor's part. To Lucian's mind, the paltry gesture did nothing to ameliorate the sheer injustice of her plight. He did not know whom he blamed more for this tragedy, her father or himself.

"I am so sorry," he murmured. A coarse brown tunic and trousers had supplanted his leather armor. The guards had not bothered to replace his collar, however; apparently, he was no longer a slave but a prisoner. The gashes left by the silver arrows had long since healed, leaving his bare throat unscratched. But his guilt tortured him without respite. *If only you had never met me!*

She shook her head. Gentle brown eyes refused to hold him accountable. "No," she said softly.

He welcomed her kindness, but was less quick to accept her forgiveness. His mind feverishly reviewed the last few days, trying to figure out how he might have averted the disasters that had befallen them. "If I had not left . . . if I had not forged that key . . . none of this would have happened. . . ."

"And you would not be who you are," she said, gently throwing his own words back at him. A brave smile offered him absolution. She glanced at the other lycans trapped in the cages around them. "You were right. No one should live a life like this. Others, both human and lycan, are free because of you. Things will never be the same because of what you have done."

Lucian nodded, seeing some truth in her words. He thought of Raze and the others making a new life for themselves in the forest, and wished his fellow rebels well. And yet knowing they were safe was small comfort when the woman he loved, and the mother of his unborn child, languished in Viktor's filthy prison, facing the wrath of her entire people.

"But I have failed you."

She shook her head once more. "No, Lucian, you have not failed me. The choices I made have led me here, not you." She spoke without regret. "You once said there were risks you were willing to take for me. As was I for you, for us."

Lucian's eyes welled with tears. His throat tightened. *When did you become so wise, so profoundly caring?* He cursed the adamantine bars that kept them apart. "You would make a fine mother."

A sharp metallic clang intruded on their communion. A squad of Death Dealers threw open the door of her cell. Sandor stomped across the cage, kicking the bowl of clotted blood aside, and roughly unchained her from the bars. "Get up!" he barked, hauling her to her feet. He shoved her toward his men, who dragged her from the cell. Sonja endured their brusque treatment with as much dignity as she could muster. The heavy manacles weighed her arms down. Her face maintained a brave front, but the trembling of her limbs betrayed her terror. Who knew what dreadful punishment awaited her?

"No . . . NO!" Lucian roared. The sight of her being led away from him, perhaps to her death, enraged him. He threw himself against the bars of his cage like a rabid animal. Baring his fangs, he railed at the undead guards. Wild eyes bulged from their sockets. He violently shook the unyielding bars. "I will kill you! ALL OF YOU!"

The soldiers laughed at the lycan's futile threats. Raising a crossbow, Sandor fired at Lucian through the bars of the cell. A bolt thudded into his shoulder with jarring force. The silver tip sank deep in his muscle. He dropped to his knees but refused to let go of the bars. A savage growl gave vent to his pain and anger.

It will take more than one arrow to keep me from your throats!

Stubbornly, he tried to climb to his feet, only to feel a second bolt pierce his side. An agonized wail tore itself from his lungs, even as he realized that the Death Dealer was deliberately avoiding any vital organs. He was shooting to subdue the prisoner, not kill him.

Viktor's not done with me yet, Lucian guessed. *He has something worse in mind.*

Unable to throw off the shock and pain, Lucian collapsed onto the floor of his cage. A third bolt struck his back, narrowly missing his spine. He writhed in agony as the caustic silver poisoned his body. The flesh around the wounds grew hot and inflamed. Pulsing veins throbbed with every heartbeat. Blood streaked the whites of his eyes. He whimpered and gnashed his fangs. The accursed silver kept him from assuming wolfen form. . . .

The door to his cell swung open, but Lucian lacked the strength to lunge at his visitors. He could only thrash helplessly upon the dirty straw while a Death Dealer crouched over him and painfully snapped off the wooden shafts protruding from his body, leaving the barbed silver points lodged in his tortured flesh, where they burned like acid. Rough hands grabbed him beneath the shoulders and dragged him from his cell. Every bump sent an excruciating spasm through his entire body. A steel gauntlet cuffed him for good measure.

"Time to pay for your crimes, you murdering mongrel," Sandor cursed at him. "Hell is waiting for you."

Lucian could have sworn he was already there.

Sonja faced her accusers in the crypt.

Her father gazed down on her from his throne, while the rest of the Council also sat in attendance. As ever, Tanis stood at the Elder's right hand; apparently he had not yet dared to ask for her seat on the Council. Sonja thought she detected a certain unease in his manner, as though he feared that she might expose his own complicity in Lucian's escape.

He need not worry on that score. The scheming scribe had upheld his end of their bargain; she had no intention of betraying him. Enough blood had been spilt already. Why should her own fall bring down anyone else?

Let Tanis escape with his miserable life.

She stood alone in the center of the mausoleum, above the buried tombs of Marcus and Amelia. The bronze circular plaques felt cold beneath her feet. Iron manacles chafed her wrists. Death Dealers were posted along the walls of the vaulted chamber to discourage any thought of escape. Silence rained over the somber proceedings, broken only by the crackling of the torches and braziers. An ornate chandelier hung above her head. Wooden shutters covered the stained-glass windows, keeping out the sunlight. Expectant eyes turned to her father, waiting for him to declare the trial under way.

Sonja wondered what he was waiting for.

The mystery was answered when, moments later, Sandor and his elite guards dragged Lucian into the crypt. Shackles bound his wrists and ankles. An involuntary gasp betrayed her dismay as she spied fresh bloodstains blossoming across his ragged brown tunic. His face looked gray and clammy. Purple shadows sagged beneath his bloodshot eyes. Distended blue veins throbbed across his brow. He seemed dazed and sick, almost in a stupor. Sonja recognized the telltale signs of silver poisoning.

Lucian, my love! What have those bastards done to you?

She glared accusingly at her father, who showed no sign of remorse. He merely nodded in satisfaction as the soldiers tossed him facedown onto the floor. They held on tightly to the ends of his chains. Fettered like a dog, Lucian wearily lifted his eyes to meet hers. Aching to comfort him, she started to step toward him, but the Death Dealers drew their swords, warning her away. It seemed this was as close together as they would be allowed to come. Clearly, Viktor intended Lucian to bear witness to her trial.

Or was he to be tortured before her eyes?

Coloman stepped forward to present the case against her. A creature of Marcus's creation, he no doubt relished the opportunity to embarrass Viktor before the Council.

"The accused has broken the laws of the coven," he proclaimed. The severity of his tone made clear the enormity of her offense. "She has consorted with animals. She has abetted in their escape. She—"

Sonja spoke out in her defense. "And I have saved this coven many times over!"

This was no idle boast. On more than one occasion, her quick wits and ready sword had spared her fellow vampires from disaster. It was she who had once rescued the Lady Amelia when the female Elder had been ambushed by a pack of werewolves. And had she not once ridden through enemy lines to secure reinforcements when the castle was under siege? And personally captured a mortal vampire hunter who had crept into the castle by daylight with mayhem on his mind? Truly, she had never shirked from her duty to protect her people. . . .

"You have killed your own kind!" Coloman asserted. But that, his darkening expression seemed to imply, was the least of her offenses. "And you have commingled bloodlines, resulting in the *thing* germinating within you."

The other council members looked appropriately appalled and horrified by this reminder of Sonja's gravid condition. They recoiled from her as though she were a leper. Orsova, of all women, sniffed in disgust. Only her father's face remained unmoved. His gaunt features were as fixed as carved granite. No one spoke up on her behalf.

"Your past glory does not excuse your present guilt," Coloman continued. "Nor does your lofty station as a member of this Council." He turned to face his peers. "The punishment for these crimes is death. How vote you?"

A chorus of "aye"s sealed her fate. A muscle twitched beneath Tanis's cheek, but he held his tongue. All eyes turned to Viktor. As the reigning Elder, he alone had the authority to pardon Sonja or reduce her sentence, perhaps to life imprisonment or banishment. Sonja had little expectation that he would do so; his scathing words upon the ramparts had made his feelings clear. Still, she looked hopefully into her father's eyes, praying for just a trace of understanding, if not mercy. He was still her father; she did not want their last moments together to be as complete strangers to each other. *Let us not part as enemies. . . .*

Lucian's appeal was less restrained. Lifting his head, he shouted frantically at Viktor. "She is your own daughter!"

But her father's eyes were as hard as sapphires.

"Aye," he said coldly.

Sonja felt like an orphan, condemned to death by a man she no longer knew.

"Take her to the chamber," Coloman commanded the guards.

"Nooo!" Lucian howled. He tugged helplessly at his chains like a dog on a leash, the fervor of his exertions reopening the wounds beneath his tunic. Fresh blood soaked through the threadbare fabric. "You cannot do this!"

Coloman raised an eyebrow at the lycan's protests. He glanced at Viktor for guidance. The Elder nodded gravely.

"And bring him," the boyar added.

The guards hauled Lucian to his feet, even as their comrades escorted Sonja toward the door. He thrashed helplessly in the Death Dealers' grip. The chains between his ankles scraped loudly against the floor. He called out desperately to the seated Elder.

"NO! VIKTOR!"

The execution chamber was hidden away in the turret of a tower overlooking the courtyard below. Cobwebs hung from the domed ceiling. Shuttered windows kept out the sunlight, at least for the time being. A large wooden post, reinforced with riveted iron supports, occupied the center of the doleful chamber. Sonja averted her eyes from the stake. She did not want to think about what the post was for.

The guards shoved the condemned prisoners into the turret. Forcing Lucian to his knees, they chained him to a pair of iron rings embedded in the floor. Exhausted by his struggles in the crypt, he was easily subdued by the armored soldiers who clubbed him into submission before turning their attention to Sonja.

Very well, she thought. *Do your duty.*

Outnumbered and unarmed, she did not fight back as they shackled her to the stout oaken column, binding her arms uncomfortably above her head. Their grim faces betrayed neither anger nor regret as they secured her bonds, then stepped away from the post. Sonja held her chin high, determined to face the end of her immortality with dignity. Her composure faltered, though, as she felt her baby stir within her. The realization that she would never look upon her child's face, and that its innocent life would be snuffed out even before it began, tore at her heart. The life inside her had been conceived in love; it was no abomination, no matter what the Covenant said. If anything, it was living proof that lycans and vampires were meant to live together in harmony.

My father is destroying more than just his own flesh and blood, she thought. *He is slaughtering the future.*

The doors opened to admit Viktor and the rest of the Council. Their velvet robes rustled like cobwebs as they entered the chamber. They spread out along the circumference of the turret, so that they surrounded both Lucian and Sonja. Viktor faced his daughter but did not address her. Instead he nodded at a burly Death Dealer by the name of Soren. Palace gossip had it that the bearded Irishman, who had been recruited into the coven generations ago, was first in line to take Kosta's place as the new overseer of the lycans.

Soren uncoiled a fearsome whip composed of forged silver vertebrae. "No!" Sonja cried out as he cracked the lash against Lucian's shoulders. The barbed vertebrae tore through his ragged tunic and made ribbons of his hide, burning his skin even as they sliced through his defenseless flesh, paring it to the bone. Hot blood streamed down his back. The scalding silver cauterized the gaping wounds before each new blow opened them anew. Steam rose from overlapping layers of throbbing scar tissue. Sonja saw Lucian brace himself for the blows, but not even his heroic heart could steel itself against the searing agony as the whip viciously lashed his back again and again, shredding meat and muscle, until he was left gasping on the bloodslick floor. Crimson welts showed through the back of his rent tunic.

Tears leaked from Sonja's eyes at the sight of her lover brought low once more. She suddenly recalled the first time she had ever laid eyes on him, when, as a mere child, she had breathlessly watched him prevail over her father's many grueling tests and trials. How young and handsome he had been then! She had been drawn to him at once, even before she was old enough to truly know what love was, as though they had always been destined to be together. The future had seemed bright and full of possibility.

How then had they come to this dismal pass?

Viktor raised his hand at last, signaling an end to the flogging. Soren lowered the whip and stepped away from the defeated lycan. Crimson globules dripped from the silver vertebrae onto the cold stone floor.

Sonja realized that her own penalty was drawing nigh.

Taking care not to step in the pooling blood, the council members filed out of the mausoleum one by one. Viktor was the last to leave; Sonja held onto the hope that he might turn and look back at her one last time. Now that the trial was over, and the other council members departed, perhaps he could spare her a kindly word or two before they were parted forever? This was their last chance to say good-bye. . . .

At first, she feared he would not even look at her. But, at the last moment, he hesitated upon the threshold and glanced back over his shoulder. Their eyes met briefly. Viktor's thin lips parted as though to bestow some final message of forgiveness, but then his jaws clenched tightly shut. Unable to speak, he left the crypt without a word.

The guards stepped forward to carry out the sentence.

The soldiers exited the crypt, leaving only Soren and one other guard to play executioner. A heavy oaken door slammed shut. The Death Dealers retreated to a shadowy alcove at the far end of the mausoleum, where a large iron wheel awaited them. Squealing metal reverberated through the cavernous vault as the ancient wheel initially refused to turn. Grunting, the vampires put their backs to it and gradually managed to crank the wheel in a clockwise direction. Every turn, Sonja knew, brought her closer to oblivion.

Timeworn gears began to squeak and grind overhead. Sonja swallowed hard as she braced herself for what was to come. Panic flooded Lucian's face as he grasped what was happening. His bloodshot eyes widened in horror.

Be brave, my love, she thought. *I wish I could spare you this.*

The relentless grinding drew her gaze upward. Directly above her, at the very apex of the domed ceiling, a circular iron hatch slowly dilated. Many yards away, the Death Dealers backed deeper into the shelter of the secluded alcove. A tiny crack of sunshine hurt Sonja's eyes, proving that, just as she had feared, it was still daylight outside.

A frightened whimper escaped her lips. Her heart pounded in fear.

"No, Sonja," Lucian called out to her. "Look at me. Keep your eyes on me!"

Averting her eyes from the blinding glare, she stared across the crypt at Lucian. Now that the fatal moment was upon her, she felt her courage evaporating. She looked to him for strength and found a measure of comfort in his caring eyes.

"I love you," he declared.

I know, she thought. His eternal devotion was the one thing she could always rely on, even in the hour of her death. "I love you." Her voice cracked as their last few seconds slipped away with heart-breaking speed. "Your face will not be there when this is over, will it?"

He tried to answer her but could not find the words. There was no way to deny the dreadful enormity of the moment. She cursed her father for forcing Lucian to witness her death; that would surely be an even more harrowing ordeal than the one she now faced. Remembering the helpless anguish and frustration she had felt when Kosta had flogged Lucian before her eyes, she suspected that she was the lucky one.

"Good-bye, my love."

Two hundred years seemed like hardly enough.

Sonja's blood still stained her bed linens. Viktor stood alone in his daughter's chambers, having dismissed Tanis and the other vampires from his sight. He wanted no eyes upon him as he endured the final moments of his daughter's life. He held onto a carved wooden bed-post for support. Unbearable sorrow weighed down his shoulders; he had not experienced pain like this since his beloved wife had perished in childbirth two centuries ago.

Thank the dark gods that she had not lived to see this day!

He knew that he should leave, that he was only tor-

turing himself by lingering here, surrounded by reminders of Sonja, yet he could not tear himself away
from his daughter's room. Despite her grievous sins, he
had been impressed and moved by Sonja's grace and
courage at the end. She had neither denied her crimes
nor groveled for mercy like a sniveling mortal. What a
magnificent Elder she might have become, had not that
vile lycan seduced her!

He will beg me to put him out of his misery!

Many floors shielded him from the sight of Sonja's
impending cremation, but he could hear the rusty
gears carrying out the lethal purpose for which they
had been engineered. Never before had this fearsome
penalty been imposed on another vampire, let alone
one of royal blood, but Viktor himself had commis-
sioned the mechanism as the ultimate deterrent for
any vampire who might dare to violate the sacred Covenant that governed them all. A clever mortal locksmith, whom Viktor had previously employed to craft
William's hidden oubliette, had installed the deathtrap
according to the Elder's specifications.

*Little did I know its first victim would be my own
daughter!*

It was not too late, he knew. He could rush in and
call a halt to the execution. The Council would be
scandalized, and he would face strident opposition
from Coloman and the rest, but Sonja would be spared.
In time she might even come to see the error of her
ways and renounce her foolish passion for that lycan
scum. She could still make him proud and become his
loving daughter once more.

286

He moved to the door. His hand fell upon the handle. White knuckles tightened around the knob.

Then he remembered the unspeakable monstrosity gestating in her womb. Her unnatural offspring was more than just a scandalous embarrassment; it was a dire threat to their very kind. It could not be allowed to exist for one more day. No matter the cost.

He took his hand away from the door.

The metal hatch opened entirely. Daylight poured through the circular gap. The golden radiance fell directly upon Sonja, who let out a blood-curling scream.

No! Lucian thought. *Not the sun! Not on her!*

He lunged forward, desperate to shield her with his own body, but the heavy chains snapped taut, holding him back. Iron shackles cut into his wrists, but he barely noticed the pain. Silver barbs, buried deep in his flesh, trapped him in human form. He strained with all his might, working himself into a lather of blood and sweat, yet there wasn't a damned thing he could do to save the woman he loved.

Sonja's pale face blackened and flaked away beneath the sun's pitiless rays. Smoking lesions popped and snapped across her delicate skin. Shrieking, she tossed her head from side to side but could not escape the unsparing sunlight as it turned her vulnerable flesh to charcoal. Smoke rose from her dark hair moments before she burst into flame, the thrashing noblewoman turning into a living torch. Her charred face contorted in agony, exposing her fangs, while her blistering arms twisted above her head. Chains rattled as she fought in vain against the manacles binding her to the post. Her ragged shift was set ablaze. The smell of burnt meat befouled the air. Her golden pendant glowed red as blood within the hellish inferno.

The scorching heat beat against Lucian's face. The devouring flames were reflected in his wild cobalt eyes. Only yards away from the blazing pyre, yet too far away to do anything but watch the corrosive sunlight consume his beloved, he bellowed like a madman. His raspy voice joined her dying screams in one final, excruciating moment of communion.

"SONJA!"

Viktor listened to his daughter die. Her agonized shrieks echoed through the castle, and ripped his ancient heart to shreds. He pressed his furrowed brow against the bedroom door, while ice-cold tears streamed down his face. Sobs shook his ageless form.

Centuries ago, when he had fought for breath upon his deathbed, Marcus had come to Viktor and offered him immortality in exchange for the mortal warlord's assistance against William and the other werewolves. Looking death in the face, Viktor had gladly accepted the vampire's bite. For centuries, he had never regretted that decision.

Until today.

He sagged against the sturdy wood, covering his ears to drown out the horrific screams coming from the execution chamber. The ghastly cries finally died away as her lungs were surely seared to ash. Viktor rammed his fist into his mouth. His fangs gnawed on his knuckles.

No one must ever speak of this again, he resolved. He

would ban all mention of Sonja and her sins, upon pain of death, and order Tanis to have her name entirely stricken from the archives. The pain of today's dark deeds would never leave him, but perhaps, in time, his daughter's disgrace would be lost to history. One more secret for him to guard throughout eternity.

The loss of his only daughter was like a stake to the heart. *First my wife,* he lamented, *and now my precious Sonja.* He was bereft of family and affection.

Now all he had left was vengeance—against Lucian and all his misbegotten breed!

Chapter Twenty-one

Lucian sprawled upon the floor of the chamber, drained of tears and emotion. Hours had passed and his spilled blood had long since dried, although the merciless silver still burned beneath his skin, trapping him in human guise. The killing sun slowly retreated from the sky and the purple glow of twilight filled the open iris in the ceiling. Storm clouds swept past the opening.

The sun's departure had not come soon enough for Sonja. All that remained of the lovely vampire warrior was a lifeless gray statue of charred bone and ash. Her powdery arms were still raised above her, held in place by the scorched iron shackles. Her lustrous hair had been completely seared away, exposing the naked contours of her skull. A look of anguished sorrow, for both herself and their unborn child, was baked onto her agonized features. Scraps of burnt linen were fused to her remains, barely protecting her modesty. Blackened bone showed through the cracked charcoal. Only a solitary golden shimmer added a touch of color to the bleak gray figure: Sonja's crest-shaped pendant, still clasped around her lifeless throat.

Even in death, there was something ineffably beautiful about her.

As the last glint of daylight vanished from the sky, the door to the chamber swung open, disturbing Lucian's grief. Viktor entered, accompanied by an honor guard of Death Dealers. Garbed as always in somber shades of black, it was impossible to tell if the malignant Elder was in mourning. Long-faced and solemn, he made his way across the chamber to the crumbling effigy that was once his daughter. If the smoldering ruin troubled him, his austere face bore no evidence of it. A polished silver broadsword hung at his side. Bits of baked skin and sinew crunched beneath the soles of his boots.

Monster! Lucian thought. Unbridled fury reawakened inside him. *Look what you did to her!*

A cold draft entered with Viktor. The wind buffeted Sonja's remains, sending swirling clouds of ash across the chamber. The flakes blew against Lucian's face. His beloved's ashes tasted bitter upon his lips.

Ignoring Lucian for the moment, Viktor contemplated the charred corpse. He reached and brushed the gilded pendant resting against Sonja's bosom. His eyes moistened briefly, and a look of genuine grief flashed across his face, but it passed quickly as his aristocratic countenance resumed a cold, distant expression. He plucked the pendant from Sonja's throat, easily snapping the delicate chain, and turned toward Lucian at last. Icy disdain and hatred smoldered in his unearthly blue eyes.

His callous inhumanity inflamed Lucian, who matched the Elder's baleful gaze with a red-hot glare of his own. His blood surged volcanically in his veins. His heart was as hard as steel, having been forged and tempered by the tragedy of his loss. A growl formed at the back of his throat.

Viktor drew his sword and raised it high above his head. Lucian rattled the chains holding him fast to the floor. It seemed the chamber was about to witness a second execution, but at the last minute, the Elder had a change of mind. He stepped back and returned his sword to its scabbard. A cruel smile made him look even more demonic than usual. "On second thought," he instructed Sandor. "Fetch me my knives."

Lucian guessed that Viktor intended to skin him alive. Part of him welcomed death and the opportunity to rejoin Sonja in the afterlife, but as his loved one's ashes continued to swirl around the chamber like macabre snowflakes, he realized that he was not ready to die just yet. Not until Viktor and all his blood-sucking vermin paid for their crimes.

I will have my revenge, he vowed. *The revenge of the wolf!*

A full moon shone down through the open hatch, renewing his strength. He pounced at Viktor, every muscle in his body quivering in feral anger. The thrice-damned chains restrained him, but he grimaced in concentration as he focused all his will on the intrusive silver barbs lodged in his back. The baneful metal kept him from changing, but his lycan flesh fought against the foreign objects, eager to answer the call of the moon. Straining muscles rippled beneath his skin, while the tendons in his neck stood out like drawn bowstrings. Hot blood pounded at his temples. His jaws clenched as tightly as his fists. His eyes flashed blue.

Waiting for his knives, Viktor chuckled in amusement at Lucian's seemingly futile exertions. The other Death Dealers jeered as well.

At first, nothing happened. Then, one by one, the suppurating wounds contracted, disgorging flattened silver points in what looked like a grotesque mockery of the miracle of birth. A single bloodstained barb clattered onto the floor, followed swiftly by two more extruded lumps of metal. The crimson fragments rolled across the uneven paving-stones. Lucian gasped in relief as, for the first time in endless hours, the silver no longer seared his flesh.

He was himself once more.

Viktor's eyes widened in alarm as he belatedly realized what was happening. He reached for his sword, but he was already too late. The change came upon Lucian instantly. In the blink of an eye, he grew to Herculean size. His bloodstained tunic and trousers came apart at the seams. Coarse black fur sprouted from his hide, covering the ugly welt marks on his back. His hearing and sense of smell heightened immeasurably, so that he could practically taste the panic in Viktor's blood as the Elder grasped his danger. A scarlet haze fogged Lucian's vision. Iron shackles snapped like dry twigs.

You should have killed me when you had the chance, Lucian gloated. *Now the beast inside me is free!*

Viktor drew his sword, but the snarling werewolf swatted the blade away with a sweep of its paw. The Elder staggered backward, knocked off balance by the force of Lucian's blow. Sonja's pendant flew from his hand. It skittered across the floor before coming to rest only inches from her torched remains. Bits of ash rained down on the pendant, dimming its polished luster. Sonja's charred toes crumbled into powder.

The werewolf slashed at Viktor with its claws, tearing the fabric of his robe. Death Dealers swarmed forward to defend the imperiled Elder. Lucian heard the distinctive click of crossbows being armed. A silver bolt whizzed past his head, ricocheting off Viktor's throne. A second bolt thudded into the wooden post supporting Sonja's corpse.

Lucian growled in anger. The wolf in him wanted nothing more than to lunge for Viktor's throat, regardless of the odds against him, but his keen mind realized that, even blessed with wolfen speed and strength, he was at a severe disadvantage. Searching for an escape route, his eyes seized on one of the shuttered stained-glass windows overlooking the crypt. His muscles tensed to spring, but a golden glint caught his eye first.

He knew he could not leave without a token of Sonja's love.

Exploding into action, he barreled past Viktor. A

shaggy paw snatched the golden pendant from the floor. Death Dealers shouted and swore in rage as hastily fired bolts missed him by inches. Sparks flashed as the silver points bounced off the granite masonry. A lighted brazier toppled over, spilling red-hot coals onto the floor. Viktor hissed in rage as he spotted the pendant in Lucian's hand. Brandishing his sword, he shoved his own men aside in his haste to recover the precious memento.

Lucian had his own scores to settle with Viktor, but not now. *Later,* he vowed, clutching Sonja's pendant in his hairy palm. He growled at his enemies one last time, then sprang through the beckoning window. Wooden shutters and tinted green glass shattered before the force of his leap, raining down onto the cobbled floor of the courtyard outside. The werewolf hit the ground a second later. He rolled nimbly across the debris before springing to his feet.

The inner bailey of the castle stretched between him and the outer walls. It was a cold, clear winter night. A full moon hung high above the mountains. His explosive escape from the mausoleum alerted the sentries upon the ramparts, who swung around and launched a volley of silver bolts at the fleeing werewolf. The flying missiles thwacked into the paving-stones all around Lucian. The guards shouted frantically at one another. A horn sounded a call to arms. Panicked ladies and servants ran for the safety of the keep.

Lucian zigzagged across the courtyard, dodging the deadly hail of arrows. His only hope was to escape over the walls. Her pendant rested securely against his hairy palm. He was halfway to the stairs when a pair of Death

Dealers burst from the base of the gatehouse to block his path. Drawn swords reflected the moonlight. Angry curses assailed him.

The werewolf neither halted nor turned tail at the sight of the guards. Instead he vaulted over the startled vampires, grabbing onto the crests of their helmets as he did so. He yanked the soldiers off their feet, carrying them over ten feet through the air, before slamming their skulls into the pavement when he landed at the base of the steps. Their steel helmets crumpled like cheap pewter. Vampire brains leaked onto the cobblestones.

Lucian had no time to savor his victory. The steps to the ramparts lay before him, but more soldiers poured out of the keep into the courtyard behind him. Soren and a Death Dealer named Radu hefted oversized crossbows armed with long silver-tipped spears. Heavy iron chains were affixed to the ends of the harpoons. Practiced hands cranked the windlasses to draw the bowstrings tight, even as ordinary silver bolts rained down from the palisade, barely missing the speeding werewolf.

Lucian found himself besieged from all directions.

Seething with anger, Viktor strode out onto the balcony overlooking the courtyard. Tanis followed nervously in his wake, no doubt happy to be far away from the fighting. Peering down from his perch, he was dismayed to see that Lucian yet lived. He gnashed his fangs in frustration. Could not all his men bring down a single werewolf?

That Lucian had purloined Sonja's precious pendant

only added to his anxiety. Beyond its sentimental value, the pendant was also a vital component of the key to William's hidden prison. Thank the gods that Lucian was unaware of its true import.

Or was he?

Viktor recalled that the mortal locksmith who had crafted the key was still breathing. That was a loose end that needed snipping once this present crisis was concluded; the temporary loss of the pendant made it clear that its secret had to be guarded even more zealously than Viktor had previously believed. *A pity,* he reflected. As he recalled, the locksmith had an enchanting young daughter. *What was her name again? Selene?*

In the courtyard below, the werewolf stubbornly ducked the Death Dealers' quarrels. Viktor's nails dug into his palms as he waited impatiently for one of his knights—just one!—to rid him of this troublesome beast. A flicker of hope flared within him as Radu and Soren emerged from the front entrance of the keep, bearing the very same chain-bearing crossbows used to capture William two centuries ago. The ingenious harpoons had finally brought an end to the first werewolf's carnivorous rampage.

He could only hope they would do the same for William's despicable successor!

A bolt smacked into the pavement only an inch away from Lucian's back paw. Another quarrel nicked a tufted ear. The werewolf knew he was tempting fate every minute he braved the lethal fusillade; it was only a matter of moments before one of the flying missiles found its mark. He launched himself up the stairs, clearing five steps in a single leap. Another spring would bring him to the top, but, before his hind legs could propel him into the air again, a harpoon came arcing across the courtyard to spear him in the arm!

He yelped out loud. Feeling a sharp, painful tug on his arm, he glanced behind him to see a length of chain stretching across the bailey to the large crossbow cradled in Radu's arms. The taut chain pulled on Lucian like a leash, tearing at the gory wound in his hide. Silver invaded his muscles, sapping his strength. The Death Dealer cranked a handle on the crossbow, reeling the werewolf back in like a fish on a line.

No! Lucian raged. *I'll not be made a captive again!*

He spun away from the pull of the chain, which cracked like a whip, flinging Radu into the arched gateway of the keep with incredible force. His bare head exploded against a looming granite column. Bone shattered like glass. Blood sprayed Soren's face and armor.

The violent motion wrenched the harpoon from the werewolf's arm. Free once more, he bolted up the stairs, only to be speared in the knee by a second harpoon. His chin cracked against the stone steps as he toppled face-forward onto the stairs. He bit down hard on his own tongue. The salty taste of blood filled his muzzle. His skewered leg felt like it was on fire. Another chain clanked against the steps behind him.

Have to keep going. Almost there . . .

Crippled and bleeding, Lucian refused to surrender. Sonja's pendant dangled from his clenched paw as he painfully clawed his way up the stairs, one step at a time. His talons scratched the well-worn stones. Gritted fangs held in the pain. He dragged his injured leg behind him, leaving a crimson trail in his wake. Every movement jarred the diabolical harpoon, causing him unbearable agony, but he kept on climbing until at last he reached the summit of the palisade. Moonlight shone down on the elevated walkway, yet the pernicious silver counteracted the energizing power of the cold white radiance. He felt his wolfen vigor draining away along with his blood. His gushing wounds declined to heal. The chain pulled against him.

Only yards away from freedom, he collapsed upon the ramparts. Death Dealers rushed across the palisade toward his fallen form. More soldiers stormed the stairway from the courtyard below. Raising his eyes from the masonry, Lucian spied Viktor upon the balcony across the way. The triumphant Elder smiled thinly at the werewolf's imminent demise.

It's not fair, Lucian despaired. *I was so close. . . .*

He threw back his head and let out an agonized howl that echoed across the castle and countryside beyond. He keened for Sonja, his child, and his own crushed hopes.

Two more silver quarrels struck him in the back.

Chapter Twenty-two

*R*aze raised his eyes to the full moon shining above the clearing. The lambent lunar orb stirred something deep within his soul. He felt the beast awakening, yearning to break free. His dark skin itched as though bristling fur was scratching at it from inside. Wiry black hairs spouted from his palms. His teeth tugged painfully at their roots. Exploring his mouth with his tongue, he found his incisors sharper and more pointed than he remembered.

Like the fangs of an animal.

Closing his eyes, he fought back against the impending change. He knew the hour would come, perhaps even tonight, when he would have to let the wolf loose, but he was not ready to surrender his human guise yet.

Let me pretend that I am still a man, he thought, *if only for a while longer.*

A fervent howl suddenly rang out across the forest. Raze's eyes snapped open and he jumped to his feet. A damp fog shrouded the clearing. All around the campsite, the other lycans and humans instantly dropped what they were doing. Sabas put down the rabbit he was skinning. Xristo lifted his head from his bedroll. Everyone was riveted by the melancholy baying, which seemed to come from the direction of the castle. Raze knew at once who was howling.

Lucian!

The other lycans turned toward Raze, worry and confusion written over their scruffy faces. In Lucian's absence, they looked to the giant African for direction. Raze wished he knew what to tell them. He had already guessed, when Lucian had not returned to them, that their leader's mission to rescue his beloved Sonja had gone tragically awry. Indeed, many of them had already given Lucian up for dead. Now his anguished howl proved that Lucian was still alive, but for how much longer?

And what can we do to save him?

Raze clenched his fists. Deep furrows creased his brow. Before he could decide on a course of action, however, an ominous rumbling came from deeper in the wilderness. Broken branches and twigs cracked beneath what sounded like a stampede of onrushing bodies. Frightened birds and bats took to the moonlit sky in fright. The dense brush rustled as though before a storm. The startled rebels shouted and looked at each other in alarm. Xristo raised his sword, and lobbed a spare hatchet over to Sabas. Raze grabbed for his ax. He spun away from the castle to see an unstoppable wave of werewolves hurtling from the misty depths of the forest!

Panic surged within Raze as he recognized the feral beasts who had attacked the caravan several nights ago. The other humans, and even most of the newly liberated lycans, gasped in terror at the charging pack. Some braced for battle, while others turned and fled for their lives. Raze hefted his ax and vowed to sell his life dearly if need be. Lycan though he was now, he could not help but fear his savage brethren. Had not Lucian himself described the wolves of the wild as mindless, ravening beasts?

So much for immortality, he thought wryly.

But, to the astonishment of both Raze and his compatriots, the werewolves swept through the camp without attacking anyone, passing the dumbfounded rebels by. Raze blinked in surprise, frankly amazed to find himself still alive. He watched the huge pack bound away from the clearing—as though answering Lucian's call.

Of course! he thought. He remembered how Lucian had turned back the rampaging werewolves the night of the ambush and realized that he had vastly underestimated his friend's influence over the untamed denizens of the forests. *The wolves weren't coming for us at all*, he realized. *They're heading for the castle!*

He shared a pointed look with Sabas and Xristo and the rest. Awareness dawned on their faces as well. A wolfish grin crossed Raze's face as he grasped the full implications of what was happening. He raised his ax above his head and answered Lucian's howl with a deep-throated roar of his own. Fear gave way to exhilaration. His lycan blood sung in his veins. Casting all doubts aside, he sprinted eagerly after the pack.

To the castle—and Lucian!

Cheering exuberantly, the entire camp followed him.

Hardened Death Dealers were shaken by the intensity of Lucian's howl. They inched slowly toward the impaled lycan, who lay sprawled atop the palisade. Although he appeared weak and vulnerable now, the former blacksmith had already slain more vampires than any werewolf since the infamous William of yore. They would take no chances with this one. . . .

The lycan's shaggy hide receded as he reverted to human form. Naked and bleeding, Lucian hung onto Sonja's pendant as he writhed in agony. The vicious harpoon still transfixed his right knee. Silver quarrels studded his back and shoulders. Despite the pain, he refused to let go of the ash-covered pendant. Viktor would have to pry it from his cold, dead fingers!

Lucian heard heavy footsteps drawing near. Clanking armor heralded a hasty end to his struggles. After missing his chance to execute him twice now, Viktor was not likely to make that mistake again. Grimacing, Lucian tried to expel the silver bolts from his body, as he had before, but he was too weak from pain and loss of blood. There was nothing to do now but wait for the Death Dealers to live up to their name at last.

Make it quick, he thought. *So I may see my Sonja again.*

But a sudden clamor, coming from beyond the castle walls, drowned out the tentative approach of the guards. At first Lucian mistook the deafening roar for another thunderstorm, but then his keen hearing made out the howls, whoops, and war cries of an oncoming army. His bleary eyes widened in surprise. Hope flared unexpectedly in his heart. Despite the harpoon and chain mercilessly nailed to his leg, he hauled himself up against the battlements. Gasping for breath, he peered out over the parapet at the breathtaking sight of dozens of frenzied werewolves and lycans charging up the mountain toward the castle. Armed lycans brandishing swords, pikes, and axes ran alongside snarling werewolves who stormed the fortress in tremendous numbers. This was no mere raiding party, Lucian realized at once. It appeared as though every werewolf and lycan in creation was rushing to his rescue. He spotted Raze in the forefront of the charge, with Sabas and Xristo following closely behind him. The rocky slope quaked beneath the stampeding horde. A chorus of belligerent growls and shouts filled the air.

"Thank you, my brothers," Lucian whispered hoarsely. He sagged against the battlements, too weak to do more than watch as the bestial invaders stormed the fortress. The chain tugging on his leg went slack as the Death Dealer at the other end of the iron links suddenly had a bigger problem to deal with. Defying gravity, an irresistible tide of werewolves crested over the outer walls, taking the outnumbered guards by surprise. They ran straight up the carved granite fortifications and bounded over the parapet onto the palisade, where they bowled over the blindsided guards. Shrieking knights were sent tumbling down the stairs. Werewolves pounced upon the fallen guards, tearing into them with slashing claws and fangs. Mangled pieces of armor were flung aside as the voracious beasts feasted on cold vampire blood and entrails. Strewn limbs and viscera littered the courtyard. Surviving the initial onslaught, a female Death Dealer made it to her feet and bolted for the keep, only to be brought down by a lunging werewolf. Pinned beneath the creature's massive paws, she barely had time to squirm before its jaws closed upon her head, crushing her skull in an explosion of blood and brains. The beast swallowed her head whole before bounding after another victim. Blood streamed across the cobblestones, forming scarlet canals between the tiles. Bones crunched like broken china. The ghastly sounds brought a pained smile to Lucian's lips. The screams of the dying vampires were like music to his ears.

Do you hear that, Viktor? he thought bitterly. *That is vengeance come calling!*

Viktor leaned out over the balcony. His jaw hung open in astonishment. He couldn't believe what he was seeing and hearing. For more than half a millennium Castle Corvinus had defied invasion. Never before had any enemy dared to breach its walls. But his seasoned Death Dealers were being torn apart by a pack of animals!

How in Perdition had this ever come to pass?

His nails dug into the railing so hard that they gouged the polished black marble. His pale face flushed with anger. Hellfire burned in his eyes.

This is all Lucian's fault, he raged. First the treacherous lycan had despoiled his daughter, now he had brought death and carnage to the very door of the keep. *Is there no end to his atrocities?*

Behind him, Viktor heard Tanis slink away. Without so much as begging his master's leave, the cowardly scribe retreated from the balcony. His furtive steps quickened as he disappeared back into the keep.

Not so fast, Viktor thought. He had need of Tanis now. There was a vital task to be carried out before the invaders could get any farther. Even before Viktor could join the battle himself.

The future of the entire coven might depend on it.

After the werewolves came the lycans. Armed men poured over the parapet, shouting and waving weapons. A pair of heavy boots landed on the ramparts beside Lucian. He looked up to see Raze gazing down at him in concern.

Welcome, my friend, Lucian thought. *I have need of your strength.*

Raze contemplated the other lycan's wounds, his gaze shifting from the arrows in Lucian's back to the bloody harpoon impaling his leg. "Be brave, lycan," his deep voice rumbled as he bent to extract the poisoned missiles from Lucian's body. Choosing to get through the ordeal as swiftly as possible, he yanked the crossbow bolts from Lucian's inflamed flash and hurled them away. His back against the battlements, Lucian gritted his fangs and tried to keep from screaming. Fresh blood streamed down his naked back as each arrow was wrenched free. He remembered Sonja doing the same for him only four nights ago, after Kosta riddled his body with silver-tipped quarrels. The memory of her death flayed his soul anew.

Raze seemed to recall the incident as well. "Your lady?"

Lucian shook his head, unable to put the blazing horror of Sonja's execution into words. He doubted that he would ever be able to speak of it, no matter if he lived unto the next millennium. Even for a lycan, some scars never healed. . . .

Raze nodded grimly. Mercifully, he did not ask to know more. Instead he turned his attention to the harpoon spearing Lucian's knee. Lucian braced himself against the damp stone battlements as Raze grabbed the shaft at both ends, then snapped it in two. Blinding pain filled Lucian's world for a heartbeat. Agony contorted his face. He gasped out loud.

But then the worst was over. Raze worked the severed ends of the spike from the wounded knee, which immediately began to scab over. He tossed them over the edge of the parapet, then rose once more to his feet. A headless Death Dealer lay prone upon the ramparts a few feet away, a thick wool cloak spread atop his body. Raze rescued the cape from the corpse, who would not be needing it any longer, and draped it over Lucian's naked body like a blanket. The cloak was only a *little* bloody.

Lucian was touched by the giant's care. Shucking the cloak aside, he tried to rise to his feet. Dizziness assailed him and he slumped against a nearby merlon to keep from falling. He closed his eyes while he struggled to keep his balance.

"Steady, my friend," Raze advised. "You need time to heal."

Lucian grasped Raze's wrist and pulled himself up. The dizziness passed and he shook his head. The wounds upon his back began to close. His punctured knee supported his weight. Already he could feel the moonlight restoring him.

"Do not worry, my friend." Lucian mustered a weak smile. "Tonight is not the day I die." He nodded at the conflict raging in the courtyard below, where a besieged band of Death Dealers was fighting a losing battle to keep the invading werewolves and lycans from the front entrance of the keep. The outmatched defenders were losing ground, and men, with every passing moment. "Now go and free the others."

Not entirely happy about leaving Lucian alone, Raze nonetheless scrambled toward the scaffolding left behind by the lycan workers. Lucian took a moment to catch his breath, but no longer. He would not wait a second more. Escape was no longer his goal.

Now is the rise of the lycans, he thought. *It is time for the vampires to taste our wrath.*

Viktor most of all.

Chapter Twenty-three

*V*iktor found Tanis in his beloved archives. Two leather saddlebags rested at the scribe's feet, packed to overflowing with rare books and manuscripts. More scrolls were tucked under his arms as he hurriedly ransacked the library. Tanis muttered under his breath, unable to make up his mind which texts to rescue.

Caught up in his dilemma, he didn't even hear the Elder approach until Viktor lunged forward and knocked an armload of heavy tomes onto the floor. Alarmed, Tanis shrank from the irate Elder. He threw up his hands in fear of another blow.

"There is more to worry about than your precious scrolls!" Viktor bellowed. He was appalled at the scribe's distorted priorities. Did he not realize that there were more important things at risk? "Get to the other Elders! Now!"

Tanis scurried to obey.

Following Lucian's orders, Raze stormed the castle's dungeons. Blood dripped from his mighty war ax. The bodies of dead and wounded guards lay in his wake. Avoiding the heavily guarded front entrance, he had climbed the scaffolding to one of the keep's upper windows, then made his way down to the dungeons. The dank subterranean corridors stirred unpleasant memories in the former prisoner, who had hoped never to return to this hellish purgatory again. Lycan slaves stared at him in alarm through the iron bars of their cages. Raze recognized some of them as survivors of the ambushed caravan who had been too frightened to escape with him and Lucian before. Already agitated by the sounds of battle seeping down from above, they greeted his unexpected appearance with startled gasps and questions. Fear and confusion showed upon their greasy faces. Moon shackles pricked their throats. Unearthly blue eyes glowed in the shadows. Like Raze, they were no longer human.

Not pausing to explain, he took hold of a barred gate with both hands. As a mortal, the forged metal would have withstood even his considerable thews, but now he brought the strength of a full-blooded lycan to bear. His powerful muscles flexed beneath his skin. Veins swelled upon his biceps and atop his shaved cranium. Straining iron creaked in protest before surrendering to the lycan's preternatural might. He ripped the heavy gate from its hinges and tossed it down the corridor, where it clattered loudly against the moldy stone floor. Ringing echoes reverberated throughout the dungeons.

He stepped away from the door to let the prisoners out. Most rushed to join him, but a timid few hesitated at the rear of the cell. They peered uncertainly at Raze, more intimidated than impressed by his prodigious feat of strength. He saw a hunger for freedom in their eyes, but also the same debilitating fear that had held them back before. This time, however, Raze had no intention of leaving any slave behind.

"You want your revenge?" he challenged them. "It is out there. GO!"

His stentorian voice overcame their doubts. The remaining prisoners rushed from their cage. Moving swiftly, Raze tore open the adjoining cells, freeing yet more lycans, until he found himself at the head of a parade of liberated slaves. Eager to put the dungeons behind them forever, he guided them up from the depths toward the battle above. The growls of the invading werewolves, and the frantic cries of the vampires, called out to him. A brilliant shaft of moonlight penetrated a lattice window at the top of the stairs, bathing Raze in the celestial glow. He suddenly felt more alive than he ever had before. His newfound power surged through his veins. Dark brown eyes turned cobalt blue.

No longer afraid of what he had become, he embraced the wolf within him. His massive frame swelled to even more gargantuan proportions. Constricting clothing was shredded by his expanding form. Thick black fur covered his nakedness. A canine snout protruded from his face. Fangs filled his gaping jaws.

Growling more deeply than any other werewolf, Raze pounced up the steps.

Satisfied that Tanis was seeing to the safety of his fellow Elders, Viktor went to war. His royal armor encased his regal form as he stalked through the keep, flanked by Captain Sandor and the rest of his honor guard. His broadsword hung in its scabbard. A pair of silver daggers were clasped to his waist. His coat-of-arms was emblazoned on his burnished steel cuirass. Blood-red rubies studded his gauntlets and the pommel of his sword. Scowling, he lowered his helmet over his livid features. Cast in the semblance of a leering death's-head, the helm gave him the skeletal aspect of an armored Grim Reaper. Sharpened fins crested his helmet and shoulder plates. Icy azure eyes peered out from behind his iron mask.

He marched out onto the balcony once more.

The situation below was even more dire than before. The front gates had been opened from within, allowing yet more enemies to penetrate the castle's defenses. Fog rolled in from outside, adding to the confusion. The hate-maddened werewolves had been joined by a throng of human-looking lycans. The escaped slaves wielded swords and axes against his knights, who were in complete disarray. Dead vampires, their immortality cut short by the rapacious animals, lay in pieces upon the blood-soaked floor of courtyard. The ravaged corpses testified to the unremitting savagery of their barbarous foes. Viktor cursed William for unleashing their vile breed upon the world—and Lucian for inspiring this heinous insurrection. Indeed, unless his eyes were deceiving him, Lucian had united William's rabid spawn and the new breed of lycans in common cause.

Such an obscene alliance could not go unchallenged a moment longer.

Viktor drew his sword. He strode to the edge of the balcony and flung himself over the rail. Dropping twenty feet to the courtyard below, his silver blade lopped off the head of an unlucky werewolf even before his boots touched down on cobblestones. Sandor and his guards leapt after him. Viktor shouted above the bloody strife.

"KILL THE DOGS!"

Lucian surveyed the battle from atop the ramparts. A leather vest, trousers, and boots, harvested from the uncomplaining body of the headless of Death Dealer, clothed his body. His bare chest was caked with sweat and blood. Sonja's pendant was safely tucked in his pants. Although his knee still ached where it had been pierced, he felt his strength returning. The full moon blessed him and his army with the power they needed to lay waste to their ancient foes and former masters. Lucian was tempted to assume his wolfen form once more, but, no, when he faced Viktor once more he wanted to do so man to man, not werewolf to vampire. He needed a human tongue to confront Viktor with his crimes.

But where was the coven's tyrannical ruler?

Gripping the dead soldier's sword in his fist, Lucian searched for his ultimate enemy. Let his valiant brethren take on Viktor's foot soldiers; the Elder's foul blood belonged to him. At first he could not spot his quarry, but then an armored figure dropped from a balcony into the fray, followed by a squad of Death Dealers. The lead vampire thrust himself into the heat of the melee, hacking and slashing with abandon at the werewolves and lycans around him. His shining sword cut a bloody swath through the invaders. Lucian recognized the ornate armor and its macabre headpiece; he had forged it himself for none other than . . .

"Viktor!"

Sword in hand, Lucian pounced from the ramparts to the floor of the courtyard. Fog swirled around his ankles. Grappling combatants, engaged in brutal hand-to-hand fighting, blocked his path to Viktor. The clash of metal competed with the primeval roars of the werewolves. Body parts crunched wetly beneath his boots. The pavement was slick with blood and spilled intestines. Swinging his sword like a berserker, he fought his way through the chaotic free-for-all toward Viktor. A foolish Death Dealer got in his way and paid for it with his life. Lucian's sword stabbed him in the face, producing a geyser of frigid vampire blood. Shrieking, the soldier reeled backward into the mist, where he was immediately disemboweled by a roaring werewolf. Lucian glimpsed Sabas and Xristo fighting side by side. A knife-wielding Death Dealer came at Xristo from behind, almost taking him unawares, but Sabas saved his boon companion by tackling the vampire from the side. Digging his nails into the soldier's throat, the burly lycan throttled the Death Dealer with his bare hands. Xristo defended Sabas in turn by holding off Viktor's men with a whirling hatchet until his friend was done strangling the vampire. Together, they exacted gory vengeance for generations of servitude.

But despite the lycans' bravery, the advent of Viktor and his reinforcements threatened to turn the tide of the battle. The embattled Death Dealers rallied around the Elder and began to hold their ground. Viktor himself slew any werewolf, lycan, or mortal peasant that came within reach of his sword. Shaggy carcasses began to join the heaps of mutilated vampires filling the bailey. Dead werewolves melted back into human guise. For a second, Lucian feared that the hated vampires were going to prevail once more. . . .

Would nothing end their undying reign of terror?

Then a host of howling lycans, led by an enormous black werewolf, burst from the front gate of the keep. Moon shackles, clamped around the throats of the lycans, identified them as the caged slaves Lucian had dispatched Raze to liberate. Peering gratefully at the hulking wolf commanding the escapees, Lucian realized that Raze had finally shed the last vestiges of his mortality. His heart surged with pride.

What a werewolf he had become!

Armed with stolen swords, axes, and picks, the freed slaves charged into the rear of the Death Dealers, breaking their ranks. Raze lifted a squirming vampire above his head and flung him into the inner wall of the fortress. The impact cratered the granite wall, sending rocky chips flying amidst a cloud of powdered stone and mortar. A crimson stain defaced the masonry as the vampire's crushed body slid lifelessly on the pavement.

Viktor whirled in surprise, caught off guard by the second wave of lycans. His blue eyes bulged behind his skull-like mask. He faltered and looked about in confusion, as though realizing for the first time that he might actually lose this conflict. Lucian wondered if the haughty Elder finally knew what fear tasted like.

If not, Lucian was ready to introduce him to the sensation. Their eyes met across the teeming battlefield. The rest of the war, with all its noise and grisly spectacle, receded from his consciousness as his primal senses locked onto his immortal enemy. All he saw now was Viktor—Sonja's murderer—caught in his sights. His fist tightened on the hilt of his sword. His unwavering eyes narrowed to vengeful blue slits.

No one had ever slain an Elder before. Not man, beast, nor vampire.

There's a first time for everything, Lucian thought.

He strode relentlessly toward his prey.

The hideous tumult of war penetrated even the many subterranean levels separating Tanis from the carnage in the courtyard. Tanis shivered beneath his robe as he stood upon a rickety wooden landing atop a forgotten staircase buried deep within the heart of the mountain. The inky waters of an underground river lapped against a slimy stone dock at the bottom of the steps. Reflected torchlight cast rippling shadows onto the walls of the cavern. Luminous green algae clung to damp limestone walls. Jagged stalactites hung above the nervous scribe's head like the fabled Sword of Damocles. Roosting bats rustled in shadows. *A shame I can't turn into a bat as the mortals suppose,* he lamented, *else I'd fly away from here as fast as my leathery wings could carry me.*

Alas, that fanciful notion was nothing but a superstitious myth.

His sweaty hands tugged on a rusty chain as he struggled with a complex block-and-tackle system hanging from the ceiling. At the other end of the chain, suspended above the murky waters below, was a polished brass sarcophagus engraved with intricate cabalistic runes. An ornate capital *A* was embossed upon the head of the heavy metal coffin. Tanis strained to hold the sarcophagus steady as he carefully lowered the casket into the ebony skiff waiting many feet below. The boat, cleverly stored beneath the castle for just such an emergency, was moored to the dimly lit pier. Tanis heard it bump gently against the dock.

The chain slipped through his fingers, causing the hanging sarcophagus to drop precipitously for a few inches before he got it back under control. Straining to support the coffin's weight, he slowed its descent to a more prudent pace.

Forgive me for disturbing you, Lady Amelia, he thought. *Viktor's orders.*

Slumbering in their tombs, oblivious to the tempestuous events raging above them, the hibernating Elders were obviously vulnerable to the werewolves' shocking attack. Tanis well understood why Viktor thought it best to have them moved to a safer location. He just wished that this nerve-racking responsibility had fallen upon anyone else.

Remind me never again to make a bargain with a lycan,

he thought bitterly. Conspiring to free Lucian from his cell had been the worst mistake Tanis had ever committed in centuries of intricate scheming and politicking. *I'll be lucky I don't end up exiled for life after this debacle.*

He let out a sigh of relief as Amelia's coffin came to rest within the skiff. He held onto the chain for a few more moments, just to make sure the boat didn't capsize, then scuttled down the stairs to where the skiff was waiting. Marcus's sarcophagus, as well as Viktor's empty coffin, were already loaded onto the boat. Stylized initials distinguished their coffins from Amelia's. The skiff rocked unnervingly as Tanis clambered aboard. The sluggish current of the hidden river coursed past its hull. A hanging lantern illuminated the pier as he scrambled to fit a pair of painted black oars into their locks. His trembling fingers required three attempts before he got the oars properly in place. He wiped the cold sweat from his brow, then hurried to make certain the sarcophagi were secure.

After all, he didn't want their coffins to topple over into the river.

Despite the mayhem all around him, Lucian kept Viktor in sight as he fought his way toward the Elder. Faceless Death Dealers fell before his sword, but the butchered vampires made no impression on his mind; they were merely inconvenient obstacles between him and his true prey. Lucian trampled over their sundered bodies. If he had his way, Viktor would not long outlive his martyred daughter and grandchild.

320

Your bloodline ends tonight, Lucian swore upon Sonja's memory. *By my hand.*

Only yards away from Viktor, however, Captain Sandor leapt into his path. The officer's determined face made it clear that he intended to defend his lord to the end. Lucian almost admired the indefatigable guardsman's devotion to his duty, not that this made his intrusion any less infuriating. If Sandor wanted to throw away his immortality for the sake of the Elder, Lucian would be happy to oblige him.

Eschewing swordplay, Sandor raised a crossbow and fired it directly at the lycan's face. The bolt leaped from the bow, whistling through the mist like one of Sonja's silver throwing stars, but Lucian had had enough of being perforated by the Death Dealers' toxic missiles. Just as he had during Viktor's test two centuries before, Lucian snatched the quarrel from the air only inches from his face. Two more bolts flew from the weapon's triple bows, only to be deflected by Lucian's flashing sword. The misdirected quarrels went flying off to the side, eliciting a gasp of disbelief from Sandor. The horrified vampire gaped at Lucian's lightning-fast reflexes. Snatching another arrow from his quiver, he hastily tried to reload the crossbow, but Lucian was even faster. Flipping the captured missile in his hand, he flung it back at Sandor with all his strength. The bolt sank deep into the captain's forehead. Blood flooded his eyes. The crossbow dropped onto the cobblestones. A death rattle gurgled from his throat.

Lucian did not even wait for Sandor's body to hit the pavement before shoving it aside. Enough with these petty skirmishes. He wanted Viktor, not his endless myrmidons. But a growl of frustration burst from his lips as he reached the blood-soaked spot where the malevolent Elder had stood only moments before. He looked in vain for the elusive object of his hatred. *Show yourself, Viktor!* he raved inwardly. *Face me like a man!*

But Sonja's father was nowhere to be seen.

Chapter Twenty-four

Coloman and the rest of the coven huddled within the Great Hall, listening anxiously to the cataclysmic battle being waged outside in the courtyard. Ashen-faced courtiers and their ladies cowered around the edges of the spacious chamber. Sobbing courtesans and concubines hid behind the looming marble columns, their filmy black apparel offering little protection against the razor-sharp claws and fangs of the marauding monsters outside. Only the bolted oak doors at the entrance of the hall stood between them and the fearsome reckoning that had descended upon Castle Corvinus.

The wolves are at our very door, Coloman thought. *Just as I warned Viktor!*

He had never been so dismayed to be proven right.

Along with the remainder of the Council, he stood

alongside Viktor's empty throne. They strove to present an image of strength and confidence to their terrified flock, albeit with mixed results. Orsova chewed nervously on her lacquered nails, until blood dripped from her mangled cuticles. Count Ulrik looked as if he was ready to bolt from the chamber at any moment. As though there was anyplace to hide from the beastly invaders! The very walls that had guarded the keep for so long now trapped the coven inside the fortress with their ancient enemies. And even if they were to escape the castle, where were they to flee? Into the very wilderness that sheltered the werewolves?

There was no escape for them. They could only pray that Viktor and his Death Dealers could defend them as they always had before. Alas, the horrific screams and ferocious roars emanating from without did little to suggest that such desperate prayers would be answered; from the ghastly sound of things, the battle was going badly against them. Glancing about the crowded hall, Coloman saw that many vampires, who had long ago discarded their mortal faith, were now feverishly crossing themselves and calling upon the mercy of a God they had not thought of for many human lifetimes. He caught Ulrik doing the same.

For himself, Coloman fought an irrational urge to rush to the crypt and awaken Marcus. As much as he craved his patron's protection, however, he realized it was too late to revive the other Elders. Neither Marcus nor Amelia would have time to recover from their long slumber before the wolves were upon them all; newly roused from generations of fasting, they would rise at first as withered mummies, lacking the strength to rescue the coven from the nightmarish calamity that had befallen them. *Damn the Chain,* he thought. For the first time in his long existence, he questioned the wisdom of having only one Elder above the ground in any given century. *Now more than ever we need the oldest and strongest of us all!*

A pounding at the doors caused him to jump backward in fright, bumping into Viktor's throne. A petrified hush erupted into a cacophony of hysterical shrieks and exclamations. Clinging to an equally distraught maidservant, Luka screamed for Sonja to save her from beyond the grave. Coloman had no sympathy for the fear-crazed lady-in-waiting; it was said that she had conspired with the treacherous noblewoman on more than one occasion. He glared murderously at the flaxen-haired vampires, who had played a fatal role in their undoing. Did she even realize that her misguided loyalty to Sonja might have doomed them all?

He was tempted to rip her throat out himself.

The double doors buckled beneath the force of the blows. Blood-chilling roars and howls left no doubt as to the identity of the besiegers. *Where are the Death Dealers?* Coloman thought truculently. *Why aren't they here to protect us?*

The wooden bolt holding the doors shut snapped in twain. The doors crashed open, revealing a pack of slathering werewolves on the threshold. Pandemonium descended on the hall as the beasts invaded the sanctuary. The elegant vampires ran like frightened rabbits but could not outrace the rampaging creatures, who fell upon the coven with predatory glee. Antique furniture was toppled and reduced to debris in the wolves' riotous hunt. Refined lords and ladies were ripped to shreds, along with their expensive silk garments. The nubile flesh of the courtesans was strewn across the floor. Werewolves raced on all fours along the walls and ceilings, dropping like avenging angels upon the fleeing vampires. Blood spattered the hanging tapestries. Gobbets of raw meat flew from the roaring jaws of the triumphant monsters.

What did we ever do to deserve this? Coloman thought. Was there something the Council might have done to avert the catastrophe? *Were we too hard on the lycans—or too soft?*

Hiding behind Viktor's throne, Coloman gazed in fascinated horror at what seemed the end of the world. Hissing like a cat, Luka leapt onto the ceiling and hung there upside-down, clinging to the stoneworks by her claws, while she bared her own fangs at the frenzied pack, even as her abandoned maidservant disappeared down the gullet of a hungry wolf. Luka's defiance failed to spare her, though, as another werewolf launched itself from the floor and ripped her from her perch with its bloody paws. She crashed screaming to the floor, where a third wolf joined in devouring her. Her perfidy came to an end amidst a fountain of blood and viscera.

Nor was the Council spared by the conquering wolves. Orsova tore open her own wrists with her teeth, choosing to end her own life rather than fall prey to their enemies. Drawing a dagger from his belt, Ulrik tried to emulate her example by stabbing himself in the heart, but could not bring himself to do more than prick his chest before an attacking wolf ripped his arm from its socket. Bright arterial blood spurted from his shoulder.

The crimson spray struck Coloman in the face, blinding him. He wiped the blood from his eyes, only to find a ravening werewolf glaring down at him from atop Viktor's throne. The beast's cobalt eyes regarded him hungrily. Drool dripped onto Coloman's upraised face. A length of flaxen hair was caught between its teeth.

Please, the trembling boyar pleaded silently. *You don't understand. In the Council, I often pleaded for leniency for your kind. I'm on your side. . . .*

The wolf tore his head off.

Sniffing the air, Lucian followed Viktor's scent into the keep. Havoc raged all around him as the werewolves and lycans ran amok throughout the venerable structure, exacting bloody retribution for centuries of unjust persecution and subjugation. Now the vampires would know what it was like to be hunted like animals by a bloodthirsty foe. Ignoring the tantalizing smells and sounds of the massacre, Lucian trailed the Elder down into the very bowels of the keep, below even the now empty dungeons. The corpses of axed guards littered the lower stairs and corridors; Raze's handiwork, no doubt. Lucian raced over the bodies as, sword in hand, he hurried after Viktor. The distressing possibility that the Elder might elude justice added wings to Lucian's heels. He was not going to let that happen.

Run all you like, Viktor, he taunted silently. *You cannot escape me! I swear it upon Sonja's soul!*

The Elder's noxious scent led him to a wooden trap-door embedded in the floor of a murky underground corridor. A crimson hand print, left behind by a gore-soaked gauntlet, revealed Viktor's escape route. Lucian yanked open the door and, without hesitation, dropped into a sloping stone tunnel that seemed to lead down into the very heart of the mountain, almost as though Viktor were seeking refuge in the depths of hell. Undaunted, Lucian raced down the tunnel.

He thought he heard water lapping somewhere ahead.

Viktor reached the stairs leading down to the dock. Many feet below, his fellow Elders waited with Tanis aboard the loaded skiff. He could sense the muffled heartbeats of Marcus and Amelia as they slumbered within their respective sarcophagi, dreaming of bygone centuries while waiting patiently to rise again, each in their turn. How in Perdition was he going to explain this disaster to Amelia when she awoke at the turn of the century?

Damn you, Marcus! This is all your subhuman brother's fault!

He removed his helmet, the better to breathe in the musty stairwell. It galled his soul to leave the fortress in the hands of the enemy, but a wise commander knew when to execute a judicious retreat. Immortality stretched before him; there would be time enough to retaliate later. For now, it was more important that the Elders of the coven escape to his estate outside Buda. *I will return with a fresh army of Death Dealers,* he vowed, *and make Lucian and his rabble pay for this atrocity, even if I have to burn down every forest in Eastern Europe!*

The block-and-tackle still hung suspended from the ceiling. Viktor took hold of the dangling chain, intending to slide down the cable to the waiting skiff. But before he could dismount from the steps, iron links snapped apart above him—and the chain plummeted down into the abysmal waters far below. He heard Tanis yelp in alarm as the chain splashed beneath the waves. The skiff pulled away from the dock, leaving the Elder behind. Viktor stared in surprise at his empty hands. He looked up the steps.

What in blazes?

Lucian pounced from the upper landing, alighting onto the stair only a few steps above Viktor. Pure animal hatred flared in his cobalt eyes. He growled like the wild animal Viktor had always treated him as. He tossed away a broken link of chain.

I have you now! he gloated. *Did you truly think you could escape me?*

Viktor met Lucian's murderous glare with one of equal loathing. Yanking his sword from its scabbard, he hurled himself up the stairs at his lycan nemesis. Their swords clashed loudly in the flickering torchlight. Frightened bats fled their roosts. Mice scurried away in panic.

The intensity of the Elder's attack staggered Lucian, forcing him backward up the steps. Sparks flew as tempered steel blades collided with preternatural force. The dueling swords engaged in a heated conversation, exchanging deadly thrusts and ripostes in a blur of motion. This was more than just a battle to the death. Their mutual hatred raised the stake beyond mere survival as each man held the other accountable for their broken hearts.

"You defiled my daughter." Viktor hissed.

Lucian refused to take the blame for Sonja's death. Parrying an angled cross from Viktor's broadsword, he launched a furious counterattack that slammed against the Elder's defenses like a hammer striking an anvil. "She was your daughter!"

"I did what needed to be done!" Viktor declared without remorse. He sneered at Lucian across their interlocked swords. Bitterness sprayed from his lips. "How did you think this would end?"

Not like this! Lucian thought. *Not for Sonja!* A glancing blow from Viktor reopened one of the arrow wounds on his shoulder. Hot blood streamed down his arm, making the grip of his sword wet and sticky. Raw anguish frayed his voice. "I loved her!"

"You *killed* her!" Viktor spat.

The accusation fanned the flames of Lucian's wrath like the bellows of his forge. The searing memory of Sonja burning alive before his eyes, her charred skin flaking away while she shrieked in agony, stoked his rage into an all-consuming blaze. Abandoning all caution and restraint, he hacked at Viktor like a maniac, driving the Elder back down the stairs. Viktor's foot slipped upon the mildewed steps. The tip of Lucian's sword sliced his cheek, drawing blood. Viktor's hand went to his face as he fought back against Lucian's feverish assault. A crimson smear glistened upon his metal gauntlet. It was, perhaps, the first time in untold centuries that Viktor had been wounded in battle.

His face curdled in disgust. He gave Lucian a withering look. "I should have crushed your skull under my heel when you were born."

"Yes," Lucian agreed. The utter coldness of Viktor's words, and an overpowering sense of destiny, fueled his determination. It felt as though they had always been moving toward this moment, ever since Viktor had callously murdered his wolfen mother two centuries ago. "You should have."

A furious exchange of blows reached its climax as a powerful swipe knocked Viktor's sword from his hand. The blade flew from the Elder's fingers. Unarmed, he lunged at Lucian, his fanged mouth opened wide.

Lucian rammed his sword down the vampire's throat.

"But you didn't," he said.

Viktor choked on the blade. A bloody froth bubbled past his lips. Lucian leaned into the thrust until their faces were only inches apart. Viktor looked back at him in pain and shocked disbelief as a crimson haze flooded his bulging blue eyes.

This is for you, Sonja, Lucian thought.

He yanked back his sword. Viktor tumbled backward off the stairs, landing with a splash into the pitch-black waters below. His pale face disappeared beneath the surface of the river, leaving behind only cloudy scarlet swirls that were rapidly carried away by the current. Within seconds, no trace of the Elder remained.

Lucian tossed his sword into the dark river. The fire within him cooled and died, giving way to sorrow and fatigue. Tears welled in his eyes as he came to the end of the longest night of his life. He retrieved Sonja's pendant and stared mournfully at the precious heirloom.

He wondered if he would ever feel whole again.

Chapter Twenty-five

*T*he dawn was rising as Lucian staggered out onto the balcony overlooking the courtyard. Radiant sunlight set the bodies of the fallen Death Dealers ablaze, so that countless small bonfires were scattered throughout the bailey. More fires burned upon the ramparts. Thick black smoke billowed from the windows of the keep, which had been laid waste by the victorious rebels. Flames consumed the stables and smithy. Torn pennants had been ripped from their spires.

He found them all celebrating their triumph. Lycans in human guise and the wild werewolves mingled freely in the blood-soaked courtyard. An enthusiastic cheer, which was seconded by the howls of the wolves, greeted Lucian as he emerged, bloodied but unbowed, from the entrance to the balcony. They raised their weapons above their heads, or flaunted charred vampire bones, as they hailed the leader who had brought them to this historic moment. Sabas and Xristo shouted as loudly as any.

The warmth of the acclamation helped to lift his spirits, which were still weighed down by tragedy. He raised his own arm in acknowledgment. Sonja's pendant hung around his neck.

If only she could have lived to see this day!

Raze came and joined him on the balcony. Lucian was glad to see that the formidable African had survived the bloodshed. Once more in human form, he clasped Lucian's arm in fellowship. An uncharacteristic smile lit up his broad features.

"It is finished," he said.

Lucian pondered his friend's words. Following Viktor's defeat, he had eventually made his way to the Elders' crypt, where he'd found the tombs of both Marcus and Amelia lying open, their ponderous sarcophagi missing. The implications of this ominous discovery were not lost on him. He knew that as long as the remaining Elders endured, the coven could rise again. And that the vampires would never forget or forgive what had transpired here tonight.

"No," he said solemnly. "This is just the beginning."

The sleek black bark sailed down the Danube toward the Black Sea. The jagged peaks of the Carpathians receded into the distance as the ship cruised away from the forbidding mountains. Fog blanketed the surface of the water. An icy winter wind filled its sails. A carved figurehead bearing the likeness of an enormous bat faced the sea. An ornate capital *V* was emblazoned upon the sails and pennants. Towed behind the bark, an empty skiff bobbed in its wake.

Deep in the hold, Tanis lashed the Elders' sarcophagi together, securing them for the long voyage ahead. He double-checked the knots before turning to the mute figure standing in the shadows.

Viktor waited silently. Blood dripped down his chin, a legacy of the wound that had nearly killed him. A black robe had replaced his lost armor. Tanis shuddered at the memory of the Elder's bleeding form bursting from the depths of the underground river as the scribe had frantically roared the skiff away from the castle. Viktor's watery resurrection had nearly caused Tanis to jump out of his skin. Truth be told, he had thought twice before pulling the Elder from the river. . . .

More dead than alive, his gaunt face as white as a ghost's, Viktor let Tanis escort him to his own sarcophagus. He settled back against the red velvet lining. Azure eyes gazed balefully inward. His fingers twitched at his sides, as though imagining Lucian's throat within his grasp. Tanis would not want to be a lycan once the Elder regained his strength. He could only imagine the bloody campaigns to come.

The lycans are no longer slaves, he realized. *Now they are our mortal enemies.*

The ship sailed forward into the future.

Epilogue

Six hundred years later . . .

Selene perched upon the roof of a sooty building, gazing down at the city below. Driving rain pelted Budapest, while the howling wind carried the memory of winters long past. A beautiful woman, with dark brown hair and alabaster skin, she resembled a long-dead noblewoman whose name and story she had never heard. Lustrous black leather clung to her lithe frame like armor. The tail of her trench coat flapped in the wind.

Heedless of both the storm and her own precarious roost upon the narrow ledge, she stared grimly into the night. Her striking chestnut eyes were fixed on the teeming streets beneath her. Her tongue traced the polished contours of her fangs. Lycans were abroad tonight, and she and her fellow Death Dealers were ready. Twin Berettas rested against her hips. Silver bullets waited to send the hated werewolves to hell, where they belonged.

More than half a millennium had passed since the infamous Lucian had embarked on his murderous crusade, but the Death Dealers' work was not yet done. Selene waited eagerly for tonight's hunt to begin.

The war continued. . . .

Acknowledgments

My fourth visit to the Underworld was made possible by the efforts of several valuable allies. Besides my able editor on this project, Ed Schlesinger, I also have to thank Margaret Clark at Pocket Books for graciously adjusting the deadline on another book to allow me to squeeze *Rise of the Lycans* into my schedule; I appreciate her patience and understanding.

Thanks also to my agents, Russ Galen and Ann Behar, for handling the business end of things, and to Sony Pictures Consumer Products, Lakeshore Entertainment, Screen Gems, the Sony Pictures Photo Department, and the filmmakers for their generous assistance. In particular, I want to thank Kevin Grevioux (aka "Raze") for sharing his own insights into the character with me.

Finally, none of this would be doable without the constant support and encouragement of my girlfriend, Karen Palinko, who makes every day a little better. And I have to give credit to our large and thriving family of four-leggers (Alex, Churchill, Henry, Sophie, and Lyla) for dragging me away from the keyboard once in a while!

About the Author

GREG COX is the *New York Times* bestselling author of numerous books and short stories. He wrote the official movie novelizations of the first two *Underworld* movies, as well as an original *Underworld* novel titled *Blood Enemy*. He has also written novelizations of such films as *Daredevil*, *Ghost Rider*, and *Death Defying Acts*. In addition, he has authored books and stories based on such popular series as *Alias*, *Batman*, *Buffy the Vampire Slayer*, *C.S.I.*, *Fantastic Four*, *Farscape*, *The 4400*, *52*, *Infinite Crisis*, *Iron Man*, *Roswell*, *Spider-Man*, *Star Trek*, *Xena*, *X-Men*, and *Zorro*. He lives in Oxford, Pennsylvania.

His official website is: www.gregcox-author.com.